OPPOSE ANY FOE

(A LUKE STONE THRILLER—BOOK 4)

JACK MARS

BOOKS BY JACK MARS

CHAPTER ONE

October 16
5:25 a.m. Mountain Daylight Time
Marble Canyon
Grand Canyon National Park, Arizona

"They're coming through on all sides!"

Luke was trying to live until daybreak, but the sun refused to rise. It was cold, and his shirt was off. He had ripped it off in the heat of combat. There was no ammo left.

Turbaned, bearded Taliban fighters poured over the walls of the outpost. Men screamed all around him.

Luke tossed his empty rifle away and pulled his handgun. He fired down the trench on his own position—it was overrun with enemies. A line of them were running this way. More came sliding, falling, jumping over the wall.

Where were his guys? Was anyone still alive?

He killed the closest man with a shot to the face. The head exploded like a cherry tomato. He grabbed the man by his tunic and held him up as a shield. The headless man was light, and Luke was raging with adrenaline—it was if the corpse were an empty suit of clothes.

He killed four men with four shots. He kept firing.

Then he was out of bullets. Again.

A Taliban charged with an AK-47, bayonet attached. Luke pushed the corpse at him, then threw his gun like a tomahawk. It bounced off the man's head, distracting him for a second. Luke used that time. He stepped into the attack, sliding along the edge of the bayonet. He plunged two fingers deep into the man's eyes, and pulled.

The man screamed. His hands went to his face. Now Luke had the AK. He bayoneted his enemy in the chest, two, three, four times. He pushed it in deep.

The man breathed his last right into Luke's face.

Luke's hands roamed the man's body. The fresh corpse had a grenade in its breast pocket. Luke took it, pulled it, and tossed it over the rampart into the oncoming hordes.

He hit the deck.

1

BOOOM.

The explosion was *right there*, spraying dirt and rock and blood and bone. The sandbagged wall half collapsed on top of him.

Luke clawed his way to his feet, deaf now, his ears ringing. He checked the AK. Empty. But he still had the bayonet.

"Come on, you bastards!" he screamed. "Come on!"

More men came over the wall, and he stabbed them in a frenzy. He ripped and tore at them with his bare hands. He shot them with their own guns.

At some point, the sun rose, but there was no warmth to it. The fighting had stopped somehow—he couldn't remember when, or how, it had ended. The ground was rugged, and hard. There were dead bodies everywhere. Skinny, bearded men lay all over the ground, with eyes wide and staring.

Nearby, he spotted one crawling back down the hill, trailing a line of blood like the trail of slime that follows a snail. He should really go out there and kill that guy, but he didn't want to risk being in the open.

Luke's chest was painted red. He was soaked in the blood of dead men. His body trembled from hunger, and from exhaustion. He stared out at the surrounding mountains, just coming into view.

How many more were out there? How long before they came?

Martinez was sprawled on his back nearby, low in the trench. He was crying. He couldn't move his legs. He'd had enough. He wanted to die. "Stone," he said. "Hey, Stone. Hey! Kill me, man. Just kill me. Hey, Stone! Listen to me, man!"

Luke was numb. He had no thoughts about Martinez's legs, or about Martinez's future. He was just tired of listening to Martinez's complaints.

"I'd gladly kill you, Martinez, just for whining like that. But I'm out of ammo. So man up... okay?"

Nearby, Murphy was sitting on an outcropping of rock, staring into space. He wasn't even trying to take cover.

"Murph! Get down here. You want a sniper to put a bullet in your head?"

Murphy turned and looked at Luke. His eyes were just... gone. He shook his head. An exhalation of air escaped from him. It sounded almost like laughter. He stayed right where he was.

If more Taliban came, they were toast. Neither one of these guys had much fight left in them, and the only weapon Stone still had was the bent bayonet in his hand. For a moment, he thought idly about picking through some of these dead guys for weapons.

He didn't know if he had the strength left to stand. He might have to crawl instead.

As he watched, a line of black insects appeared in the sky far away. He knew what they were in an instant. Helicopters. United States military helicopters, probably Black Hawks. The cavalry was coming. Luke didn't feel good about that, or bad. He felt nothing. Emptiness was an occupational hazard. He felt nothing at all....

Luke was awakened by his ringing phone. He lay there and blinked.

He tried to orient himself. He was in a tent, he realized, at the bottom of the Grand Canyon.

It was just before first light, and he was in the tent he shared with his son, Gunner. He stared into the black night, listening to the sound of his son's deep breathing nearby.

His phone kept ringing.

It vibrated against his leg, and made the annoying buzzing sound that phones set to vibrate make. He didn't want to wake Gunner, but this was probably a call he needed to take. Very few people had this number, and they were people who wouldn't just call to shoot the breeze.

He glanced at his watch: five thirty a.m.

Luke unzipped the tent, slid out, then zipped it up again. Nearby, in the first pale light of the gathering day, Luke saw the other two tents—Ed Newsam in one, Mark Swann in the other. The remains of last night's fire were in the circle of stones at the center of the camp—there were still a few coals glowing red.

The air was cool and crisp—Luke wore only boxer shorts and a T-shirt. Goosebumps popped up along his arms and on his legs. He kicked his feet into a pair of sandals and walked down to the river, past where the raft was tied up. He wanted to get far enough away from the campsite so that he didn't wake anyone.

He sat on a boulder and gazed at the rising walls of the canyon. Just below him, although he could barely see it, was the sound of trickling water. Downriver, maybe half a mile away, he could hear the rushing of the next set of rapids.

He looked at the phone. He knew the number by heart. It was Becca. Probably the last person he wanted to hear from right now. He'd had Gunner for five days, which was perfectly legal, according to their agreement. Yes, Gunner had been out of school during that time, but the kid was some kind of genius—there was talk of him skipping grades, not falling behind.

To Luke's mind, getting him out into the wild, enjoying nature and testing himself both physically and mentally, was good for him—and probably more important than anything he might get up to at home. Kids nowadays—they spent a lot of time staring into video screens. It had its place—those screens were powerful tools, but let's limit it to that. Let's not allow them to take the place of family, physicality, fun, or imagination. Let's not pretend that real adventure, or even experience, took place inside of a computer.

He called her back, his mind alert, but open. Whatever game she tried to play, he would stay calm and be as reasonable as he could.

The phone rang once.

"Luke?"

"Hi, Becca," he said, his voice low and friendly, acting like it was the most normal thing in the world to call someone back before sunrise. "How are you?"

"I'm okay," she said. Her speech with him was always abrupt, tense. His life with her was over—he recognized that. But his life with his son was just beginning, and he was firm that he would navigate any roadblocks she might try to put in his way.

He waited.

"What is Gunner doing?" she said.

"He's sleeping. It's still pretty early here. The sun's not even quite up yet."

"Right," she said. "I forgot about the time difference."

"Don't worry about it," he said. "I was awake anyway." He paused for a few seconds. The first glint of real sun was appearing in the east, a ray of light which peeked over the rim of the canyon and played on the cliff wall to the west, turning it pink and orange.

"So what can I do for you?"

She didn't hesitate. "I need Gunner to come home right away."

"Becca—"

"Don't fight me on this, Luke. You know it won't hold any water with the judge. A special operations agent with diagnosed post traumatic stress disorder and a history of violence wants to take his young son on outdoor adventures, which, by the way, causes his son to miss entire weeks of school. I can't believe I even agreed to this in the first place. I've been so distracted that I—"

He interrupted her. "Becca, we're in the Grand Canyon. We're rafting. You do realize that, don't you? Unless a helicopter lands down here to pick us up, we are probably three days from reaching

4

the South Rim. Then a night in the lodge there, and a full day's drive down to Phoenix. Which sounds about right, because as I recall it, our plane tickets back are scheduled for the twenty-second. And by the way, this whole PTSD diagnosis isn't real. It never happened. No doctor has ever even suggested it. It's just something that you've manufactured in your—"

"Luke, I have cancer."

That stopped him in his tracks. In recent days, she had been more agitated than he'd ever seen her before. Of course he had noticed this, but mostly ignored it. It was typical of her, and the amount of pressure she put on herself. Becca was a Grade A stress case. But this was different.

Luke's eyes watered, and a thick lump formed in his throat. Could it be true? Whatever had happened between them, this was the woman he had fallen in love with. This was the woman who had carried his child. At one time, he had loved her more than anything in this world, certainly more than he loved himself.

"Jesus, Becca. I'm so sorry. When did that happen?"

"I was feeling sick all summer. I lost some weight. At first, it was no big deal, but then it became a surprising amount of weight. I thought it was from all the anxiety, everything that's happened in the past year—the kidnapping, the train crash, all the time you've been away. But things have calmed down a lot, and the sickness didn't stop. I went for tests starting a couple weeks ago. I had been vomiting. I didn't want to tell you until I knew more. Now I know more. I saw my doctor yesterday, and she told me everything."

"What is it?" he said, though he was not sure he wanted to hear the answer.

"It's pancreatic," she said, dropping perhaps the worst bomb he could have imagined. "Stage Four. Luke, it's already metastasized. It's in my colon, in my brain. It's in my bones…" Her voice trailed off, and he could hear her sob two thousand miles away.

"I've been crying all night," she said, her voice breaking. "I can't seem to stop."

As bad as he felt, Luke found that his thoughts suddenly weren't with her—they were with Gunner. "How long?" he said. "Did they give you a timeframe?"

"Three months," Becca said. "Maybe six. She told me not to hang my hat on that. A lot of people die very quickly. Sometimes there's a miracle and the patient lives on and on indefinitely. Either way, she told me I need to get my affairs in order."

She paused. "Luke, I'm so afraid."

He nodded. "I know you are. We'll be there as soon as we can. I'm not going to tell Gunner."

"Good. I don't want you to. We can tell him together."

"Okay," Luke said. "I'll see you soon. I'm very sorry."

The hang-up was awkward. If only they hadn't been fighting all these months. If only she hadn't been so hostile to him. If these things hadn't happened, maybe he could have found a way to comfort her, even from this distance. He had become hardened against her, and he didn't know if there was any softness left.

He sat on the boulder for several minutes. Light began to fill the sky. He didn't reminisce about the good memories with her. He didn't go over all the battles they'd fought this past year, and how vicious and dug in she'd been. His mind was a blank. That was for the best. He needed a way out of this canyon, and he needed to break the news to Ed and Swann that he and Gunner were leaving.

He pushed off the rock and walked back to camp. Ed was awake and crouched by the fire. He had started it up again and had put the coffee pot on. He was shirtless, wearing nothing but a pair of red boxer briefs and flip-flops. His body was thick rippling muscle and ropey veins, hardly an ounce of fat on him—he looked like a martial arts fighter about to enter the cage. He watched Luke approach, then gestured to the west.

Over there, the sky was still cobalt blue, the night retreating, being chased away by the light coming from the east. At the very top, the towering walls of the canyon were lit by a sliver of sun now, setting their striations aflame in red, pink, yellow, and orange.

"Damn, that's pretty," Ed said.

"Ed," Luke said. "I've got bad news."

CHAPTER TWO

**9:15 p.m. Greenwich Mean Time
(4:15 p.m. Eastern Daylight Time)
Molenbeek Suburb
Brussels, Belgium**

The thin man could speak Dutch.

"*Ga weg*," he said under his breath. Go away.

His name was not Jamal. But that was the name he sometimes gave to people, and the name that many, many people had come to know him by. Most people called him Jamal. Some called him the Phantom.

He stood in the shadows near an overflowing garbage can, just inside a narrow cobblestone street, smoking a cigarette and watching a police car parked on the main avenue. The street he was on was little more than an alleyway, and as he stood back in the shadows, he felt certain no one could see him there. The empty boulevards and sidewalks and alleys of the infamous Muslim slum were wet from a hard, chilly rain that had stopped maybe ten minutes before.

The place was a ghost town tonight.

On the boulevard, the police car pulled out from the curb and rolled quietly down the street. There was no other traffic.

A tickle of excitement—it was almost fear—went through Jamal's body as he watched the police. They had no reason to harass him. He wasn't breaking any laws. He was a well-dressed man in a dark suit and Italian leather shoes, with a clean-shaven face. He could be a businessman, or the owner of these low-rise tenement buildings all around him. He wasn't the type for the police to randomly stop and search. Even so, Jamal had fallen into the hands of the authorities before—not here in Belgium, but in other places. His experiences were unpleasant, to put it mildly. He had once spent twelve hours listening to himself scream in agony.

He shook his head to clear the dark thoughts, finished his cigarette in three deep inhales, ignored the garbage can, and pitched the butt on the ground. He turned back down the alley. He passed a round red sign with a horizontal white stripe—DO NOT ENTER. The street was too narrow for car traffic. If the police suddenly decided they wanted to pursue him, they'd be forced to do so on foot. Either that, or circle around several blocks. By the time they returned, he'd be gone.

After fifty meters, he turned quickly and unlocked the entrance to a particularly dilapidated building. He climbed a narrow stairwell three stories until it dead-ended at a thick, steel-reinforced door. The stairs were old, made of wood and crazily warped. The whole stairwell seemed to twist this way and that like taffy, giving it the feeling of a carnival funhouse.

Jamal made a fist and hammered on the heavy door, his knocks coming in a careful sequence:

BANG-BANG. BANG-BANG.

He paused a few seconds.

BANG.

A gun-hole slid open and an eye appeared there. The man on the other side grunted as he verified who it was. Jamal listened to the guard turn keys in locks, then remove the steel t-bar wedged into the floor at the bottom of the door. The police would have a very hard time entering this apartment, if their suspicion ever fell upon it.

"*As salaam alaikum*," Jamal said as he entered.

"*Wa alailkum salaam*," the man who opened the door said. He was a tall, burly man. He wore a grimy sleeveless T-shirt, work pants, and boots. A thick unkempt beard covered his face, meeting the mass of curly black hair on his scalp. His eyes were dull. He was everything the thin man was not.

"How do they seem?" Jamal said in French.

The big man shrugged. "Good, I think."

Jamal passed through a beaded curtain, down a short hallway, and entered a small room—what would have been the living room if a family were occupying this place. The dingy room was crowded with young men, most wearing T-shirts, jerseys from their favorite European football teams, track pants, and sneakers. It was hot and humid in the room, perhaps from the proximity of all the bodies in a small space. It smelled like wet socks mingled with body odor in there.

In the center of the room, on a wide wooden table, sat a bullet-shaped device made of silver metal. It was about a meter long and less than half a meter wide. Jamal had spent time in Germany and Austria, and the device reminded him of a small beer keg. In fact, except for its weight—it was quite light—it was a very close replica of an American W80 nuclear warhead.

Two young men were at the table while the others circled around and watched. One stood in front of a small laptop computer mounted inside a steel suitcase. The suitcase had a panel which ran alongside the laptop—there were two switches, two LED lights (one red and one green), and a dial built into the panel. A wire ran from the case to another panel along the side of the warhead. The entire device—the suitcase and the laptop inside it—were known as a UC 1583 controller. It was a device designed for one task only—to communicate with a nuclear weapon.

The second man was bent over a white envelope on the table. He wore an expensive digital microscope affixed to his eye, and slowly scanned the envelope, looking for what he knew must be there—a tiny dot, no larger than the period at the end of a sentence, in which there was embedded the code that would arm and activate the warhead.

Jamal moved closer to watch.

The young man with the microscope slowly scanned the envelope. Every few seconds, he covered the microscope with his hand and took a larger scale view with his uncovered eye, looking for ink spots, blemishes, any dots that were likely suspects. Then he dove back in with the microscope.

"Wait," he whispered under his breath. "Wait..."

"Come on," his partner said, an air of impatience in his voice. They were being judged not just for accuracy, but for time. When their moment came, they would be forced to act very quickly.

"Got it."

Now it was the partner who was on the spot. From memory, the young man typed in a sequence that enabled the laptop to accept an arming code. His hands shook as he did so. He was nervous enough that he botched the sequence on the first attempt, canceled, and started over.

"Okay," he said. "Give it to me."

Very slowly and clearly, the man with the microscope read a sequence of twelve numbers. The other man typed each number as it was spoken. After twelve, the first man said "Done."

Now the man at the laptop went through another short sequence, flipped the two switches, and turned the dial. The green LED light on the panel popped on.

The young man smiled and turned to his instructor.

"Armed and ready to launch," he said. "God willing."

Jamal also smiled. He was an observer here—he had come to see how the recruits were progressing. They were true believers, preparing for what was likely a suicide mission. If the codes were entered incorrectly, the warheads might simply shut themselves down—they might also self-destruct, dispersing a deadly cloud of radiation and killing everyone in the vicinity.

No one was sure what would happen in the event of an incorrect code. It was all hearsay and speculation. The Americans kept those secrets closely held. But it didn't matter. These young men were willing to die, and that's probably what they would do. Regardless of the codes, when the USA discovered that their precious nuclear weapons had been stolen, they weren't going to respond kindly. No. The giant beast would lash out, its tentacles flying, destroying everything in its path.

Jamal nodded and recited a silent prayer of thanks. It had been quite a task pulling together this project. They had the mujahideen necessary—but then, young men willing to die for their faith were easy to acquire.

The other elements were more challenging. They would soon have the launch platforms and the missiles—Jamal would see to that himself. The codes had been promised, and he was certain they would receive them as described. Then all they would need were the warheads themselves.

And soon, if it was Allah's will, they would have those as well.

CHAPTER THREE

October 19
1:15 p.m. Eastern Daylight Time
Fairfax County, Virginia—Suburbs of Washington, DC

Luke had hired a chopper to take himself and Gunner out of the canyon. He had finagled a new flight for them, and driven like the devil to make it to Phoenix in time to catch the plane. All the while, he had fended off Gunner's questions about why they had left so abruptly.

"Your mom just wants you home, Monster. She misses you, and she doesn't like you skipping all this school."

In the passenger seat, the highway zooming by his window, Luke could see Gunner's antennae twitching like crazy. He was a smart kid. He was already learning to catch people lying. Luke hated—*hated!*—that he had to be one of the first people Gunner would catch.

"I thought you worked all that out with Mom before we left."

"I did," Luke said with a shrug. "But it got unworked out. Listen, we'll all talk about it when we get there, okay?"

"Okay, Dad."

But Luke could see that it was not okay. Soon, it would be a lot less okay.

Now, two days later, here he sat, on the big plush sofa in the living room of his former house. Gunner was at school.

Luke glanced around the place. Once upon a time, he and Becca had had a great life here. It was a beautiful home, modern, like something out of an architectural magazine. The living room, with its floor to ceiling windows, was like a glass box. He pictured Christmas time—just sitting in this stunning sunken living room, the tree in the corner, the fireplace lit, the snow coming down all around as if they were outside, but they were inside, warm and cozy.

God, it was nice. But those days were gone.

Becca bustled around, cleaning up, dusting, putting various things away. At one point in the conversation, she took the vacuum cleaner out of the closet and let it rip. She was in a very bad place psychologically. He had tried to hug her when he first arrived, but she had gone wooden, her arms at her sides.

"I was over you, did you know that?" she said now. "I was ready to move on with my life. I even went on a few coffee dates when you had Gunner with you this summer. Why not? I'm still young, right?"

She shook her head bitterly. Luke said nothing. What was there to say?

"Do you want to know something about yourself, Luke? The first one I met, he was a teacher on his summer vacation, nice guy, and he asked me what you do for a living. I told him the truth. Oh, my ex-husband's some kind of secret assassin for the government. He used to be in Delta Force. You know what happened after that? I'll tell you. Nothing happened. It was the last I ever heard from him. He heard Delta Force and he disappeared. You frighten people, Luke. That's my point."

Luke shrugged. "Why don't you just tell them I do something else? It's not like I'm going to—"

"I did. Once I caught on, I started telling people you're a lawyer."

.For a second, Luke wondered what the plural "people" meant. Was she going on dates every day? Two a day? He shook his head. It was none of his business anymore, as long as she was safe. And even that... she was dying. She would never be safe again, and there was nothing he could do about it.

A long paused passed between them.

"Do you want to get a second opinion?"

She nodded. She looked numb, in shock, like the survivors of disasters and atrocities Luke had seen so many times. The amazing thing was that she also looked perfectly healthy. A little thinner than usual, but no one would ever guess that she had cancer. They would probably think she'd been on a diet.

It's the chemo that makes them look sick. Half the time, it's also what kills them.

"I've already gotten a second opinion from an old colleague of mine. I'm going for a third opinion early next week. If it's consistent with what I've already heard, then by Thursday, I'll begin the protocols."

"Is surgery an option?" Luke said.

She shook her head. "It's too late for that. The cancer is everywhere..." Her voice trailed off. "Everywhere. Chemotherapy is the only option. If I exhaust the approved chemo drugs, then maybe clinical trials, if I'm even still alive."

12

She started crying again. She stood in the middle of the living room, abjectly, her face buried in her hands, her body shaking with the sobs. To Luke, she looked just like a little girl. It stung him to see her reduced to this. He had been around death a lot in his life, seen too much of it, but this? It couldn't be true. He stood, and went to her then. He would comfort her if he could.

She pushed him away, violently, like a child in a playground fight.

"Don't touch me! Get away from me!" She pointed at him, her face a raging mask of anger. "It's you!" she shrieked. "You make people sick, don't you realize that? You steal all the oxygen in the room. You and your superhero garbage."

She bobbed her head from side to side, mocking him. "Oh, I'm sorry, honey," she said in a caricature of a low masculine voice. "I've got to run off and save the world. No telling if I'll be alive or dead three days from now. Raise the boy for me, won't you? Just doing my patriotic duty."

She was seething. Her voice went back to normal. "You do it because it's fun, Luke. You do it because you're irresponsible. You enjoy it. For you, there are no consequences. You don't care if you live or die anyway, and everybody else has to deal with the fallout and the stress."

She burst into tears. "I'm done with you. I'm just done." She waved her hand at him. "I'm sure you can find your own way out of here. So just go. Okay? Go away. Let me die in peace."

With that, she left the room. A moment of silence passed, and then he heard her down the hall in the master bedroom, sobbing.

He stood there for a long moment, not sure what to do. Gunner would be home in a couple of hours. It wasn't a good idea to leave him here with Becca, but he didn't know if he had much choice. She had custody. He had visitation rights. If he took Gunner with him now, without her permission, it was technically kidnapping.

He sighed. When had the legalities of a situation stopped him before?

Luke was at a loss. He felt his energy draining away. And they still hadn't explained anything about this to the child yet. Maybe he should call Becca's parents and talk to them. The truth was Becca had handled nearly all the domestic details during their relationship. Maybe she was right about him—he was a lot more comfortable out in the world, playing cops and robbers with very dangerous people. Other people worried about him, he knew, but he didn't worry.

What kind of person lived like that? Maybe one who had never grown up.

On the glass table near the sofa, his telephone began to ring. He glanced at it. As it often did, it seemed almost like it was alive, a viper, dangerous to touch.

He picked it up. "Stone."

A male voice was on the line.

"Hold for the President of the United States."

He glanced up, and Becca hovered in the doorway now. Apparently, she had heard his phone ring. She was back again, ready to listen to his conversation and confirm all of her worst feelings about him. For a split second, he felt real hatred for her—she was going to be right about him, no matter what. All the way into her grave, she was going to have him nailed.

Now the voice of Susan Hopkins came on.

"Luke, are you there?"

"Hi, Susan."

"Long time, no see, Agent Stone. How are you doing?"

"I'm fine," he said. "You?"

"Good," she said, but the tone of her voice said something else. "Everything is okay. Listen, I need your help."

"Susan…" he started.

"It's a one-day thing, but it's very important. I need someone who can put it to bed quickly, and with complete discretion."

"What is it?"

"I can't talk about this over the telephone," she said. "Can you come in?"

His shoulders sagged. *Ah, man.*

"All right."

"How soon can you be here?"

He glanced at his watch. Gunner would be home in an hour and a half. If he wanted to spend time with his son, the meeting would have to wait. If he went to the meeting…

He sighed.

"I'll be there as soon as I can."

"Good. I'll make sure they bring you straight to me."

He hung up. He looked at Becca. There was something cruel and mocking inside her eyes. There was a demon in there, dancing on a lake of fire.

"Where are you going, Luke?"

"You know where I'm going."

"Oh, you're not going to stay and have a nice time with your son? You're not going to be a good daddy? That's a surprise. Gee, I would have thought—"

"Becca, stop it. Okay? I'm sorry that you're—"

"You're going to lose custody of Gunner, Luke. You go off on missions all the time, right? Well, guess what. I'm going to make you *my* mission. You're not even going to see that boy. With my dying breath, I'm going to make it happen. My parents are going to raise him, and you're not even going to have access to him. You know why?"

Luke headed to the door.

"Good-bye, Becca. Have a nice day."

"I'll tell you why, Luke. Because my parents are rich! They love Gunner. And they don't like you. You think you can outlast my parents in a legal battle, Luke? I don't think so."

He was halfway outside, but he stopped and turned around.

"Is this what you want to do with the time you have left?" he said. "Is this who you want to be?"

She stared at him.

"Yes."

He shook his head.

He didn't know her anymore, if he ever did.

And with that, he left.

CHAPTER FOUR

11:50 p.m. Eastern European Time
(5:50 p.m. Eastern Daylight Time)
Alexandroupoli, Greece

They were thirty miles from the Turkish border. The man checked his watch. Almost midnight.

Soon, soon.

The man's name was Brown. It was a name that was not a name, for someone who had disappeared a long time ago. Brown was a ghost. He had a thick scar across his left cheek—a bullet that had just missed. He wore a flattop haircut. He was big and strong, and had the sharp features of someone who had spent his entire adult life in special operations.

Once, Brown was known by a different name—his real name. As time passed, his name had changed. At this point, he'd gone by so many names he couldn't remember them all. This latest one was his favorite: Brown. No first name, no last name. Just Brown. Brown was good enough. It was an evocative name. It reminded him of dead things. Dead leaves in late fall. Dead trees after a nuclear test. Wide open and staring dead brown eyes of the many, many people he'd killed.

Technically, Brown was on the run. He had ended up on the wrong side of history about six months ago, on a job that hadn't even been explained to him. He'd had to leave his home country in a hurry and go underground. But after a period of uncertainty, he was back on his feet again. And as always, there was plenty of business to do, especially for a man with the kind of bounce-back ability he had.

Now, just before midnight, he stood outside a warehouse in a rundown section of this seafaring town's port district. The warehouse was surrounded by a high fence topped with razor wire, but the gate was open. A chilly fog rolled in off the Mediterranean Sea.

Two men stood with him, both wearing leather jackets, and both with Uzi submachine guns strapped over their shoulders, and stocks extended. The guys would be nearly identical, except one of them had shaved his head completely bald.

Out on the street, headlights approached.

"Eyes open," Brown said. "Here come the holy warriors now."

A small box truck drove up along the deserted boulevard. There was a giant image of oranges along the side of it, with one sliced in half and showing the bright reddish-orange meat of the fruit. There were words on the side of the truck in Greek, probably a company name, but Brown didn't read Greek.

The truck reached the gate and pulled straight into the yard. One of Brown's men walked over and slid the gate shut along its track, then locked it with a heavy padlock.

As soon as the truck stopped, two men climbed out of the cab of the truck. The rear door opened, and three more clambered out. The men were dark-skinned, probably Arab, but clean-shaven. Their uniform consisted of blue jeans, light windbreaker jackets, and sneakers.

One man carried a large canvas bag, like a hockey equipment bag, over either shoulder. The weight of the satchels pulled the man's shoulders down. Three of the men carried Uzis.

We have Uzis, they have Uzis. It's an Uzi party.

The fourth man, the driver of the truck, was empty-handed. He approached Brown. His eyes were blue, and his skin was very dark. His hair was jet black. The combination of blue eyes and dark skin gave his face an odd effect, as if he wasn't quite real.

The two men shook hands.

"Jamal," Brown said. "I thought I told you to come with only three men."

Jamal shrugged. "I needed one to carry the money. And I don't count toward the total, right? So I did bring three. Three gunmen."

Brown shook his head and smiled. It hardly mattered how many people Jamal brought. The two men with Brown could kill a busload of gunmen.

"Okay, let's go," Brown said. "The trucks are inside."

One of Brown's men—he called himself Mr. Jones—pulled an automatic opener from his pocket, and the garage door of the warehouse slowly rattled open. The eight men walked into the cavernous space. The warehouse was mostly empty, except for heavy green tarps thrown over two giant vehicles. Brown walked to the closest one and yanked the tarp halfway off.

"Voila!" he said. What he revealed was the front half of a large tractor-trailer, painted in green, brown, and tan camouflage colors. Jones yanked the tarp off near the rear of the truck, revealing a flat, four-cylinder missile launch platform. The two parts of the truck were separate and independent of each other, but were attached by hydraulics in the middle.

The trucks were called transporter-erector-launchers, or TELs, relics of the Cold War, mobile attack stations that NATO had used to target the old Soviet Union. The launchers fired smaller variants of the Tomahawk cruise missile, and the missiles could be outfitted with small thermonuclear warheads. These weapons were for a limited tactical nuclear strike—the kind that would take out a medium-sized city, or totally destroy a military base and its surrounding countryside, but maybe not bring about the apocalypse. Of course, once you started launching nukes at people, all bets were off.

In the old days, they called this missile system the "Gryphon," after the ancient mythical creature with the legs and body of a lion, and the wings, head, and talons of an eagle—the protector of the divine. Brown got a kick out of that.

The system was decommissioned in 1991, and all of these units were supposed to have been destroyed. But there were still a few of them in existence. There were *always* weapons floating around somewhere. Brown had never heard of a missile class or a weapons system that had been entirely dismantled—there was too much money to be made misplacing them and having them turn up later. Retail stores called it "shrinkage." Walmart and Home Depot experienced it. So did the military.

In fact, here were two of the mobile platforms, just parked in a warehouse in a Greek port city all this time, very close to Turkey, and less than a mile from the docks. Sitting snug inside each of the launch cylinders was a Tomahawk missile, each one operational, or likely to become operational with a little tender loving care.

Why, it was almost as if you could drive these trucks out of here and right onto a freighter or a ferry, then sail away for parts unknown. They were conventional weapons, certainly, but surely there were still nuclear warheads somewhere that would fit these missiles.

Then again, obtaining warheads wasn't Brown's department. That was Jamal's problem. He was a capable guy, and Brown imagined he already knew where he might find some loose nukes. Brown wasn't sure how he felt about that. Jamal was playing a dangerous game.

"It's beautiful," Jamal said.

"God is great," said one of his men.

Brown winced. As a rule, he frowned on religious talk. And beautiful was a relative term. These trucks were two of the ugliest war machines Brown had ever seen. But they would pack a wallop—that much was certain.

"You like?" Brown said to Jamal.

Jamal nodded. "Very much.

"Then let's see the money."

The man with the heavy satchels came forward. He dropped them from his shoulders and onto the stone floor of the warehouse. He knelt and unzipped them, each in turn.

"A million dollars in cash in each bag," Jamal said.

Brown gestured with his head to his other man, the bald one.

"Mr. Clean, check it."

Clean knelt by the bags. He pulled random rubber-banded stacks of money from various sections of each bag. He took a small, flat digital scanner from his pocket and began to remove bills from each stack. He turned on the scanner's UV LED light and placed the bills on the scanner window one at a time, revealing the UV security strip on each bill. Then he ran a light pen over each bill, revealing the hidden watermarks. It was a cumbersome process.

As Clean worked, Brown slipped a hand inside his jacket, touching his gun there. He made eye contact his man Jones, who nodded. If something funny was coming, it would happen now. The body language of the Arabs didn't change—they just looked on impassively. Brown took that as a good sign. They were really here to *buy* the trucks.

Mr. Clean dropped a stack of money on the floor. "Good." He picked up another stack, began riffling through it, checking bills with the device. Time crawled by.

"Good." He dropped that stack and picked up another one. More time passed.

"Good." He kept going.

After a while, it started to grow boring. The money was real. In ten minutes or so, Brown turned to Jamal.

"Okay, I believe you. That's two million."

Jamal shrugged. He opened his jacket and pulled out a large velvet purse. "Two million in cash, two million in diamonds, as we agreed."

"Clean," Brown said.

Mr. Clean stood and took the purse from Jamal. Clean was the money and valuables expert on this little team. He pulled a different electronic device from his pocket—a small black square with a needle tip. The device had lights on the side, and Brown knew it tested the heat dispersal and electrical conductivity of the stones.

Clean began to take stones one at a time from the bag and gently press the needle tip to them. Each time he did one, a warm tone would sound. He had done about a dozen before Brown said another word to him.

"Clean?"

Clean looked at Brown. He grinned.

"They're good so far," he said. "All diamonds."

He tested another one. Then another.

Another.

Brown turned to Jamal, who was already gesturing to his men to pull the tarps and board the trucks.

"It was a pleasure doing business with you, Jamal."

Jamal barely glanced at him. "Likewise." He was preoccupied with his men, and the trucks. The next part of their journey had already begun. Getting two mobile nuclear missile launch platforms with missiles included to the Middle East was probably not an easy proposition.

Brown raised a finger. "Hey, Jamal!"

The thin man turned back to him. He made an impatient hand gesture, as if to say, "What?"

"If you get caught with those things…"

Now Jamal did smile. "I know. You and I never met." He backed away toward the nearest of the two trucks.

Brown turned to Mr. Jones and Mr. Clean. Jones was on one knee, stuffing the money back into the heavy bag. Clean was still testing diamonds from the velvet bag, handling them one at a time, the needle device still in his hand.

They had made one whale of a score. Things were looking up finally, after the fiasco that had run Brown out of his own country. He smiled.

All in a day's work.

And yet, something about the scene here disturbed Brown. His guys were not paying attention to their environment—they were distracted by all the money. They had let their guard down, badly. And so had he. On a different operation, that could come back to bite them. Not everyone was as trustworthy as Jamal.

He turned to look at the Arabs again.

Jamal was there, near the truck, holding one of the Uzis. Two of his guys were with him. They stood in a line, pointing their guns at Brown and his men.

Jamal smiled.

"Clean!" Brown shouted.

Jamal fired, and his men did the same. There came the ugly blat of automatic gunfire. To Brown, it seemed like they were almost spraying him with a fire hose. He felt the bullets piercing him, biting into him like stinging bees. His body did an involuntary dance, and he struggled against it, to no avail. It was almost as if the bullets were holding him up, pinning him in an upright position, making him jitter and jive.

For a moment, he lost consciousness. Everything went black. Then he was lying on his back, on the concrete floor of the warehouse. He could feel the blood flowing from him. He could feel that the floor was wet where he lay. A puddle was spreading around him. He was in a lot of pain.

He glanced over at Mr. Clean and Mr. Jones. They were both dead, their bodies riddled, their heads half gone. Only Brown was still alive.

It occurred to him that he had always been a survivor. Hell, he had always been a winner. There was no way, after more than two decades of combat, madcap adventures, and narrow escapes, that he was going to die now, like this. It was impossible. He was too good at his job. So many men had tried to kill him before now, and failed. His life wouldn't end like this. It couldn't.

He tried to reach inside his jacket for his gun, but his arm didn't seem work right. Then he noticed something else. Despite all the pain, he couldn't feel his legs.

He could feel the burning in his gut where he had been shot. He could feel the ringing pain in his head where he had smacked it on the stone floor when he fell down. He swallowed, then lifted his head and stared down at his feet. Everything was still down there and still attached—he just couldn't feel any of it.

The bullets severed my spine.

No thought had ever caused him such horror. Valuable seconds passed as he saw his future—rolling in a wheelchair, trying to climb from the chair to the driver's seat of his handicapped accessible car, emptying the colostomy bag that drained the shit from his useless digestive system.

No. He shook his head. There was no time for that. There was only time for action. Clean's gun was above his head and behind him somewhere. He reached back there—it hurt just to raise his arms like that—but he couldn't find it. He started crawling backwards, dragging his legs after him.

Something caught his eye. He looked up and here came Jamal, swaggering toward him. The bastard was grinning.

As he approached he raised his gun. He pointed it at Brown. Now Brown noticed Jamal's two men were with him.

"Don't try to do anything, Brown. Just lay still."

Jamal's men took the big heavy bag with the money, and the small purse with the diamonds. Then they turned and headed back to the trucks. They climbed into the cab of the lead truck. The headlights came on. The engine farted and belched, black smoke pouring from a stack on the driver's side.

"I like you," Jamal said. "But business is business, you know? We're not leaving any loose ends on this one. Sorry about that. I really am."

Brown tried to say something, but he didn't seem to have his voice. All he could do was gurgle in response.

Jamal raised the gun again.

"Do you want a moment to pray?"

Brown nearly laughed. He shook his head. "You know something, Jamal? You crack me up. You and your religion are a joke. Do I want to pray? Pray to what? There is no God, and you'll find that out as soon as you—"

Brown saw fire lick the end of the gun's barrel. Then he was flat on his back, staring up at the ceiling of the warehouse high above his head.

CHAPTER FIVE

9:45 p.m. Mountain Daylight Time
(11:45 p.m. Eastern Daylight Time)
Florence ADX Federal Penitentiary
(Supermax)—Florence, Colorado

"This is it," the guard said. "Home sweet home."

Luke walked the white cinderblock hallways of the most secure prison in the United States. The two tall, heavyset guards in brown uniforms flanked him. They were nearly identical, these guards, with military recruit-style crew cuts, big shoulders and arms, and even bigger midsections. They moved along, their bodies stiff and top-heavy, like offensive linemen from a football team who had been out of the sport for a while.

They were not fit in any traditional sense of that word, but Luke mused that they were the perfect size and shape for their jobs. In close quarters, they could put a lot of weight on a resistant prisoner.

Footfalls echoed on the stone floor as the three men passed the closed, windowless steel doors of dozens of cells. Each cell door had a narrow opening near the bottom, like a mail slot, through which the guards could shove meals to the prisoners. Each also had two small windows with steel-reinforced glass facing the walkway. Luke didn't glance into any of the windows they passed.

Somewhere on this hallway, a man was screaming. It sounded like agony. It went on and on, no sign of ending. It was night, soon it would be lights out, and a man was shrieking. Luke thought he could almost make out words embedded in the sound.

He glanced at one of the guards.

"He's okay," the guard said. "Really. He's not in any pain. He just howls like that."

The other guard chimed in. "The solitude drives some of them insane."

"Solitude?" Luke said. "You mean isolation?"

The guard shrugged. "Yeah." It was semantics to him. He went home at the end of his shift. Ate at Denny's, by the looks of him, and chatted the people up. He wore a wedding band on the ring finger of his thick left hand. He had a wife, probably kids. The man had a life outside these walls. The prisoners? Not so much.

A who's who of rogues and baddies had stayed here, Luke knew. The Unabomber Ted Kaczynski was a current resident, as was Dzhokhar Tsarnaev, the surviving brother of the two Boston Marathon bombers. The mob boss John Gotti had lived here for years, as had his violent enforcer, Sammy "The Bull" Gravano.

It was a breach of facility rules to allow Luke past the visiting room, but it wasn't exactly visiting hours, and this was a special case. A prisoner here had intelligence to offer, but he insisted on seeing Luke personally—not on a telephone with a thick glass partition between them, but face to face, and man to man, in the cell. The President of the United States herself had asked Luke to take this meeting.

They came to a stop in front of a white door, one among many. Luke felt his heart skip a beat. He was nervous, just a little bit. He didn't try to catch a glimpse of the man through the tiny windows. He didn't want to see him that way, like a mouse living in a shoebox. He wanted the man to be legendary, larger than life.

"It's my duty to inform you," one of the guards began, "that the prisoners here are considered among the most violent and dangerous currently in the United States federal corrections system. If you choose to enter this cell and you decline personal..."

Luke raised a hand. "Save it. I know the risks."

The guard shrugged again. "Suit yourself."

"For the record, I don't want this conversation recorded," Luke said.

"All cells are filmed by surveillance cameras twenty-four hours a day," the guard said now. "But there is no audio."

Luke nodded. He didn't believe a word of it. "Good. I'll scream if I need any help."

The guard smiled. "We won't hear it."

"Then I'll wave frantically."

Both guards laughed. "I'll be down the end of the hall," one of them said. "Bang on the door when you want to come out again."

The door clanged as it unlocked, then slid open of its own accord. Somewhere, someone was indeed watching them.

As the door slid away, it revealed a tiny, dismal cell. The first thing Luke noticed was the metal toilet. It had a water faucet at the top of it, an odd combination, but one which made logical sense, he supposed. Everything else was made of stone, and in a fixed location. A narrow stone desk extended from the cinderblock wall, with a rounded stone stool like a small peg coming out of the floor in front of it.

24

The desk was piled with papers, a few books, and four or five stubby pencils like the ones golfers use to keep score. Like the desk, the bed was narrow and made of stone. A thin mattress covered it and there was one green blanket that looked to be made of wool serge, or some equally itchy material. There was a narrow window in the far wall, framed in green, perhaps two feet tall and six inches wide. It was dark outside that window, except for a sickly yellow light that streamed into the cell from a nearby sodium arc lamp mounted on the outside wall. There was no way to cover the window.

The prisoner stood in an orange jumpsuit, his broad back to them.

"Morris," the guard said. "Here's your visitor. Do me a favor and don't kill him."

Don Morris, former United States Army colonel and Delta Force commander, founder and former director of the FBI Special Response Team, turned around slowly. His face seemed more lined than before and his salt and pepper hair had gone entirely white. But his eyes were deep-set, sharp, and alert, and his chest, arms, legs, and shoulders looked as strong as they ever had.

His mouth made something almost like a smile, but it didn't reach his eyes.

"Luke," he said. "Thanks for coming. Welcome to my home. Eighty-seven square feet, approximately seven and a half by twelve."

"Hi, Don," Luke said. "I love what you've done with the place."

"Last chance to change your mind," one of the guards said behind him.

Luke shook his head. "I think I'll be okay."

Don's eyes fell upon the guards. "You know who this man is, don't you?"

"We do. Yes."

"Then I guess," Don said, "you can imagine how little danger I present to him."

The door clanged shut. Luke had a moment, as they stared at each other across the cell—he might call it nostalgia. Don had been his commanding officer and his mentor in Delta. When Don started the Special Response Team, he had hired Luke as his first agent. In a lot of ways, and for more than ten years, Don had been like a father to him.

25

But not anymore. Don had been one of the plotters in the conspiracy to kill the President of the United States and take over the government. He'd been complicit in the kidnapping of Luke's own wife and child. He'd had foreknowledge of the bombing that killed more than three hundred people at Mount Weather. Don was facing the death penalty, and Luke couldn't think of anyone more worthy of that fate.

The two men shook hands, and Don placed a hand on Luke's shoulder, just for a second. It was an awkward gesture by a man no longer accustomed to human contact. Luke knew that Supermax prisoners rarely touched another human being.

"Thanks for all the visits you've made and the letters you've sent," Don said. "It's been a comfort to know my welfare is such a priority for you."

Luke shook his head. He almost smiled. "Don, until yesterday afternoon, I didn't even know where they were holding you. And I didn't care. It could have been a hole in the ground. It could have been at the bottom of Mount Weather."

Don nodded. "When you lose, they can do whatever they want with you."

"Richly deserved, in this case."

Don gestured at the stone peg sprouting like a mushroom out of the ground. "Won't you have a seat?"

"I'll stand. Thanks."

Don stared at Luke, his head leaning quizzically to the side. "I don't have much hospitality to offer, Luke. This is it."

"Why would I accept your hospitality, Don?"

Don's eyes did not look away. "Are you joking? For old times' sake. As a gesture of thanks for mentoring you through Delta, and giving you your current job. Think of a reason, son."

"Exactly my point, Don. When I think of you, I think of my own son, and my wife, who you had kidnapped."

Don raised his hands. "I had nothing to do with that. I promise you. If it were up to me, I would never allow harm to come to Gunner or Becca. They're like my blood, like my own family. I warned you because I wanted to *protect* them, Luke. I found out after it had already happened. I'm sorry that happened. There's nothing in my long career that I regret more."

Luke scanned Don's eyes, his body language, looking for… something. Was he lying? Was he telling the truth? What did Don even believe? Who was this man, whom Luke once thought he loved?

Luke sighed. He would take the man's meager hospitality. He would give him that much, and lie awake tonight wondering why he had.

He squatted on the low stone.

Don sat on the bed. A pause stretched out between them. There was nothing comfortable about it.

"How's the SRT?" Don said finally. "I suppose they made you director?"

"They offered, but I declined. The SRT is gone, scattered to the winds. Most of the agents were absorbed back into the Bureau proper. Ed Newsam is on the Hostage Rescue Team. Mark Swann went to NSA. I keep in pretty close touch with those guys—I borrow them for an operation from time to time."

Luke saw something flash in Don's eyes, and disappear almost before it was there. His baby, the FBI Special Response Team, the culmination of his life's work, had been dismantled. Had he not known that? Luke supposed he hadn't.

"Trudy Wellington has disappeared," Luke said.

Something else appeared in Don's eyes, and this time it stayed there. If it lingered, it meant Don wanted him to see it. Luke couldn't tell if it was an emotion, a memory, or some piece of knowledge. He was good at reading people, but Don was an old spy. His mind and his heart were closed books.

"You wouldn't know anything about that, would you, Don?"

Don shrugged, offered half a smile. "The Trudy I knew was very smart. She had her ear to the ground. If I had to guess, she heard a distant rumble that disturbed her, and she ran away before it could come closer."

"Did you speak to her?"

Don didn't answer.

"Don, there's no sense thinking you're going to stonewall me about anything. I can make a phone call and find out who you've talked to, who's written to you, and what was in the letter. You have no privacy. Did you talk to Trudy or didn't you?"

"I did, yes."

"And what did you tell her?" Luke said.

"I told her that her life was in danger."

"Based on what?"

Don looked at the ceiling for a moment. "Luke, you know what you know, and that's good. You also don't know what you don't know. If you have any limitations, that's certainly one of them. What you don't know in this case, because you don't involve yourself in politics, is there's been a quiet war going on behind the scenes for the past six months. The attack at Mount Weather? A lot of high-profile people died that night. And a lot of low-profile people have died since then. I'd say at least as many who died in the original attack. Trudy wasn't involved in the plot against Thomas Hayes, but not everyone believes that. There are people out there seeking retribution."

"So she ran on your say-so?"

"I think so, yes."

"Do you know where she is?"

Don shrugged. "I wouldn't tell you if I did. One day, if she wants you to know where she is, I'm sure she'll be the first to tell you."

Luke had the urge to ask if she was okay, but he controlled himself. He wasn't going to give Don that kind of power—it would be just what the old man wanted. Instead, another pause stretched out between them. The two men sat in the tiny space, staring into each other's eyes. Eventually Don broke the silence.

"So who are you working for, if not the SRT? I have trouble picturing Luke Stone out of work for very long."

Luke shrugged. "I guess you'd say I'm a freelancer, but I only have one client. I work directly for the President, on the rare occasions she calls me. Like she did earlier today, asking me to come out here and see you."

Don raised an eyebrow. "A freelancer? Do they still pay you your salary and benefits?"

"They gave me a raise," Luke said. "As a matter of fact, I think they gave me your old salary."

"Government waste," Don said, taking on his agency administrator persona and shaking his head. "But it suits you. You never were the Monday to Friday type."

Luke didn't answer. From this angle, he could see the view that the window afforded. Nothing—the cinderblock wall of another wing of the building, with a sliver of dark sky visible above.

It was an insidious design. The facility was located in the Rocky Mountains—when Luke arrived tonight, beyond the guard towers and the concrete and the razor wire, he was struck by the vista of the tall peaks that surrounded this place. The air was cold and the mountains were lightly salted with early snow. Even at night, you might say the location was beautiful.

The prisoners would never see it. Luke would bet five dollars that every cell in this prison enjoyed the same vista as every other— a blank wall.

"So what do you want, Don? Susan told me you've got a piece of intelligence you're eager to share, but only with me. I've got a lot going on in my life at this moment, but I came out here because that's my duty. I'm not sure how you obtained this intel, given your current circumstances…"

Don smiled. His eyes were completely divorced from whatever emotion his mouth tried to convey. They seemed like the eyes of an alien, lizard-like, with no empathy, no concern, not even any interest. The eyes of something that might eat you or run from you, but feel nothing while doing so.

"There are some very clever men in here," he said. "You wouldn't believe how intricate the communication system is among the prisoners. I'd love to describe it to you—I think you'd be fascinated—but I also don't want to jeopardize it or put myself at risk. I will give you an example of what I'm talking about, though. Did you hear the man screaming before?"

"Yeah," Luke said. "I didn't catch what it was all about. The guards told me he had gone insane…" His voice trailed off.

Of course. The man had been saying something, if you had the ears to hear it.

"Right," Don said. "The town crier. That's what I call him. He's not the only one, and that's not the only method. Not even close."

"So what do you have?" Luke said.

"There's a plot," Don said, his voice dropping to just above a whisper. "As you know, many of the men in here are affiliated with terrorist networks. They have their own ways of communicating. What I've heard is there's a group in Belgium targeting the old Cold War nukes stored there. The warheads are lightly guarded on a Belgian NATO base. The security is a joke. The terrorists, I'm not sure who, are going to try to steal a warhead, or perhaps a missile, or more than one."

Luke thought about it for a moment. "What good would that do? Without the nuclear codes the warheads aren't even operational. They must be aware of that. It's like risking your life to steal a giant paperweight."

"I'd assume they have the codes," Don said. "They either have access to the codes themselves, or they've discovered a way to generate them."

Luke stared at him. "They have no way to launch a warhead. Without the delivery system, they'll never generate the energy to detonate. This isn't Bugs Bunny. It's not like you can hit the thing with a hammer."

Don shrugged. "Believe what you want to believe, Luke. All I'm telling you is what I heard."

"Is that everything?" Luke said.

"It is."

"So why are you choosing to share it? If someone found out you were passing secrets you picked up in here… well, my guess is that communicating isn't the only thing these guys can do."

Anger flashed across Don's face now, like a brief summer squall on the high seas. Everything became dark for a moment, the storm appeared, then passed. He took a deep breath, apparently to calm himself.

"Why wouldn't I share intelligence that I have? I'm concerned you've got me all wrong, Luke. I'm a patriot, as much as you are, if not more. I was risking my life for the United States before you were even born. I did what I did because I love my country, and not for any other reason. Not everyone agrees it was the right thing to do, and that's why I'm in here. But please don't question my loyalty, and don't question my courage, either. There isn't a man in this facility who frightens me, and that includes you."

Luke was still skeptical. "And you don't want anything in return for this?"

Don didn't say anything for a long moment. He gestured at the messy desk. Then he smiled. There was no humor in it.

"I do want something. It's not a lot to ask." He paused, and looked around the tiny cell. "I don't mind it in here, Luke. Some men really do go crazy—they're the uneducated ones. They have no access to the life of the mind. But I do. To you, it seems like I'm locked away behind cinderblock walls, but to me, it's almost like I'm on sabbatical. I was running for forty years straight, without a chance to take a break. These walls don't imprison me. I've lived enough life for a dozen men, and all of it is still up here."

He tapped himself on the forehead.

"I'm thinking a lot about the old times, the old missions. I've started working on my memoirs. I think it will make for fascinating reading one day."

He stopped. A faraway look entered his eyes. He stared at the wall, but he was seeing something else. "Remember the time in Delta, when they sent us into the Congo to go after the warlord calling himself Prince Joseph? The one with all the child soldiers? Heaven's Army."

Luke nodded. "I remember. The brass at JSOC didn't want you to go. They thought—"

"I was too old. That's right. But I went anyway. And we dropped in there at night, you, me, who else? Simpson—"

"Montgomery," Luke said. "A couple others."

Don's eyes were very alive. "Right. The pilot screwed the pooch and dropped us into the river, one of the tributaries. We all hit the water with forty-pound rucks on."

"I don't like to think about it," Luke said. "I shot that rhinoceros."

Don pointed at him. "That's right. I forgot about that. The rhino charged us. I can still see it in the moonlight. But we crawled up there, soaking wet, and slit that murderous bastard's throat— decapitated his whole team in one swift and decisive strike. And we didn't split a hair on one child's head. I was proud of my men that night. I was proud to be an American."

Luke nodded again, almost smiled. "That was a long time ago."

"For me, it was yesterday," Don said. "I just started writing that one. Tomorrow I'll add the rhino."

Luke didn't say anything. It was a mission, one of many. Don's memoir was going to be one long book.

"So that's my whole point," Don said. "It's not bad in here. The food isn't even bad—well, not as bad as you might expect. I have my memories. I have a life. I've put together a workout routine, most of which I can do right here in the cell. Squats, pushups, chins, even yoga and tai chi moves. I have a sequence, and I move through it for hours each day, change it up, reverse it. It has a mindfulness component to it as well. I believe it would start a fitness craze if people knew about it. I'd like to trademark it— Prison Power. It's put me in much better shape than when I was out in the world and free to do whatever I pleased."

"Okay, Don," Luke said. "This is your retirement villa. That's nice."

Don raised a hand. "I want to live, that's what I'm telling you. They're going to give me the needle. You know it and I know it. I don't want the needle. Listen, I'm realistic. I know I'm not going to get a pardon, not in the current political environment. But if the intelligence I've given you pans out, I want the President to commute my sentence to life in prison without possibility of parole."

Luke was frustrated by their meeting. Don Morris was sitting in what amounted to a stone bathroom, writing his memoirs and developing what he hoped would become an exercise fad. It was pathetic. Luke had once thought of Don as a great American.

The control knob on Luke's blood turned from simmer to boil. He had his own problems, and his own life, but of course Don didn't care much about that. Don had become the center of his own universe in here.

"Why'd you do it, Don?" He gestured at the cell. "I mean..." He shook his head. "Look at this place."

Don didn't hesitate. "I did it to save my country, and I'd do it again. Thomas Hayes was the worst President since Herbert Hoover. Of that, I have no doubt. He was running us into the ground. He had no idea how to project American power in the world, and no inclination to do so. He thought the world took care of itself. He was wrong. The world does NOT take care of itself. We have dark forces arrayed against us—they run amok if for one second we're not watching them. They step into any power vacuum we leave them. They victimize the weak and defenseless. Our friends lose faith. I could no longer stand by and let these things happen."

"And what did you get?" Luke said. "Hayes's vice president is running the country."

Don nodded. "Right. And she has a bigger pair of cojones than he ever did. People surprise you sometimes. I'm not unhappy with Susan Hopkins as President."

"Great," Luke said. "I'll tell her that. I'm sure she'll be delighted to hear it. Don Morris is not unhappy with your presidency." He stood. He was ready to go. This little encounter was going to be a lot to chew on.

Don jumped off the bed. He put his hand on Luke's shoulder again. For a second, Luke thought Don was going to blurt out something emotional, something Luke would find embarrassing, like, "Don't go!"

But Don didn't do that.

"Don't discount what I told you," he said. "If it's real, then we've got trouble. Just one nuclear weapon in the hands of the terrorists would be the worst thing you could dream of. They won't hesitate to use it. One successful launch and the genie is out of the bottle. Who gets hit? Israel? Who do they hit back with their own nukes? Iran? How do you put the brakes on that? Call a time-out? I doubt it. What if we get hit? Or the Russians? Or both? What if automatic retaliatory strikes get triggered? Fear. Confusion. Zero trust. Men in silos, their fingers getting itchy, lingering over that button. There are *a lot* of nuclear weapons left on Earth, Luke. Once they start launching, there's no good reason for them to stop."

CHAPTER SIX

October 20
3:30 a.m.
Georgetown, Washington, DC

A black pickup truck was following him.

Luke had taken a late flight back. Now he was tired—exhausted—and yet still wired and awake. He didn't know when he would sleep again.

The taxi had dropped him off in front of a row of handsome brownstones. The tree-lined streets were quiet and empty. They seemed to shimmer in the light from the ornate overhead lamps. As the cab pulled away, he stood in the street and soaked up the cool night. The trees were losing their leaves—they were all over the ground. As he watched, a few more drifted down.

He had come straight from the airport to Trudy's place. The shades were drawn but at least one light was on in the street level apartment. No one was home—the lights were clearly on a timer, and probably a cheap one from a department store. The pattern was always the same. Trudy must have set it before she left.

She still owned the place—Luke knew that much. Swann had hacked her bank account. There were automatic payments in place for her mortgage, her association fees, and her electricity. She had paid two years of estimated real estate taxes upfront.

She had disappeared, but the apartment was here, going right along by itself as if nothing had happened.

Why did he keep coming here? Did he think she would suddenly be home one night? Did he think these past months would have erased themselves?

He paused for just a few seconds, facing away from the pickup truck, picturing it back there, remembering it from when he had walked passed it just a moment ago.

It was large, heavy duty, the kind of truck you saw on construction sites. The windows in its cab were smoked, making it impossible to see much inside. Even so, he had the sense that there were two silhouettes behind those windows. The truck's headlights had been off when he walked past, and they were still off—there had been no approaching lights to tip him off. What had given the truck away was sound. He could hear its engine rumbling.

There was a gas station and convenience store at the bottom of the hill. It was lit up on the outside above the pumps, but the store itself looked to be closed. Luke walked down the middle of the street, toward the beckoning light.

He glanced to his left and his right without turning his head. On either side, expensive cars were parked nose to tail against the curb in unbroken lines. This was a crowded neighborhood, and there wasn't much parking. There was no obvious way to get off the street and onto the sidewalk.

He broke into a sprint.

He did it without warning. He didn't accelerate gradually from a walk to a run. One moment he was walking, and a heartbeat later he was running as fast as he could. Behind him, the pickup roared into life. Its tires burned rubber on the pavement, the shriek of the wheels tearing open the quiet night.

Luke dove to his right, sliding head first over the hood of a white Lexus. He slid off the car and tumbled onto the sidewalk, landing on his back, rolling into a sitting position while pulling his Glock from the shoulder holster inside his jacket, all in one move.

The Lexus started to disintegrate behind him. The truck had stopped, and its passenger side window was down. A man in a ski mask was there, firing a submachine gun with a giant sound suppressor. The gun had a drum magazine attached to the bottom, probably twelve dozen rounds. Luke absorbed all of this information in an instant, before his conscious mind was even aware of it.

The windows of the Lexus shattered, the tires popped and the car sank to the ground. THUNK, THUNK, THUNK—bullets punched through its side panels. Steam rose from under its hood. The man in the truck was spraying it with machine gun fire.

Luke ran forward, ducking low. The bullets followed him, shattering the next car as it had the Lexus. Glass sprayed all over him.

A car alarm went off, rang for five seconds, then stopped as the bullets pierced the vehicle and destroyed the alarm system.

Luke kept running, his breath hot in his lungs. He reached the gas station and bolted across its wide open yard. The overhead lights cast eerie shadows—the gas pumps seemed like looming monsters. The pickup truck skidded into the lot behind him. Luke glanced back and saw it bounce over the curb and take the corner hard.

He raced down another side street, then darted left into an alley. It was an old cobblestone street. He stumbled over the rough and pitted surface. The truck's engine squealed, very close. Luke didn't look. A grinding, crunching sound came as the truck bounced over the cobblestones.

Luke felt it there—the truck was one second behind him.

His heart pounded in his chest. It was no use. He turned his head and there was the truck, right behind him. Its massive grille barreled forward, growing bigger and bigger as it came. It looked like a huge, grinning mouth. The hood of the truck was nearly as high as his head.

To Luke's left there was a dumpster. He sensed it more than saw it. He dove behind it, falling to the cobblestones, landing hard in a tiny alcove. The impact rattled his bones, and he pressed himself against the wall, as tight as his body would go.

An instant later, the pickup rammed the dumpster, crushing it against the wall of the alley. The truck passed, just missing Luke, dragging the dumpster with it. It skidded to a halt in the alleyway fifty feet past the alcove. Its brake lights shone red. The dumpster was crushed between the driver's side door and the wall.

Luke could retake the initiative, but to do so, he had *to move.*

"Get up," he said.

He hauled himself to his feet, gun in hand, and wedged his body into the alcove. Two-handed, he aimed at the back window of the truck.

BLAM, BLAM, BLAM, BLAM.

The window shattered. The noise of his gun was deafening. It echoed down the alleyway and out into the silent city streets. If he wanted attention, and he did, this would bring it.

The truck's tires screamed and shredded on the cobblestones, the driver trying to get free of that dumpster.

The passenger—the shooter—used the butt of his gun to smash out the remains of the back window. He was going to try for a shot.

Perfect.

BLAM.

Luke shot him, dead center in the forehead.

The man slumped, his head hanging out the back window, his gun clattering uselessly into the pickup's bed.

The truck skidded sideways, its grille sliding along the wall, the driver's side facing Luke now. Luke would take the driver too, if he could, but not with a kill shot. He would keep him alive to answer questions.

The driver was good—better than his friend. His window had been shattered by the collision, but he had ducked way down below it. Luke couldn't see him.

BLAM, BLAM, BLAM.

Luke put three shots into the driver's side door. The sound was hollow, metallic, as the bullets punched through. The driver screamed. He was hit.

Suddenly, the truck skidded sideways to the right, like a joyrider doing donuts in the snow. The pickup bed swung around and rammed the wall. But the truck had broken loose from the dumpster. If the driver was still able, he was free to make a run for it.

Luke aimed at the rear left tire. BLAM.

The tire popped, but the truck squealed out and peeled off down the alley. It bounced out onto the street, skidded, and went left. Gone.

Nearby, sirens were already approaching. Luke could hear them coming from several different directions. He holstered his gun and limped out of the alley, his knee already stiffening. He had scraped it falling to the cobblestones.

A DC police interceptor roared up, lights flashing, throwing crazy blue shadows against the surrounding buildings. Luke already had the badge out for them, the old badge from the defunct FBI Special Response Team. It still had a year left before it expired. He raised his arms high in the air, the badge in his right hand.

"Federal agent!" he shouted at the cops who burst from the car, guns drawn and trained on him.

"On the ground!" they told him.

He did exactly as they said, moving slow and deliberately, no threat to anyone.

"What's going on here?" one of the cops said as he snatched the badge from Luke's outstretched hand.

Luke shrugged.

"Somebody's trying to kill me."

CHAPTER SEVEN

10:20 a.m.
The White House, Washington, DC

It was like a state funeral, the grand opening of a used car lot, and an amateur comedy show rolled into one.

Susan Hopkins, the President of the United States, and wearing a blue dress and shawl made especially for this occasion by the designer Etta Chang, looked out across the South Lawn at the gathered dignitaries and journalists. It was a select group, and the hardest invitation to score in town for the past month. On a bright sunny autumn day, under blue skies, the White House—one of the most enduring symbols of America—was rebuilt and ready to go.

Secret Service men towered behind and just in front of Susan, taking any shooting angles away—she felt almost like she was lost in a forest of tall men. Washington, DC, Virginia, and Maryland were restricted flight zones this morning. If you hadn't flown in by 7 a.m., you were out of luck.

The ceremony was running long. It had started just after 9 a.m., and already it was pushing toward 10:30. Between the opening military procession with the bugler playing Taps and the riderless horse in honor of Thomas Hayes, the release of a flock of white doves to symbolize the many others who had died that day and that night, the fighter jet flyover, the children's choir, and the various speeches and blessings...

Oh yes, the blessings.

The rebuilt house had been blessed, in turn, by an Orthodox rabbi from Philadelphia, a Muslim imam, the Catholic Archbishop of Washington, DC, the minister of the North Capitol Street AME Zion Church, and the famous Buddhist monk and peace activist Thich Nhat Hanh.

The wrangling that had gone into picking the religious dignitaries—that alone had soured Susan's taste for this event. An Orthodox rabbi? The Women of Reform Judaism were vocal with their annoyance—they had pushed for a female rabbi. Sunni or Shiite for the imam—there was no pleasing both. In fact, Kat Lopez had stuck a finger in both their eyes and gone with a Sufi.

Catholic groups were not thrilled about Pierre. The First Gentleman of the USA was gay? And married to a woman? Cats

38

and dogs were lying down together. That question was resolved when Pierre decided to take a miss and watch the event from the apartment in San Francisco.

Pierre and the girls had largely disappeared from public life since the scandal. It was right to keep the girls away from the spotlight after everything that had happened, but this was an important event and Pierre hadn't even wanted to come. That worried Susan a little. Really, more than a little. And of course, now the gay rights activists were furious with him for what they saw as his bowing to pressure from the Catholic Church.

At the podium, Karen White, the new Speaker of the House, was just finishing her speech. Karen was eccentric, to say the least—she wore a hat with a large paper sunflower on it. The hat was more appropriate for a children's Easter egg hunt than for today's event. If Etta Chang saw that hat, it would be time for a fashion makeover.

Karen's remarks had been short on jabs at the liberals in government—thank God, because the special elections to re-constitute the decimated Congress were two weeks away. The campaigns had turned into a mindless hate-filled scramble—historians enjoyed going on CNN and FOX News to claim that the civil discourse in the country had reached its lowest ebb since the Civil War.

What Karen White lacked in offensive rhetoric on the domestic front, she more than made up for on the world stage. Her speech seemed to suggest—to the gasps of many in the audience—that the White House had been destroyed not by rogue elements of the conservative movement and the military here in the USA, but by foreign operatives, possibly from Iran or Russia. During one string of tortured logic, the special envoy from Iran had stood up and stormed away, two of his senior diplomats in tow.

"It's fine," Kurt Kimball, the National Security Advisor, said in Susan's ear. "They all know Karen's a little nutty. I mean, look at her hat. We'll have someone from the State Department make it up to them."

"How?" Susan said.

He shrugged. "I don't know. We'll figure something out."

On the stage, Kat had given Susan the nod. They were ready for her. She stepped onto the stage as Secret Service agents moved into position around her. The podium was surrounded on three sides by clear bulletproof glass. She stood for a moment and surveyed the assembled crowd. She wasn't nervous at all. Talking to the people had always been one of her strong points.

"Good morning," she said. Her voice echoed out over the lawn.

"Good morning," a few wisecrackers shouted back.

She launched comfortably into her prepared speech. It was a good one. She spoke to them about shared sacrifice, and about loss, and about resilience. She told them about the greatness of the American experiment—something they already knew. She told them about the valor of the men who had saved her life that night, and she recognized Chuck Berg—who was now the head of her home security detail, and was standing on stage with her—and Walter Brenna, who was an honored guest in the front row. Both men raised their hands and received thunderous applause.

She told them she was moving into the White House this very day—which brought a standing ovation—and she welcomed them inside after her remarks, to take a tour and see what she'd done with the old place.

She finished with a flourish, echoing that great hero of hers, and of everyone, John Fitzgerald Kennedy.

"Nearly sixty years ago, John Fitzgerald Kennedy was elected President. His inaugural address is one of the greatest and most quoted speeches ever delivered. All of you know that he told us in that speech to ask not what our country could do for us, but what we could do for our country. But you know? There's another part of that speech, less well known, that I enjoy just as much. It seems particularly appropriate for today's events, and I want to leave you with it. What Kennedy said was this."

She took a deep breath, hearing in her mind the pauses that Kennedy had taken. She wanted to get his phrasing exactly right.

"Let every nation know," she said, "whether it wishes us well or ill... that we shall pay any price... bear any burden..."

In the crowd, the cheering had already begun. She waved a hand, but it was no use. They were just going to do it, and her job now was to meet the rising swell of their outburst, somehow get ahead of it and above it, and race it to the finish line.

"Meet any hardship..." she shouted.

"Yes!" someone screamed, somehow cutting through the noise.

"Support any friend," Susan said, and raised her fist in the air. "And oppose any foe... to assure the survival and the success of liberty!"

The crowd had come to its feet. The ovation went on and on.

"This much we pledge," Susan said. "And more." She paused again. "Thank you, my friends. Thank you."

* * *

The inside of the building gave her chills.

Susan moved through the hallways with her Secret Service contingent, Kat Lopez, and two assistants trailing close behind. The group passed through the doors to the Oval Office. Just being in here had a strange effect on her. She'd felt it before, just a week ago, when they'd first given her a tour of the renovated White House. There was something surreal about it.

Almost nothing had changed. That was part of it. The Oval Office seemed just the same as the last time she had seen it—the day it was attacked and destroyed, the day Thomas Hayes and more than three hundred people died. Three tall windows, with drapes pulled back, still looked out on the Rose Garden. Near the center of the office, a comfortable sitting area was situated on top of a lush carpet adorned with the Seal of the President. Even the Resolute Desk—a long-ago gift from the British people—was still there in its customary spot.

Of course, it wasn't the same desk. It had been re-crafted from the original drawings sometime in the past three months in a woodworking shop in the Welsh countryside. But that was her point—everything looked exactly the same. It was almost as if President Thomas Hayes—taller than everyone around him by at least four or five inches—would walk in any minute and give her his customary frown.

Was she traumatized? Was this building a trigger for her?

She knew that she would prefer to live at the Naval Observatory. That grand old house had been her home for the past five years. It was light, open, and airy. She was comfortable there. In comparison, the White House—especially the residence—was creaky, cranky, dreary, and drafty in the winter, with bad light.

It was a big place, but the rooms felt cramped. And there was... something... about the place. You felt like you might turn any corner and run into a ghost. She used to think it would be the ghost of Lincoln or McKinley or even Kennedy. But now she knew it would be Thomas Hayes.

She would move back to the Naval Observatory house in a heartbeat—if only she hadn't given it away. Her new Vice

President, Marybeth Horning, was due to move in there during the next few days. She smiled when she thought of Marybeth—the ultra-liberal senator from Rhode Island—who had been on a fact-finding tour of human rights violations at egg farms in Iowa on the day of the Mount Weather attack. Marybeth was a firebrand for workers' rights, for women's rights, for the environment, for everything Susan cared about.

Elevating her to Vice President had actually been Kat Lopez's idea. It was perfect—Marybeth was such an outspoken leftist that no one on the right would ever want to see Susan killed. They'd just wind up with their worst nightmare as President. And under the new Secret Service rules, Susan and Marybeth would never be in the same place at the same time for the rest of Susan's term—hence Marybeth's absence from the festivities today. That was kind of a shame because Susan liked Marybeth.

Susan sighed and glanced around the office again. Her mind wandered. She remembered the day of the attack. She and Thomas had been estranged for a couple of years. Susan didn't really mind. She was having fun being Vice President, and David Halstram—Thomas's chief-of-staff—made sure her schedule was kept busy with events far away from the President.

But that day, David had asked her to fly in and be by the President's side. Thomas's approval ratings had cratered, and the Speaker of the House had just called for his impeachment. He was under siege, all because he didn't want to go to war with Iran. Of course, the Speaker was Bill Ryan, one of the leaders of the coup, who at this moment was in a federal prison, preparing to be transferred to death row.

She remembered how she and Thomas were poring over a map of the Middle East right in this office. They weren't talking about anything, just bantering about this or that. It was a photo op, not an actual strategy meeting.

Suddenly, two men burst in.

"FBI!" one of them screamed. "I have an important message for the President."

One of those men was Agent Luke Stone.

Her life had changed in that instant, and had not returned to normal since then. Her previous life might never come back, she realized. Her marriage had nearly been destroyed by scandal. Her daughter had been kidnapped. Susan had aged ten years in six months, as she weathered one terrorist or political attack after another.

Now she was faced with sleeping in this drafty old house, alone. They had spent a billion dollars renovating the place, and she did not want to live here. Hmmm. She would have to talk to Kat, or someone, about this.

"Susan?"

She looked up. It was Kurt Kimball. His sudden appearance snapped her back to reality. Kurt was tall and broad, with a head as round and smooth as a cue ball. His eyes were bright and alert. He was the picture of vitality and health at fifty-three. He was one of the people who thought fifty was the new thirty. Until she became President, Susan would have agreed with him. Now she wasn't so sure. She was two years shy of half a century herself. If things kept up the way they had been going, by the time she got there, fifty was going to be the new sixty.

"Hello again, Kurt."

"Susan, Agent Stone is here. He interviewed Don Morris in Colorado last night. He thinks he may have intelligence we want to hear. I haven't spoken with him yet, but my people tell me he was involved in an incident when he arrived back in Washington early this morning."

"An incident? What does that mean?" It didn't sound good. But then again, when *wasn't* Agent Stone involved in an incident?

"There was a shootout in Georgetown. Two men in a truck apparently tried to murder him. Luke killed one. The other escaped."

Susan stared at Kurt. "Was it related to Don Morris?"

Kurt shook his head. "We don't know. But it happened about two blocks from the apartment of Trudy Wellington. Wellington has disappeared, as you know, but it seems that Stone went to her apartment as soon as he landed from interviewing Morris. The whole thing is very… unusual."

Susan took a deep breath. Stone had saved her life more than once. He had rescued her daughter from the kidnappers. He had saved countless lives during the Ebola crisis, and during the North Korean crisis. He had even done the world a favor and assassinated the dictator of North Korea while he was there. He was an invaluable asset to Susan's administration. More than that, he was Susan's secret weapon. But he was also unstable, he was violent, and he appeared to involve himself in things that he shouldn't.

"Anyway," Kurt said. "We have him here, and he has a report to give. I think we should break in the new Situation Room right away and debrief him."

43

Susan nodded. It was almost a relief to have something to sink her teeth into. The Situation Room here at the White House was a dedicated space, nothing like the converted conference room they had been using at the Naval Observatory. It was a totally renovated and updated command center, with the latest in high-tech wizardry. It would expand their strategic capabilities tremendously—or so she was told.

The only problem? It was underground, and Susan liked windows.

"Give me a few moments to get changed, okay?" Susan indicated the fancy, one-of-a-kind designer dress she wore. "I don't know if this thing works for an intelligence meeting."

Kurt smiled. He made a show of looking her up and down.

"Nah. Come on. You look great. People will be impressed—you came right in from the dedication and went to work."

* * *

Luke rode the elevator with a crowd of people in suits, down to the Situation Room. He was tired—he had spent two hours being interviewed by the DC cops, then caught a few hours of fitful sleep. He had missed the dedication ceremony entirely.

Things like the rebuilt White House and its reopening just weren't on his mind. He barely noticed the place, or the crowds ooohing and ahhhing over it. He was lost in a forest of dark thoughts—about himself and his life, about Becca and Gunner, and about Don Morris, his choices and the end to which he had come. Luke had also killed a man last night, and he still had no idea why.

The elevator opened into the egg-shaped Situation Room. It was smaller and more cramped than the former conference room they'd been using over at the Naval Observatory. It was also less ad hoc, less tossed together. The place looked like the command module on a Hollywood spaceship. It was set up for maximum use of the space, with large screens embedded in the walls every couple of feet, and a giant projection screen on the far wall at the end of the table. Tablet computers and slim microphones rose from slots out of the conference table—they could be dropped back into the table if the attendee wanted to use their own device.

Every plush leather seat at the table was occupied—mostly with middle-aged, overweight decision makers. The seats along the walls were filled with young aides and even younger assistants, most of them tapping messages into tablets, or speaking into telephones.

Susan Hopkins sat in a chair at the closest end of the oblong table. At the far end stood Kurt Kimball, Susan's National Security Advisor. A sprawl of usual suspects took up the seats in between them.

Kurt noticed Luke enter and clapped his big hands. It made a sound like a heavy book dropping to a stone floor. "Order, everybody! Come to order, please."

The place quieted down. A few aides continued to talk along the wall.

Kurt clapped his hands again.

CLAP. CLAP.

The room went dead quiet.

"Hi, Kurt," Luke said. "I like your new command center."

Kurt nodded. "Agent Stone."

Susan turned to Luke and they shook hands. Luke's big hand swallowed her tiny one. "Madam President," he said. "Good to see you again."

"Welcome, Luke," she said. "What do you have for us?"

He looked at Kurt. "Are you ready for my report?"

Kurt shrugged. "That's why we're here. If it weren't for you, we'd all be upstairs enjoying the festivities."

Luke nodded. It had been a long day, and it was still early. He wanted to finish this up and go out to the country house he had once shared with Becca. Everything was too much right now, and what he most wanted to do was take a nap. Just nap on the couch, and maybe later, in the late afternoon, sit outside with a coffee and watch the sun set over the water. He had a lot to think about, and a lot of planning to do. An image of Gunner appeared in his mind.

All eyes were on him. He took a deep breath. He repeated what Don had told him. Islamic terrorists were going to steal nuclear weapons from an air base in Belgium.

A tall heavyset man with blond hair raised a hand. "Agent Stone?"

"Yes."

"Haley Lawrence. Secretary of Defense."

Luke had known that. But until this moment, he had forgotten it.

"Mr. Secretary," he said. "What can I do for you?"

The man gave a slight smile, almost a smirk. "Please share with us how you think Don Morris obtained this intelligence. He's

45

in a federal high-security facility, the highest security we currently have, held in isolation in his cell twenty-three hours a day, and has no direct contact with anyone except the guards."

Luke smiled. "I think that's a question for the guards to answer."

A ripple of laughter went around the room.

"I've known Don Morris a long time," Luke said. "He's probably one of the most resourceful people alive in the United States at this moment. I have no doubt that he receives intelligence, even in his current location. Is it accurate intelligence? I have no idea, nor does he. He doesn't have any way to confirm it or discredit it. I guess that's our job."

He gave Kurt a sidelong glance. "Those are all the details I have. Any thoughts?"

Kurt paused for a moment, then nodded. "Sure. This will be a little bit on the fly, but mostly accurate. Belgium has been much on my mind in recent years, for obvious reasons." He turned to an aide standing behind him. "Amy, can you bring us up a map of Belgium? Key in on Molenbeek and Kleine Brogel, if you don't mind."

The young woman fiddled with her tablet, while another aide turned on the main display monitor behind Kurt. A few seconds passed. The monitor ran through a few internal tests, then showed a blue desktop. A quiet buzz of conversation started again.

Kurt watched his aide. She nodded to him, and then he looked at the President.

"Susan, are you ready?"

"Ready when you are."

A map of Europe appeared on the screen behind him. It quickly zoomed in to focus on Western Europe, and then Belgium.

"Okay. Behind me, you see a map of Belgium. There are two locations in that country I want to call your attention to. The first is the capital city, Brussels."

Behind him, the map zoomed again. Now it showed the dense grid of a city, with a ring highway circling it. The map moved to the upper left-hand corner, and several photographs of cobblestone streets, a government building from the nineteenth century, and a stately and ornate bridge over a canal.

He turned to his aide. "Bring up Molenbeek, please."

The map zoomed again, and more photos of streets appeared. In one, a group of bearded men marched carrying a white banner, fists pumping the air. The top of the banner had Arabic characters written in black. Below that was the apparent English translation:

No to Democracy!

"Molenbeek is a suburb of about ninety-five thousand people. It is the most densely populated section of Brussels, and parts of it run as high as eighty percent Muslim, mostly of Turkish and Moroccan descent. It's a hotbed of extremism. The weapons used in the *Charlie Hebdo* magazine attack were cached beforehand in Molenbeek. The 2015 Paris terror attacks were planned there, and the perpetrators of that crime are all men who grew up and lived in Molenbeek."

Kurt looked around the room. "In short, if there are terror attacks being planned in Europe, and we can safely assume there are, there's a pretty good chance that the planning is taking place in Molenbeek. Are we clear on this?"

A ripple of agreement went through the room.

"Okay, let's see Kleine Brogel."

On the screen, the map zoomed out, scrolled to the right a short distance, then zoomed in again. Luke could make out runways and buildings at a rural airfield not far from a small town.

"Kleine Brogel Air Base," Kurt said. "It's a Belgian military airfield located about sixty miles east of Brussels. The village you see there is the municipality of Kleine Brogel, hence the name of the base. The base is home to the Belgian Tenth Tactical Wing. They fly F-16 Falcons, supersonic jet fighters, which among other capabilities, can deliver B61 nuclear bombs."

On the screen, the map disappeared and an image materialized. It was of a missile-shaped bomb, mounted on a wheeled trundle and parked beneath the fuselage of a fighter jet. The bomb was long and sleek, gray with a black tip.

"Here you see the B61," Kurt said. "Not quite twelve feet long, about thirty inches in diameter, and weighing in at about seven hundred pounds. It's a variable yield weapon that can put as many as three hundred forty kilotons on a target—roughly twenty times the magnitude of the Hiroshima explosion. Compare that yield to the megatons of the large ballistic missiles, and you can see that the B61 is a small tactical nuke. It's designed to be carried by fast airplanes, like the F-16. You'll note its streamlined shape— that's so it can withstand the speeds its delivery craft are likely to reach. These are American-made bombs, and we share them with Belgium as part of our NATO agreements."

"So the bombs are onsite there?" Susan said.

Kurt nodded. "Yes. I'd say about thirty of them. I can get you the exact figure, if we need it."

Another ripple went through the gathered crowd.

Kurt raised his hand. "It gets better. Kleine Brogel is a political football in Belgium. Many Belgians hate the fact that the bombs are there, and want them out of the country. In 2009, a group of Belgian peace activists decided to show everyone how unsafe the bombs were. They breached the security of the base."

The map reappeared on the screen. Kurt indicated an area along the bottom edge of the base. "To the south of the airfield there are some dairy farms. The activists walked across the farmland, then climbed the fence. They wandered around the base for at least forty-five minutes before anyone noticed they were there. When they were finally intercepted—by a Belgian airman with an unloaded rifle, by the way—they were standing right outside a bunker where some of the bombs were stored. They had already spray-painted slogans on the bunker and put up some of their stickers."

Chatter erupted in the room again, louder and more pronounced this time.

"Okay, okay. It was a serious lapse in security. But before we get carried away, let's recognize a few things. For one, the bunkers were locked—there was no danger the activists were going to get inside. Also, the bombs are stacked in chambers underground—even if the activists did somehow make it inside, they wouldn't have been able to operate the hydraulic lifts to bring the bombs to the surface. The activists were on foot, so even if they managed to operate the lifts, they wouldn't have gotten very far carrying a weapon that weighs seven hundred pounds."

"So, with all that in mind, what is your assessment of the risk level?" Haley Lawrence said.

Kurt took a long pause. He seemed to stare at something very far away for a moment. To Luke, it was if Kurt's mind was a calculator, currently attaching numbers to the various elements he had just described, then adding, subtracting, multiplying, and dividing them.

"High," he said.

"High?"

Kurt nodded. "Yes, of course. It's a high-level threat. Could a group be planning to steal a bomb from Kleine Brogel? Sure. This isn't the first time we've heard this idea—it arises from time to time in terrorist network chatter that NSA and the Pentagon pick up. A terror cell in Brussels might have a contact or contacts at the airbase who can help them—in fact, this is a very likely scenario. Yes, the bombs aren't operational without the nuclear codes, and yes, they're meant to be delivered by supersonic aircraft. But what if the Iranians want the bombs simply to reverse engineer them, or even just to mine them for the nuclear material? The militants in Molenbeek tend to be Sunnis, and they hate Iran. Our militants could be mercenaries, willing to hire themselves out to the highest bidder.

"Or consider this," Kurt continued. "The Somali air force has a handful of obsolete supersonic jets. Most are in disrepair, but I bet one or two could still get airborne. The Somali government is weak, under constant attack from radical Islam, and teetering on the verge of collapse. What if militant Islamists commandeer one of these aircraft, mount a bomb on it, and crash the entire plane in a nuclear suicide attack?"

"Didn't you just say the bombs won't work without the codes?" Susan said.

Kurt shrugged. "Nuclear codes are among the most advanced encryption on the planet. To our knowledge, they've never been broken, leaked, or stolen. But that doesn't mean they won't be. In worst-case-scenario planning, I'd say the safest assumption is that one day the codes will be broken, if they aren't already."

"So what do you suggest we do?"

Kurt didn't hesitate. "Beef up security at Kleine Brogel Airbase. Do it immediately. We have troops there, but they're in a constant state of tension with the Belgians. To get any meaningful increase in security, we're going to have to step on some toes. I'd also reexamine security measures at the other NATO bases where American nuclear weapons are stored. I think we'll find that these are in pretty good shape. For lax security, the Belgians really take the cake.

"Finally, I'd do something that I've wanted to do for a while—put a few special operatives on the ground in Brussels, specifically Molenbeek. Have them poke around and ask some questions. This is the kind of thing the Belgians should be doing on a regular basis, but don't. It wouldn't necessarily have to be a secret operation—it might even be better if it isn't. Just have the right agents go in there, ones who don't normally take no for an answer, and lean hard on a few people."

Nearly exhausted, Luke was only half-listening. He was mostly trying to hang on until the meeting ended. Slowly, he became aware that many of the people in the room were staring at him.

He raised his palms and leaned back.

"Thanks," he said, "but no."

* * *

"So who's trying to kill you?" Susan said.

Luke sat in a high-backed leather chair in the sitting area of the Oval Office. Beneath his feet was the Seal of the President of the United States. The last time he was here, the Secret Service had him face-down against that seal. But of course, that was a different carpet—although it looked identical, this was an entirely new room. The other one had been destroyed. For a moment, he had forgotten that.

Man, he was tired.

An aide had brought Luke a cup of coffee in a Styrofoam cup. Maybe that would help him wake up. He sipped it—the President's coffee was always good.

"I don't know," he said. "Last I heard, they were running some DNA and fingerprint tests on the dead guy."

Luke studied Susan's face. She had aged. The lines in her skin had deepened and become creases. The skin itself was not as firm and buoyant. Somehow, she had kept her adolescent beauty well into middle age, but in six months as President, time had caught up with her.

Luke thought of the youthful, middle-aged Abraham Lincoln becoming President, a man so energetic and physically powerful he was renowned for his parlor trick feats of strength. Four years later, just before he was assassinated, the stress of the Civil War had turned him into a frail and wizened old man.

Susan was still beautiful, but it was different now. She looked almost *weathered.* He wondered what she thought about it, or if she had even noticed it yet. Then he answered his own question—of course she had noticed it. She was a former supermodel. She probably noticed the smallest changes to her appearance. For the first time, he noticed the dress she was wearing. It was deep blue, very fancy, and clung perfectly to her shape. The neckline was ruffles—there, but understated.

"Hey, nice dress," he said.

She gestured at it with mock disdain. "This old thing? It's just something I threw on. You did know we were having a ceremony today, didn't you?"

Luke nodded. He knew. "It's amazing," he said. "The way they put this place back together exactly the way it was before."

"It's a little creepy if you ask me," Susan said. She glanced around at the high-ceilinged room. "I lived at the Naval Observatory for five years. I love that house. I wouldn't mind living there the rest of my life. This place is going to take some getting used to."

They lapsed into silence. Luke was here simply to pay his respects. In another minute, he was going to ask her for a car, or preferably a helicopter, to take him out to the Eastern Shore.

"So what do you think?" she said.

"What do I think? About what?"

"About the meeting we just had."

Luke yawned. He was tired. "I don't know what to think. Do we have nuclear weapons in Europe? Yes. Are they vulnerable? It sounds like they could be more secure than they are. Beyond that…"

He trailed off.

"Will you go?" she said.

Luke almost laughed. "You don't need me in Belgium, Susan. Just put an extra security detail at the base there, preferably Americans, and preferably carrying loaded weapons. That should do the trick."

Susan shook her head. "If it's a credible threat, we should get to the source of it. Listen, we've been playing footsie with the Belgians far too long. There have been too many attacks coming out of Brussels, and I'd like to break those networks. It's beyond the pale that after the Paris attacks they didn't put all of Molenbeek on lockdown. Sometimes I wonder whose side they're on."

Luke raised his hands. "Susan…"

"Luke," she said. "I need you to do this. There's something that didn't get covered in the meeting. It makes all of this a lot more urgent than you might think. Kurt knows about it, I know about it, but no one else who was there knows."

"What is it?"

She hesitated. "Luke…"

"Susan, you called me yesterday and had me fly out to Colorado on two hours' notice. I did as you asked. Now you want me to go to Belgium. You say it's important, but you don't want to tell me why. You know my wife has cancer? I only mention that so you know exactly what you're asking me to do."

For a second, he thought he was going to tell her more, maybe tell her everything. He and his wife had split up. She was from a wealthy family, but Luke didn't want any money from her. He just wanted to see his son on a regular basis, and Becca was threatening that. She had been gearing up for a custody battle, but now, suddenly, she had cancer. She was probably going to die. And still she wanted to fight. The whole thing had knocked Luke off his feet. He had no idea what to do or where to turn. He felt completely lost.

"Luke, I'm so sorry."

"Thank you. It's hard. We've been having a lot of problems, and now this."

She was staring directly into his eyes. "If it helps any, I understand. My parents died when I was young. My husband seems to have checked out of our marriage, and become a recluse. I don't even blame him. Who would want more of what they've been putting him through? But he's taken my girls with him. I know what it's like to feel alone—I guess that's what I'm saying."

Luke was surprised that she would open up to him like that. It made him realize how much she trusted him, and made him want to help her even more.

"Okay," Luke said. "Then tell me why this so important."

"There's been a data breach at the Department of Energy. No one knows the extent of it yet, whether it was accident or was planned. No one knows anything. A lot of information is just gone, including thousands of legacy nuclear codes. No one can even say whether that matters—would they even still work? It's going to take some time to get this sorted out, but in the meantime, the last thing we can afford is to lose a nuclear weapon."

He sat back. He would go. With any luck, he would get over there, knock a couple of heads together, tighten up the security protocols and be back in a couple of days. In his mind's eye, he saw Gunner in the backyard shooting baskets.

By himself.

"Okay," Luke said. "I'll need my team. Ed Newsam, Mark Swann. And I'm down a member. I need an intel officer to replace Trudy Wellington. Somebody good."

Susan nodded and flashed a smile of gratitude.

"Whatever you need."

CHAPTER EIGHT

5:15 p.m. (Eastern Daylight Time)
The Skies Above the Atlantic Ocean

"Are we ready for this, kids?"

The six-seat Learjet screamed north and east across the afternoon sky. The jet was dark blue with the Secret Service seal on the side. Behind it, the sun began to set. Luke gazed out his window to the east. It was already dark ahead of them—it was late fall, and the days were getting shorter. Far below, the ocean was vast, endless, and deep green.

Luke used his typical psych-up lingo, but it was rote. He didn't feel it. He'd been awake too long. He had too much weighing on him. And he had taken on a job that he probably didn't need to take.

He and his team used the front four passenger seats as their meeting area. They stowed their luggage, and their gear, in the seats at the back.

In the seat across the aisle from him sat big Ed Newsam, in khaki cargo pants, a long-sleeved T-shirt, and a light jacket. He dropped his sunglasses over his eyes, against the sun streaming in his window. When he was relaxed, as he seemed right now, all of the muscle tension would go out of Ed's brawny, hyper-athletic body. He was like a flat tire draped across the seat. Ed was weapons and tactics, and Luke had rarely met a man more qualified—Ed himself was about as devastating a weapon as you could ask for.

Across from Luke and to the left, facing him, was Mark Swann. He was tall and thin, with long sandy hair pulled into a ponytail and fancy black-framed rectangular glasses—Calvin Klein. He stretched his long legs out into the aisle. He wore an old pair of faded jeans and a pair of big black Doc Marten combat boots. The boots made Luke smile—the man had never seen a minute of actual combat in his life, not that Luke would want him to. Swann was information systems—a wisecracking former hacker who got busted and joined the government to avoid a long prison sentence.

Swann and Newsam had come back from the Grand Canyon a couple days early—they said it wasn't the same without Luke and Gunner.

"Babysitting some out-of-date nukes?" Swann said now. "I suppose I'm ready."

"Worse," Luke said. "We're going to babysit some Belgians while they babysit some out-of-date nukes."

"You really think that's all there is to this, man?" Ed said.

Luke shook his head. "No. I think it's deceptive. I think we need to keep our eyes wide open and our heads—"

"On a swivel," Swann said.

They were playing their roles, and that was good. Swann and Newsam were tiptoeing around the news of Becca's cancer. Other than offering their condolences when they first climbed on board, they hadn't said anything about it, and he didn't blame them. It was a hard thing to talk about.

Directly across from Luke sat the newest member of the team—in fact, she wasn't even really a member yet. This was her first time with them. The Secret Service had borrowed her from the FBI on the recommendation of her superiors. She had barely said a word since they'd boarded the plane. Luke turned his attention to her now.

He had seen her dossier. Her name was Mika Dolan. She had been born in China, but given up for adoption by her parents, who had wanted a boy. She was adopted by a couple of aging hippies who realized late in life that they wanted a child. She grew up first on the coast in far northern California, then in Marin County, just outside San Francisco. She was young—probably too young. Twenty-one years old and already a year out of MIT; 4.0 grade point average, graduated magna cum laude. Tested IQ of 169—genius level, Albert Einstein territory.

Hobbies? She liked to surf. That part blew Luke's mind a little—she was a tiny little person, with big round glasses, and looked like she had barely been out of the house, never mind out on the water. But apparently, her dad loved to surf the big waves along the Pacific coast, and had his daughter on a board starting at the age of three.

Mika was the science and intel officer, starting her second year at the FBI, and now on loan to Luke. Whatever Mika's natural gifts were, she had big shoes to fill. Trudy Wellington was a lot of things—emotional, secretive, and quietly dangerous came to mind—but she had developed extensive networks in less than ten years, could access data no one else seemed to have, and was the best scenario spinner that Luke had ever worked with. Trudy was

MIT, just like Mika. They had probably given him Mika for that reason.

"Well, Mika?" Luke said. "Would you like to start?"

"Okay," she said, struggling to maintain eye contact with him. She lifted her tablet computer from the seat beside her. "I'm a little nervous. You guys might not know this, but you're kind of legendary in my office."

"Oh yeah?" Ed Newsam said, apparently pleased. "What do they say about us?"

Mika suppressed a smile. "They say you're a bunch of cowboys. And they told me to try not to get killed while I'm with you."

Ed shook his head. "They're teasing you. Not everybody who comes with us gets killed."

"Only about four in ten," Swann said. "The rest live, although a high percentage of those are maimed for life. You'll probably be okay. The Bureau has a pretty good disability package, as I recall. "

Luke smiled, but didn't join in. Mika was very pretty, and the guys were flirting with her. He would let it go for another minute. It was a good way to break the ice, and maybe set her at ease a bit. This could be a hard-nosed group.

Luke himself felt wistful, not great. He doubted he could join in the banter if he wanted to. He had called Becca before they left. The conversation hadn't gone well. It had barely gone at all. He had told her he was leaving.

"Where are you going?" she said.

"Belgium. Outside Brussels. There's some concern about nuclear weapons stored on a NATO air base there. A terrorist cell is apparently going to—"

"So you're just going to leave?" she said.

"I'll be gone two or three days. I'm just going to inspect the security measures in place, implement some upgrades if necessary, then go into Brussels and question a few people of interest."

"Torture them?"

"Becca, I don't—"

"I have a Secret Service agent standing here in my living room, Luke. He just appeared on my doorstep this afternoon. Another one picked Gunner up at school today. Apparently, he walked right into the classroom before the children were even dismissed."

"Someone tried to kill me last night," Luke said. "The Secret Service are there for your—"

"Protection, yes, I know. Luke, I have cancer. We were going to break this news to Gunner together. You agreed to that. Now you're fleeing the country."

"Someone tried to kill me last night," Luke said again.

"Yes, I heard that part. Did it surprise you? Par for the course, I'd say. Meanwhile, my life is in actual danger, you made a commitment to me and more importantly to your son, and now you're running away. Again."

Luke took a deep breath. "Becca, I want to help you. I want to… do everything I can. But you kicked me out of the house the last time I saw you. And the time before that, come to think of it. When I picked up Gunner last time, I met you in a supermarket parking lot because you didn't want me to come to the house. And I'm not fleeing the country. I'm going to be gone a few days. I assume you'll still be alive when I—"

She hung up on that line, and he didn't blame her. It was a horrible thing to say. But she had gone out of her way to make his life a living hell the past several months. Now she was probably dying. Luke was sorry about that. He felt terrible about it, and about their relationship. He felt like a failure in every way—as a father, as a husband, as a person. But the way she was acting wasn't helping.

Now, aboard the plane, he shook his head to clear it. He had to compartmentalize. He was having problems, yes. He could recognize that he was in deep, deep trouble. He didn't know how to help his wife. He did not know how to fix any of this. But he also couldn't bring it with him to Europe. It would distract him from what he was doing, and then he'd become a danger to himself and the people with him. His focus on the job had to be total.

He glanced out the window. Far away, three F-18 fighter jets streaked across the sky, moving fast. Below Luke, white clouds skidded by in the last of the day's light. He took a deep breath. He looked at Mika again.

"How do you want to do this?" she said.

He made a two-handed gesture that seemed to draw a circle around the group. "The way we normally do it is you give us everything, every piece of intelligence you have, organized in order of importance, unless you have a compelling reason to go in another direction. Assume that we have no prior knowledge about the case at all—that way everybody ends up on the same page, no matter how much intel they came in with."

She nodded, then looked back down at her tablet. "I can do that."

"Let's start with the issue nearest and dearest to my heart," Luke said. "Who tried to kill me last night?"

"The man's name was Azab Mu'ayyad," Mika said. "Or at least that's what his current passport says. His papers indicate that he's a graduate student from Jordan and is thirty-two years old. But the man we believe him to be has at least ten aliases, and passports from four other countries. His name in Arabic means 'traveler blessed by God,' and it's likely this is just another self-applied alias."

"So who was he, really?" Luke said.

She was conferring with her tablet. She gazed into its glowing face, her thumbs moving in a blur. "NSA believes he was a Tunisian mujahid and hitman by the name of Abu Mossaui, which itself is another alias. He's probably closer to forty years old than thirty, a soldier for hire, and an enforcer among hardline Sunni groups. He was thought to have been active in Sub-Saharan Africa. He may have been involved in the kidnapping and execution of the Somali warlord Fatah al-Malik. There is data to suggest he was in Tanzania in 2011 at the time a beachfront resort there was bombed, killing thirteen members of an Israeli tour group."

"What kind of data?" Swann said.

Mika shrugged. "Flight records of a man arriving in Dar es Salaam with a name very similar to one of his known aliases. Surveillance photographs of a man in the old city who might have been him."

"Photographs that might be him," Ed Newsam said. "A man who had a similar name. Basically, you're saying nobody is sure who or what this guy was. He was a ghost, in other words."

Mika nodded. "He was a ghost, if you like."

"I do like. And he tried to kill Luke hours after our boy interviewed Don Morris in prison, and found out about a nuke plot in Europe. So they brought in a hitter—"

She raised a finger. "Careful. Luke has a long history of fighting Islamic terror groups, any number of which might want him eliminated, or want to take revenge on him. The two events could be unrelated."

"Who owns the pickup truck?" Luke said.

"No one owns it," she said.

"No one?"

"The original truck was a 2009 Ford F-350. It was totaled in a fatal accident three years ago. The owner, who was driving, was thrown through the windshield when the truck flipped in rainy and snowy conditions on a highway in western Pennsylvania. The truck was taken to a salvage yard, where it was sold for parts in a cash transaction to a mechanic allegedly based in Youngstown, Ohio. The mechanic was operating under an assumed identity. There's a city-owned vacant lot where his garage is supposed to be. The lot is a brownfield left over from a nineteenth-century leather tannery. The site received federal Superfund money in the late 1980s, but was apparently never mitigated. There has never been an auto mechanic shop located there."

"The truck is a ghost, too," Swann said. "The mechanic is a ghost. Even the garage is a ghost."

"And the Superfund money got ghosted," Ed said.

"Naturally."

The two men tapped each other's hands.

"The truck was rebuilt from junked parts of other trucks," Mika said. "Who did this is unknown. The license plates were stolen from a car stashed in long-term parking at BWI Airport. The registration is a fake, and the construction company it's registered to is a fake. The insurance cards are also clever forgeries."

"And the driver from last night?" Luke said.

Mika shrugged. "He abandoned the truck and escaped. There were no identifiable fingerprints—he must have been wearing gloves."

"I shot him, probably three times."

She nodded. "You definitely shot him. There was blood all over the driver's seat, and spatters of blood led away from the truck. The FBI lab took DNA from the blood, and has begun searching it against databases throughout the United States and Europe, with no matches thus far. We've also sent DNA samples to the Pakistani, Turkish, Saudi Arabian, and Egyptian intelligence services, but if we'll ever get a response, or if we'll believe the response we get, is anybody's guess."

"What about emergency rooms?" Luke said.

"Nine men received treatment for gunshot wounds in DC area hospitals last night, all of whom had accounts of their injuries that were corroborated by eyewitnesses. If your driver was treated for his wounds, it wasn't in a Metro hospital."

"Other areas?" Luke said.

"Baltimore, Philadelphia, Richmond, Norfolk Virginia, and Wilmington, Delaware. It's all the same story. No unexplained gunshot wounds walked in the door last night."

Luke was reasonably impressed. She was young, but she was good at tracking down details. She had taken this about as far as could be expected before reaching a dead end. Of course, Trudy Wellington would have checked hospitals as far away as the New York metro region and Boston, and probably would have sent agents to interview DC area doctors who had lost their licenses and were treating criminal gangs at under-the-radar trauma clinics, but Luke wasn't sure that was a fair comparison. Trudy was thirty years old and had been with the FBI eight years—Mika was just starting.

"So we've got a corpse who might have been a Tunisian hitman, and we've got a truck that disappeared, then reappeared, and belongs to no one. We've got a getaway driver who was shot, and also disappeared. I'm willing to guess that this hit was in some way related to my conversation with Don. It's theoretically true that some terror group or another might want to murder me for revenge, but it just doesn't happen. People don't try to kill me that often— especially not while I'm out minding my own business."

"Is that what you were doing?" Swann said.

Luke looked at him.

Swann shrugged. "I know where the shootout happened. You were two blocks from Trudy's apartment. I'd hardly call that minding your own business. Either they followed you there, or they were already there, watching her place. Considering everything that's happened with Trudy and with Don—"

"All of which would confirm my point, wouldn't it? That it's related in some way to my conversation with Don?"

"I guess. Is this case all you talked about with him?"

Luke shook his head. "No."

"Care to elaborate?" Ed Newsam said.

Luke grunted. "Okay. Sure. Don and I talked at length about an exercise program he's developing. How to stay fit and strong while living in a seven-by-twelve-foot box. He wants to call it Prison Power. I wish I was joking."

He looked at Mika again. She had flushed crimson. The location of the shootout was something she had apparently known, but was reluctant to bring up. Or maybe the tension between team members embarrassed her. It didn't matter—she'd get over it, or she wouldn't.

"Let's move on, shall we?" Luke said. "Give us what else you've got."

He drifted a bit as Mika launched into the details of the Cold War nukes stored in Belgium, about the peace activists who had breached security there, and about the Brussels-based terrorist networks likely being harbored in the Islamic enclave of Molenbeek. He had gotten it all at the White House briefing, but Swann and Newsam hadn't, and it was important they hear it.

When it was over, Luke asked what to him was the million-dollar question:

"So what does your gut say?" he said.

Mika seemed confused. "My gut?"

He nodded. "Sure. You've got all this data, and I imagine you've digested it to some extent. What thoughts do you have? Are the nukes really in danger, or is something else happening? Will the attack come from Molenbeek? Is there any merit to this at all?"

Mika gave him a blank stare. This was where Trudy normally earned her keep—really, any smart person with proficiency in government databases and slicing through red tape could track down the data. The gold was in deciding what the data meant.

These were the moments when Trudy would bring in an idea straight from left field, or work backwards from a hypothesis that no one else had even considered. She would make bold, half-crazy assertions that couldn't be true—and then demonstrate step-by-step why they were not only plausible, but in fact the most likely possibility.

Mika slowly shook her head, clearly disappointed she was letting them down.

"I have no idea," she said.

CHAPTER NINE

"I need you guys, that's all I'm saying. I can't do this all by myself. I can't be this person, and also be alone. I don't have the strength."

Susan pressed her phone to her ear as she talked. She had changed into a pair of old blue jeans, faded and ripped and sprung in all the right spots. She wore a hooded sweatshirt pulled over a wife-beater T-shirt she'd had since forever. She was wearing flip-flops and socks at the same time. If the photographers could only see her now. But she was stuck in this big scary house for the night, so she might as well be comfortable.

She sat alone at the alcove table in the family kitchen, taking her dinner. It was a room she had been in only a handful of times when Thomas Hayes was President. She reminded herself, for the umpteenth time, that it was not the same place. The entire Residence had been blown to smithereens—she remembered a giant chunk of it flying into the sky while she was escaping by helicopter.

It was a different kitchen—it just looked the same. Maybe it was a little roomier, brighter, with a more efficient use of space. But still, you'd never notice.

"I know that, sweetheart," Pierre was saying. "I want to be there for you. I hate it that I'm not. But I want to protect the girls. I want them to grow up safe from all this... insanity."

"I know," Susan said. "I know it. I want that for them, too. More than anything."

She took a bite of the chicken salad the chef had made at her request. She just wanted something light and simple—chicken salad, grapes, some crusty bread, and a little white wine—after a long, ridiculous day. But of course the chef had outdone himself. It was the best chicken salad she'd tasted in probably the past ten years—the tiniest bit tart, with raisins and walnut pieces embedded in it.

God, that was good.

"They're happy here," Pierre said. "They're away from all those pressures, all that scrutiny. They're free to be normal kids."

Susan smiled and shook her head. Pierre had a slightly skewed idea of what it meant to be normal. She loved her beautiful twin daughters more than anything, but these were two girls who bounced between an oceanfront mansion in Malibu, a thirty-million-dollar, ten-bedroom penthouse apartment in San Francisco, and a country house on a private island northwest of Seattle. They traveled everywhere in armored limousines and Secret Service jets, and their various teachers, tutors, and best friends of the moment traveled with them. The pop star Adrianna had played a thirty-minute set at their birthday party in September. They weren't normal kids.

"And you?" Susan said.

"I'm happier here, too. And I'm safer. You know I'm not an extrovert like you are." His voice took on a hard edge. "It just doesn't appeal to me to have all these TV talking heads dissecting my private life for the world to see. It doesn't appeal to me to have every angry, homophobic, xenophobic radio talk show host in America taking me down a peg for laughs. It's not fair, I didn't ask for it…"

"Pierre," she said.

"… and it's humiliating, Susan."

"I know it is. It's my private life, too."

"No, it isn't," he said.

She was about to speak, but he rushed ahead of her. "It's not your life. You're the President of the United States. I'm the overly sensitive, reclusive, gay computer geek who happened to get lucky during the dotcom era—that's my narrative now. Meanwhile, you get to be the smart, sexy leader of the free world. You're like Tomb Raider and Golda Meir wrapped in a tortilla. Every girl in America, from third grade through high school, wants to be you when they grow up.

"You know what TMZ is talking about this evening? The actor Tommy Zales, fifteen years your junior, was at the White House dedication today—he was photographed chatting *very* closely with you. He was also at National Press Club dinner two weeks ago, sitting one table away from you. He's a ladies' man, and he's a heartbreaker—what's going on? Is he trying to bed the President?"

Susan rolled her eyes. "Pierre, there's nothing going on between me and Tommy Zales. I don't even know him. I chatted closely with at least two hundred people today."

"That's not the point, Susan. Every week, there's a new interview with some disgruntled ex-employee of mine, talking about how secretive I am, how demanding I am, how I throw tantrums, and theorizing about what men at the company I might have had closeted relationships with—half of the people talking have never even met me. Do you know how many ex-employees I have? More than ten thousand. Are they going to put every single one of them on television?"

There was a long pause before he spoke again.

"Art asked me today if I was thinking about resigning."

Art Sayles was the chairman of Pierre's board, and a major stockholder. That was a bad sign. Susan really did feel bad about all of this. It had been going on in the background for months, and she just hadn't had time to focus on it or try to put a stop to it. The media was making Pierre into some kind of fall guy. Why?

"Pierre, I'm so sorry. What did you tell him?"

"I told him no! I built this company. The only way they're taking me out is in an ambulance."

The wide double doors to the kitchen opened. A Secret Service man held the doors and Kat Lopez stepped into the room. Kat was still wearing her conservative blue suit from earlier today. She looked tired. Her brown hair was slightly askew.

"Pierre, can you hold on?" Susan put her hand over the mouthpiece of the phone. "Kat, what are you still doing here? Go home."

"Susan, there's been another coup attempt in Turkey. It started in the past half an hour. The power is knocked out across half the country, and we've lost touch with the Presidential Palace. There's chaos in the streets. A massive crowd gathered in a public square in Istanbul, and the military has been firing on them—no one even knows which side the troops are on. Kurt Kimball is still here, and he's assembling a skeleton crew of staff. He's got an Army four-star from the Pentagon on the way, and Haley Lawrence says he can be back here in forty-five minutes."

"Who's behind it?" Susan said.

Kat shrugged.

"Kurt thinks that it's homegrown radical Islamists, possibly with an assist from outside actors. But the details are sketchy. At this point, no one knows if the Turkish government is going to last the night."

Kat paused. "If Turkey goes, we're going to take a lot of criticism. The implications on the world stage are bad enough, but keep in mind we've also got the Congressional elections in two weeks. Our opponents are going to say we were sleeping while the—"

Susan held up a hand, stopping her chief-of-staff in mid-sentence.

"Pierre," she said into the telephone. "I have to call you back."

"Susan, you can't just hang up the telephone every time someone—"

"Honey, I don't have a choice right now," Susan said.

"What does that say about our relationship, or my place in your life? I can tell you that the implications don't look good."

"I'm going to make it right," she said. "We're in a crisis at this moment, but we'll get past it. And I am going to make it up to you, and the girls."

She felt it as she was saying it, and she wanted so badly for it to be true. But in her heart, she knew how far she was from making it happen.

"Good night, Susan," Pierre said. "Enjoy your meeting."

CHAPTER TEN

October 21
3:30 a.m. Eastern European Time
(9:30 p.m. Eastern Daylight Time)
Incirlik Air Base
Adana, Turkey

They had been digging this tunnel beneath the air force base for six months—it was the perfect infiltration method.

Jamal marveled at the work that had been done. Twenty-four hours a day, shifts of men had been down here, four stories below the ground, working by hand. They had hammered away with pickaxes and shovels, tearing at the stone and packed earth, hauling the remains away in wheelbarrows, and bringing it to the surface using an elaborate pulley system.

Finally, it was done.

Jamal took it all in as he walked through the tunnel now with a group of thirty heavily-armed men, mujahideen prepared to sacrifice their lives. He was very tired—he had been working constantly for days and days, and strong Turkish coffee was the only thing keeping him moving. Even his excitement would otherwise not be enough—he felt as if he could fall asleep on his feet.

The tunnel was jagged and narrow, with sharp edges and sudden turns. The walls and floor were wet with trickling water. A cave-in was not out of the question. Every fifty meters, a battery-operated flashlight hung suspended from the ceiling, casting a weak light in the darkness, and throwing strange, sinister shadows against the walls.

As they grew closer to their destination, Jamal began to hear the rumble of heavy weaponry. It sounded like far away thunder. Right on cue, the fighting for the base had begun.

Soon the light changed. Briefly, it got much darker, and the tunnel became narrower. The ceiling was lower. For a time, they were forced to walk nearly in a squat, while moving through pitch-darkness.

Suddenly, the tunnel opened up. Jamal stepped through a narrow crack in the wall and came out into an area cordoned off behind a heavy canvas screen. He stepped past the screen into a thin corridor. It was dimly lit, but compared to the darkness of the tunnel, it felt like staring directly into the midday sun. It was a utility and power grid maintenance area below the base. The lights flickered overhead.

A group of mujahideen were congregated here. They seemed uncertain, confused. The bombing was closer now, louder. Jamal grabbed the squad leader by the shoulder.

"Move your men along the hall," he barked. "Let's go. There's no time to waste."

They climbed an ironwork stairway several flights, then emerged into a wide hangar area. The ceiling was at least three stories above their heads. A half dozen men in the green and tan camouflage uniforms of the Turkish air force stood waiting. The oldest was a tall man with a slight paunch. Despite his gut, he stood ramrod straight. His hair was salt and pepper, and he had a thick mustache. He watched Jamal approach.

"*As salaam alaikum,*" Jamal said as he shook the man's hand. Peace be upon you.

"*Wa alailkum salaam,*" the officer said. And upon you, peace.

"Colonel, this is the night we have long prayed for."

The colonel nodded. "Yes, it is. We must hurry."

His eyes narrowed as the mujahideen began to appear behind Jamal. In the clear light, the holy warriors seemed as if from another race. They were wide-bodied and strong, with long, thick beards and curly hair. Their eyes were hard. They carried heavy submachine guns and grenade launchers. One man had a flamethrower.

They wore ammunition belts looped over their shoulders, and suicide belts strapped around their waists. Their vest pockets were stuffed with grenades. These were fearless fighters, men who lived with death every day. They had relinquished the life of this world, surrendering it for the other life, in paradise.

"Jamal?" the colonel said. "These are the men you've gathered?"

"These men are the best of the best. God willing, they will create a diversion long enough for the trucks to escape."

Jamal didn't say it, but he imagined they would create a much longer diversion than that. With thirty more men like these, they could practically overrun the base—the Turkish half of it, anyway.

The colonel walked Jamal to an area on the far side of the hangar. The hangar door opened and four tractor trailers pulled in. They were followed by a large construction vehicle with a rear-mounted crane. That truck was a giant, a beast from the netherworld. It was the truck that would ram through the front gates.

Jamal felt, rather than heard, a missile incoming. He almost forgot himself and flinched. The missile hit outside with a whistle and a heavy WHUMP.

The ground under their feet trembled the slightest amount.

A digital command module was embedded in the wall. The colonel said something to one of his men under his breath. The man went to the command module and flipped a switch, bringing it to life. A numeric keypad lit up, and the man entered a sequence of numbers. Behind them, a section of the floor slowly slid away, revealing a hidden bay.

The man entered another code, and the squeal of hydraulics began. An ancient lift creaked toward the surface. It took several minutes for the lift to reach surface level. It continued until it was flush with the flooring that had slid aside—it was now as if the open bay had never been there.

Jamal stared at the items on the lift. Around him, the men murmured excitedly among themselves.

There were four thick iron racks in a line. On each long rack were mounted four small W84 nuclear warheads, very much like the replicas Jamal had seen the men working with in Brussels.

Jamal's breath caught in his throat. He had never been in the presence of a nuclear weapon—now he was standing in the same room with sixteen of them. Behind the W84 warheads were two B61 nuclear missiles, mounted side by side on wheeled bomb loaders. Jamal barely noticed them—he had no supersonic jet fighters, and he wasn't going to have any. Those bombs were of no use to him.

But the warheads—that was all he needed.

"*La ilaha illa Allah*," he whispered. There is no god, but God.

CHAPTER ELEVEN

3:15 a.m. Greenwich Mean Time
(10:15 p.m. Eastern Daylight Time)
Kleine Brogel Air Base
Kleine Brogel, Belgium

There was a delay getting off the plane.

Luke sat and stared out the window. Nearby were the flashing yellow lights of an equipment truck. The control tower was about half a mile away, with office lights on at the top level. Besides the runway lights, the rest of the base was dark.

"What do Belgians look like?" he said to Ed Newsam.

Newsam shrugged his big shoulders. "Like regular white people, I'd say."

Luke nodded. "I'm going to shoot the first white person I see."

There had been nothing but delays since they entered Belgian airspace. The tower had made them circle for forty-five minutes before landing. Supposedly, the Belgians misunderstood Luke's intentions—they thought an American Secret Service airplane, with important business at the base, was going to land at the Brussels international airport instead. Then its personnel were going to stay at a hotel in the capital, and in the morning, travel by car an extra hour to the base.

Where did they get these ideas?

Luke's plan had always been to come straight to the air base—he and his team would be tired from the flight, but showing up in the middle of the night would give him a sense of how tightly locked down the base was, and how vulnerable it might be.

No good. The Belgians weren't having it. He would have to wait. They claimed they'd had to awaken a general so the old man could give them permission to allow the plane to land. Luke didn't believe a word of it.

He had fallen into a restless doze during the flight. His dreams had been strange, dark, nightmarish. He couldn't remember any of them, and that was good. What was bad was he felt like he hadn't gotten any rest—he felt instead like someone had covered his head with a heavy pillow and smacked him repeatedly with a brick.

He had been awakened by air turbulence—the lights were out and the rest of his team was asleep, sprawled out in various parts of

68

the darkened cabin. Luke had gone upfront to talk to the pilots and see where they were. He was surprised to see nothing but darkness out the cockpit windshield—they were out over the Atlantic Ocean, waiting for the Belgians to tell them it was okay to come down.

Now, sitting on the tarmac, the situation was even more frustrating—not a single plane had taken off or landed since they'd been here. There was nothing going on. They could have come in with no delay at all, and gotten right off the plane.

The team was fully awake, gathering their things, but there was no word on when they could leave.

A knock came on the cabin door.

Luke pulled the hydraulic latch from left to right and pushed open the door. A man stood on the tarmac, at the bottom of the plane's fold-out steps. He wore the blue dress uniform of the United States Air Force.

"May I speak with Agent Stone?"

"That's what you're doing."

"I'm Major Dwight of the USAF. I'm a public relations officer attached to the American NATO contingent here at Kleine Brogel. May I come in?"

Luke stepped aside and gestured to enter. He felt a little like a housewife inviting a traveling vacuum salesman into the house. The man literally had his hat in his hand.

"How can we help you, Major Dwight?"

"Well, there's a problem with getting on the base tonight."

"We noticed."

"This is how it goes," Dwight said. "If you annoy them, they go into passive-aggressive mode. Everything takes forever. If you insist on your own agenda, we'll be lucky to get you off this airplane before first light."

"How did we annoy them?" Ed Newsam said. "We just got here, and we haven't even seen them yet."

"Not you personally," Dwight said. "The United States annoyed them by sending you guys over here to double-check on them. They feel they've got it under control. They don't need people looking over their shoulder, deciding they're not being diligent enough. This is Belgium. Diligence is a dirty word here."

"They *are* aware," Luke said, "aren't they, that we have intelligence to suggest the base is the target of a—"

Dwight nodded. "They feel certain they are prepared for any contingency."

"There are nuclear weapons on this base," Luke said.

"They don't like to address that issue," Dwight said. "It's a very unpopular thing—not just in this country, but all over Western Europe. Many people believe that the presence of nuclear weapons here would make this entire region a target of Russian strategic missiles, which of course it would do."

"You're saying *would* as if you don't know there are nukes here," Ed Newsam said. "That's kind of funny, isn't it?"

Dwight shook his head. "The Belgian Air Force's public stance is that there are no nukes on site, but even if there were, the weapons are disarmed through the use of encryption codes, and securely stored in underground bunkers that are impossible for unauthorized personnel to access."

"If we disembark this plane ourselves," Luke said, "will they try to stop us?"

Dwight made a pained face. "Agent Stone, I don't recommend you do that. Where are you going to go? You're dealing with international relations here. This is a touchy situation, and it requires a certain amount of tact, and some patience, to deal with it. It's not like shoving your way off the plane is going to gain you access to the bombs. It won't. All it will do is create more bad feelings. If you're concerned, I can tell you that we do already have American airmen on this base. If you look out your windows, you'll see that the base isn't currently under attack by terrorists. The nukes are perfectly safe. There is no rush."

Luke glanced out the window again. There was nothing out there—just flashing yellow lights. A little bit of rain began to spit against the glass now.

"What do they want us to do?"

Now Dwight nodded. A ghost of a smile passed across his face. He seemed pleased. "They want to put you and your gear into a passenger van and take you off the base. The village of Kleine Brogel is just a few minutes away. There is a very nice boutique hotel there that can accommodate all of you. It's located at a restored traveler's inn originally built in the late 1700s. The rooms are lovely. The place serves a hot breakfast in the morning, and the owner is a retired chef—the food is wonderful, certainly better than you'll get here."

"They want us to…"

"Yes. Leave the base, and stay the night in town. Sleep in, relax, and enjoy your breakfast in the morning. Maybe tour the historic village center, if you feel up to it. Then come back here later in the day. You'll meet the base commander personally, and he'll walk you through the security measures in place."

Luke stared at Major Dwight.

"The President of the United States sent us here," Luke said. "They do know that, don't they?"

CHAPTER TWELVE

4:30 a.m. Eastern European Time
(10:30 p.m. Eastern Daylight Time)
Incirlik Air Base
Adana, Turkey

"Slowly! Slowly! Be careful."

Jamal paced the floor of the large hangar. He was beginning to feel frenzied. The entire project, everything they had worked for, could be undone just because they were going too slow. Yet the engineer overseeing the transfer of the warheads kept insisting that they go even slower.

The sun would rise in less than three hours. They had to be far, far away from here before that happened. When daylight came they would be too vulnerable to move.

A squat, heavy crane was loading the final bombs onto the last truck in line. The crane operator moved each bomb with exquisite care, his movements so slow that his crane almost seemed to be standing still. He had arrived at this steady state because of the beseeching of the engineer.

The engineer's name was John, after the writer of the Christian scriptures, Jamal supposed, or perhaps John the Baptist. He was very thin, even frail, with thick glasses and a goatee. His eyes were wide and goggling behind his glasses. His mother was from Saudi Arabia. He had grown up in London, studied chemistry and physics, and had spent four years in the Royal Air Force. He knew about as much as a person could know about storing and safely transporting nuclear weapons.

John was working carefully, guiding the nuclear warheads with his own hands as the bomb loader moved them through the air. His touch was almost a caress. John was not a man in the same way the mujahideen fighters were—but clearly he felt passion, and even love. He was in love with the bombs.

He scrambled onto the truck as the workmen bolted the warheads into position.

"Careful, careful," Jamal heard him murmur.

"John!" Jamal shouted. "May I speak with you a moment?"

The man looked up from his communion with the warhead. He seemed disturbed by the interruption. When he saw it was Jamal who had shouted, he jumped from the truck and walked over to him.

"Your men need to be more careful," he said. "The bombs won't go off on their own. Nothing like that. But they are very sensitive to changes in their environment. This is by design. If they are being moved in a way that's inconsistent with the intentions of their creators, it is possible they will disable themselves. Yes, there are mechanisms built in for this purpose. Small, shaped charges that can destroy the detonator. Regulators that will disperse the plutonium, rendering the weapon useless. Would you like to be standing here when the plutonium is dispersed into this chamber?"

Jamal smiled. They were stealing sixteen warheads, only one of which needed to be operational when the time came. Everything after that was a bonus. What if they managed to keep four of them intact and functioning? Jamal sometimes tantalized himself with fantasies like that. Four warheads, each one with ten times the payload of the Hiroshima bomb? He nearly laughed in delight at the thought of it.

"John, I'm glad that you came. Your assistance has been invaluable. But I want to tell you something. We're leaving as soon as that last warhead is loaded, and we're going to have to fight our way out of here. It's going to be quite dangerous."

John nodded. "Fine. Will someone escort me back through the tunnel?"

Jamal gently shook his head. "I'm afraid that's impossible. The tunnel has to be destroyed. It's already wired for detonation. It will blow as soon as the mujahideen start the attack."

Now John seemed puzzled. "So I'm to stay here, then?"

"No. We can't risk your capture. Our opponents will surely torture you, and learn everything about this operation."

John stared at Jamal, his eyes darting like startled fish behind his glasses.

Jamal pulled his sidearm from its holster. He took a sound suppressor from his pocket and slowly screwed it to the barrel of the gun. There was no threat from John and no real danger of the man attempting to run—he seemed perfectly frozen in place. His body began to tremble. Jamal felt that this was a time for complete honesty.

"There's no reason to be afraid," he said. "I pray that the Holiest of the Holy will accept your sacrifice as jihad, and I believe very strongly that he will do this."

For a moment, he directed his comments away from John and to Allah Himself. "Heavenly One, I humbly ask you to throw open the gates of paradise to my brother John this very night."

He lifted the gun and held it to John's face.

"Wait!" John said. He lifted his hands, as if the fragile flesh and bones would block the bullet. "Don't!"

Jamal pulled the trigger. The same instant, John crumpled to the ground. Blood ran onto the stone floor.

Two of the Turkish soldiers came running over.

"Dispose of the body," Jamal said. "I want no one to find it or identify it. And tell those men I want the warheads loaded and locked down in the next five minutes. There is no more time to waste."

Along the far wall of the cavernous chamber, about twenty mujahideen lounged, relaxing against their supply packs and their weapons. Some were checking their weapons. A few smoked cigarettes and chatted quietly.

Jamal approached them. If they noticed that he had just murdered the engineer, they made no indication of it. They lived with death every day.

These were fierce men. Jamal had great respect for them, but he did not fear them. He went directly to their leader, a man with a thick, graying beard. The man's face was deeply grooved. His left arm was gone at the elbow. He had fought, and survived, for many years.

"Abdullah," Jamal said. "Are your men ready?"

Abdullah sat crossed-legged on the floor. "The men you see here, and the others with us, are the bravest, most experienced fighters alive. There is no fear in their hearts. They are always ready to die. If you had seen them holding the line against the infidels at Tikrit… it was a beautiful thing to witness."

"I have no doubt of this," Jamal said. "The trucks will be loaded any moment. Once you launch your attack, we will make our run for the gates. I wish you peace, and if Allah wills it, that you look upon His face today, and for all eternity."

Abdullah nodded. "I know who you are. The nameless one, the rumor, the one they call the Phantom." The man seemed almost like he would laugh, but he didn't. His hard eyes stared into Jamal's.

"Some say Allah protects you. Some say the Devil. It's a strange feeling to see you with my own eyes—until today, I was not sure you were even real. If it pleases Allah, I would wish you everything you would bestow upon me. But I think the Great One has other plans."

Jamal didn't answer for a long moment. "Five minutes," he said. "Then I would like the shooting to begin."

Now Abdullah smiled. There was a black gap where many years before, his right front tooth had been. He climbed to his feet. "Five minutes. We'll be ready. And perhaps you and I will meet again, in Heaven, or maybe in Hell."

Jamal turned and walked to the lead truck. He climbed into the passenger seat. A submachine gun leaned against the seat, waiting for him. He looked at the driver, a young man nervously smoking a cigarette.

"Let's go," Jamal said.

CHAPTER THIRTEEN

"Turkey has fallen into chaos."

Susan sat at the head of the conference table. She hadn't bothered to change out of her jeans and sweatshirt. She stared as Kurt Kimball made one dire assessment after another. After months of unrest, Turkey appeared to be collapsing at lightning speed.

On the screen behind him, images of violence were interspersed with maps of the country. "We have street fighting in a dozen cities. The army is attempting to impose martial law, but we haven't even been able to determine which units are loyal to the President, and which are in on the coup attempt. The Presidential Palace has been the site of a vicious firefight. There are tanks lined up on the plaza outside the Palace."

"Any word from the president himself?" Haley Lawrence said.

Kurt shook his head. "There was an announcement that the president was going to go on national TV to reassure the people, but the power has been out in most of the country for over an hour. The TV stations are down. The internet is down."

Susan thought of the president, Ismet Batur. She had hosted him one afternoon about three months ago. He seemed like a kind man. They'd had lunch together, one of those "long-time allies, discussing issues of mutual interest and concern" meetings. The Russians had just seized three Turkish islands in the Black Sea without firing a shot. Outside of lodging a complaint, there wasn't much to be done. Apocalyptic wars didn't happen over islands with three thousand people on them—not in Susan's world.

"What about Incirlik Air Base?"

Kurt nodded. "It seems okay at the moment. Our Thirty-ninth Air Wing is stationed there. We share it with the Turkish Air Force, and a small contingent of the Royal Air Force, each group in their own section. The power has been cut off at the base, and all flights are grounded, both in and out. There have been sporadic attacks on the base during the past couple of hours, so far easily repelled. We've sustained a few minor injuries, and inflicted what appear to be heavy losses on the attacking force."

"Who is the attacking force?" Susan said.

Kurt shrugged. "We don't know yet. Rogue elements of the Turkish military? An Islamist militia? The fighting has been in total darkness. In the morning, we should be able to discover more."

"Does it concern you," Haley said, "that there are nuclear weapons on that base?"

"Very much so," Kurt said. "Fully twenty-five percent of our stockpile in Europe is stored at Incirlik. Perhaps a hundred B61 missiles, and also some obsolete W84 warheads."

Now Susan stared. "I thought those weapons were safe, off the table, so to speak."

"They should be," Kurt said. "We have five thousand troops stationed at that base. They don't control the entire base, but the likelihood of any part of that base being overrun, and the weapons stolen, with that number of American troops onsite, is pretty low. A massive force would have to attack that base to defeat our troops, and it's clear that nothing of the sort is happening."

Susan got a sinking feeling in her gut from this talk. "Is it possible," she said, "that this is the attack Don Morris was talking about? That he had it wrong—the attack wasn't against the base in Belgium, it was against the base in Turkey?"

"It's possible," Kurt said. "But unlikely. Coup attempt or not, Incirlik really is a hard target."

"What is the status of Luke Stone's mission to Belgium?" Susan said. "He should be there by now, shouldn't he? Have we gotten any kind of communication or report from him? It would be nice to know, in the context of everything else happening, if he thinks Kleine Brogel is vulnerable."

Kurt looked at one of his aides. "Amy, can you contact the Secret Service plane that went to Belgium earlier today? If the pilots are still at Kleine Brogel, ask them to put Agent Stone in touch with us."

The young woman nodded and headed out the door, already on her telephone.

Almost as soon as she left, a young man along the wall with a headset on raised his hand. "Kurt?"

"Yes?"

"I'm getting a report right now, relayed to me from Air Force headquarters at the Pentagon. In the past ten minutes, an attack at Incirlik has broken through the defenses on the Turkish side of the base. I repeat, an attack has broken through. A hostile unit of unknown size and origin is on the base, inside the perimeter, fighting against Turkish forces there. The attack was a surprise and may represent a mutiny of units garrisoned at the base."

Kurt looked at another aide. "Can you bring us up some real-time satellite footage of what it happening there? Also, get us on the phone with our base commander."

"Will do."

The young woman named Amy came back into the room. She held her smartphone out to Kurt. "I have Agent Stone on my telephone. He says he's stuck on the tarmac at Kleine Brogel—the Belgians won't let him get off the plane."

CHAPTER FOURTEEN

**4:39 a.m. Eastern European Time
(10:39 p.m. Eastern Daylight Time)
Incirlik Air Base
Adana, Turkey**

"Don't slow down," Jamal shouted into the radio. "Go! Go! Go!"

The heavy construction vehicle was just ahead of them, bare feet away. The driver had slowed as they approached the gates. A squad of soldiers was massed there to hold the gates against invaders. They were facing the wrong way.

To his right, Jamal saw the silhouettes of two mujahideen in the darkness. One held a rocket launcher on his shoulder. The other prepared the launcher for firing. A stream of bright light ripped from the launcher, streaking on a flat plane across the night. WHOOOOSH.

"Go faster," Jamal said to his own driver. "Push them if you have to."

The rocket hit the guard station. BOOOM.

The sound was low, like the rumble of an earthquake—it went on and on, and reminded Jamal of heavy paper being crunched into a ball. The squat building exploded outward, shards of it flying. Troops ran in all directions. A man stumbled out of the ruins of the building, his body in flames, like a torch doused in gasoline.

The construction vehicle slowed down again. Who was that driver? He was putting the whole line of trucks at risk.

"Go!" Jamal screamed into the radio. "Do your job!"

Finally, some bit of courage must have risen up within him. The construction truck accelerated, gathering speed for the run at the gate. There was a slight curve in the road just before the gates. The big truck took the curve, leaning dangerously. The payload arm swung wildly at the end of its tether.

The truck skidded, but didn't slow down. The driver was committed now. He had probably said his prayers. He was going for it.

Machine gun fire came from either side. Bullet holes ripped up the hood of Jamal's truck. His driver grunted in fear, like an animal.

"Steady," Jamal said.

A rocket sizzled out from the right, from behind the burning wreck of the guard house. It hit the construction vehicle dead in the front. A direct hit. The cab blew up in a giant fireball, glass and steel and the bodies of the two men inside flying up into the darkness.

The truck kept going, driverless, barely losing momentum. It crashed into the heavy front gates at full speed, blasting through them, a rolling, burning twenty-ton juggernaut. The steel gates shrieked from the impact.

The rear of the truck flew into the air, a backwards wheelie, and for an instant Jamal thought the truck would stall right at the gate, leaving them sitting ducks for the gunfire of the guards. But no. The truck barreled through, sliding sideways now, pulling fifty meters of fencing with it on either side. The top weight became too much, and the ruined truck tumbled onto its side, sliding to a flaming halt on the road just outside the gates.

Jamal's truck rolled past the fiery carnage of the guardhouse, seconds behind the wrecked construction vehicle. There was just enough room outside the gate to make a sharp right and escape along the edge of the base.

A burst of automatic fire came from their left. Jamal ducked as the driver's window shattered inward, spraying the inside of the cab with glass. The driver made another animal noise and grabbed the side of his neck. This time the sound he made was little more than an exhalation, hardly louder than a whisper.

"Unh."

He looked at Jamal. Blood jetted from under the left side of his chin, pulsing out and streaming down his neck to his shirt. His shirt became spattered, then soaked. His eyes were bright, alert and terrified.

As Jamal watched, the color seemed to drain from the man's face. An instant later, his eyes became calm, then vacant and dazed. He was bleeding out. His jaw hung slack. He didn't speak again.

The truck was still rolling. Jamal reached across the driver, opened his door, and pushed him out. The man was still alive, but offered no resistance. He tumbled backwards out onto the roadway.

Jamal slid into the driver's seat, wrenched the steering wheel to the right, and slammed on the brakes. The truck sideswiped the burning construction vehicle and skidded to a halt. Gunfire strafed the trailer, where the warheads were stored.

Thunk, thunk, thunk, thunk thunk, as bullets punched through the metal.

Another truck roared through the gates, turned hard to the right, and rolled onto its side. Jamal flinched as the giant truck slid across the road toward him.

He braced.

CRUNCH. The impact jostled him hard, nearly tossing him through the open driver's side door. He clung to the steering wheel.

He had to get moving. If the trucks piled up here, all the plans, months of preparation, were for nothing.

He yanked the door closed. He shoved the truck into gear and stomped on the gas pedal, tires spinning on pavement for several seconds, squealing as rubber was laid down, acrid black smoke rising behind him. The truck wouldn't move—it was wedged between the two others.

He whispered feverishly, not even sure what he was saying, begging the Prophet to intervene. No. Demanding it.

"Come on! Help me!"

A rocket hit the undercarriage of the truck that had fallen over. *That truck was carrying nuclear weapons!* Not good. The explosion was deafening, so loud it was like a wall of sound. It blew out the bottom of that truck, sending debris flying away from Jamal, back toward the front gates of the base. Flames engulfed the trailer.

If he stayed here much longer, he was going to die.

Suddenly, his truck wrenched free. He fought with the steering wheel as the trailer jackknifed behind him.

Now, the third truck in line barreled through the gates, its headlights blinding him. It turned a sharp right and collided with Jamal's truck. The two trucks scraped each other's sides as they plunged together down the roadway.

The new truck roared ahead of Jamal, and he let it go. He glanced back. The fourth truck in line was on fire. That was the last one. It had rolled to a stop just short of the gates. Armed men were spraying it with machine gun fire.

Behind there, a massive explosion ripped open the dark night. A huge red fireball flew on a straight line into the air.

The mujahideen were attacking.

Jamal turned to face the blackened roadway again. The other truck had raced far ahead. That was good. It was important that they separate.

Two trucks had escaped the base. Two out of four.

Eight warheads.

Jamal turned left at the next road, away from the dwindling lights of the other truck. In a few moments, he had entered an empty highway. There were no lights on anywhere. He was not being pursued. The truck's radiator was steaming, but otherwise it seemed to be functioning normally.

On the horizon, he could still see the orange flames of the firefight against the night sky. A large helicopter gunship roared by just overhead, rushing to the battle—Jamal felt it more than saw it.

He drove directly south, bringing the truck first to the rendezvous point.

And then, Syria.

CHAPTER FIFTEEN

6:05 a.m. Greenwich Mean Time
(1:05 a.m. Eastern Daylight Time)
Kleine Brogel Air Base
Kleine Brogel, Belgium

"As you can see, there is nothing to worry about."

Luke could see that.

The base commander, Colonel Wenders, had been yanked from his bed in the middle of the night by a call from the Belgian prime minister. The President of the United States had directly requested a tour of the facilities for her agent. It could not wait until after the waffles were served in the morning.

Now Wenders stood with Luke, his team, and Major Dwight in a cavernous hangar with a rounded ceiling three stories above their heads. In front of them were three B61 nuclear bombs—long and sleek, they looked like they could be launched from the ground. Luke knew they were designed to be carried aboard fighter craft traveling very fast—they were air to surface weapons.

Wenders had walked them through all of the hardened concrete bunkers that housed the B61 nuclear missiles. There were twenty-one missiles in all, stored in groups of three, in seven different bunkers.

The bunkers were situated in clusters—one group of four and one group of three. Each bunker had double-steel bay doors with digital locks that required a key card to be swiped. Once swiped, the locking mechanism became activated and required an eight-digit code in order to continue. Once the correct code was input, the doors then required a physical key to open the lock.

Personnel were not allowed to carry both the digital swipe card and the physical key—in essence, it took two men to open the door to the bunker. Further, each bunker required a different key card, a different code, and a different physical key. And when the key card was swiped, it sounded an alarm in the night watch station, where the guards could then monitor the progress of the personnel accessing the bunkers. Gaining entry to the bunkers was, all by itself, a monstrously cumbersome process.

Once inside, the bombs were stored in bays that were under the floor of the bunker. To bring them to the surface required yet another key card, yet another code, and yet another physical key. The kicker here was that there were three different lock mechanisms at a command module inside the bunker. If the person trying to reach the nukes happened to use the wrong lock mechanism, the system would shut itself off, an another alarm would sound, and the bunker would lock from the outside. The thieves who made the mistake would have nothing to do except wait for the Belgian airmen to arrive, likely sometime after brunch.

Once the correct lock mechanism was accessed in the correct way, it would activate a hydraulic lift—the floor would slide away and the bombs would creak slowly to the surface. Swann timed how long it took from turning the physical key in the lock to the nukes parked on the floor of the bunker, and no longer moving—fourteen minutes. No terrorists who had made it this far would be likely to have that kind of time to spare.

"Is there any way to short-circuit this process?" Luke said.

Wenders—stiff, tall, and straight as a ram—made an exaggerated face designed to convey confusion, or perhaps disgust. "Short-circuit? What is this, please?"

"Go around it," Luke said.

"Break it," Ed Newsam offered. "Blow up that door. Hot-wire this lift. Steal the bombs."

The colonel laughed. "Impossible. If the doors are tampered with, the lift deactivates. The code and the keys will not even start it. You could detonate the doors, then stand here waiting to be apprehended."

"Can anyone at the guard station open these locks?" Luke said.

Wenders shook his head. "They can remotely shut down the electronic system here in this building, but they cannot access the locks or the hydraulic. Those are on a local network inside the bunker, making them impossible to hack from the guard station or from the larger world."

"So it would really take an inside job to steal the bombs," Swann said. "Someone on the base, who has access to the keys and the codes, and who has a friend at the guard station willing to look the other way."

Luke nearly laughed. Swann was not known for his charm, or his tact. The colonel gave a pained smile.

"I assure you," he said, "nothing like this is possible here. And even if it were, even if there were several people interested in taking the bombs, and they were all stationed at this base at the same time, keen to help each other… even then, it still wouldn't work. As you must know, these bombs are useless without the codes that arm and activate them. Those codes are not stored on this base. I am the commander, and I don't have access to them. Even if we needed these bombs, and we mounted them on our fighter planes, we could not get them to work because we do not have the codes."

"Who has the codes?" Mika said.

The colonel shrugged. "The Americans, perhaps. Maybe the prime minister, or someone else in government. All I know is I don't have them."

"So why have the bombs," Ed Newsam said, "if you can't use them?"

Colonel Wenders shook his head. "Maybe that is a better question for the politicians."

* * *

"What do you think?" Luke said.

By 8 a.m., they were back at the boutique hotel in Kleine Brogel that Major Dwight had warned them about. It seemed that even after the nuclear war tour, they were still not welcome at the base.

That was fine with Luke. He was tired. He was wrung out. He would be happy to take a shower and go to sleep on a large bed in a private room, rather than a cot in a barracks, or even an officer's cabin. The four of them sat in the guest living room of the hotel, doing a quick postmortem before Luke dismissed them all until this afternoon.

Their jobs here were done, as far as he was concerned.

"Looks pretty hard to me," Ed said. "The base seems tight enough, and getting to the bombs is a pain. Maybe some disgruntled ex-soldiers could make a play for them, but I doubt they'd get very far."

"The colonel told me they randomly generate new access codes every day," Swann said. "If that's really true, then a code that a thief stole yesterday is already no good. You'd have to have some way to steal the access codes on the fly, for both the outside door and the hydraulic lift, assuming you'd been able to steal the key card and the keys. Then you'd have to go straight to the bunker and get the bombs. If you took any time for extra planning at all, by the next time you arrived, the codes would have been changed."

"And the bombs themselves are useless without the permissive action link codes," Mika said. "Which the colonel said he doesn't have."

"And what would you do if you did manage to steal a bomb?" Swann said. "Would you then steal a supersonic jet? Which, by the way, is located in a different hangar on the other side of the base. And that's assuming you got on the base in the first place. He also told me they changed the fences—they're twenty feet high and topped with razor wire all the way around."

"This looks like a bust, man," Ed said. "We came out here to look at their security measures, and they look pretty good. I don't think anyone is going to get these bombs."

Luke nodded. "I feel the same way. Okay, let's call that good news. We can all get some shut-eye. We'll call it free time today, and in the evening, maybe we'll go in to Brussels for some chow on the President's dime. Tomorrow morning, we can head back to the States. We'll call it a thirty-six-hour working vacation. Sound okay?"

Around the table, the group nodded.

Luke's satellite phone started to ring. He glanced at it, hoping it wasn't Becca. It wasn't. Just the President calling him, probably to ask for his report. He would try to wrap it up quickly with her.

He held the phone to his ear.

"Hold for the President of the United States."

He waited. In another moment, she came on.

"Luke?"

"Susan. Hi. Are you guys waiting for my report? We just finished up with the colonel, ah"—Luke glanced at his watch—"ten minutes ago."

Ed shook his head and smiled.

"What's the status?" she said.

"Here? Good. Everyone on the team is in agreement. There is a negligible chance that terrorists could infiltrate this base and get to the bombs. The base itself is secure, and the process to access the bombs is positively Byzantine."

"Okay," Susan said. "I have you on speaker. We all heard that, and it's duly noted."

Luke caught the note of strain in her voice.

"We've got a problem," she said.

Luke's team were staring at him now. He shrugged, his ear pressed to the phone. "Tell me."

"Luke, this is Kurt Kimball. There is an ongoing attempt to overthrow the government in Turkey. It's happening now. As part of that, someone attacked Incirlik Air Base in Turkey last night and early this morning. It was an infiltration, an inside job. A group of irregular fighters, possibly jihadis, launched from inside the base. That unit has either been entirely destroyed, or a few may have escaped in the confusion and darkness. But that isn't the issue. The entire offensive appears to have been a cover. During the battle, another group of men infiltrated the base and attempted to steal at least sixteen W84 nuclear warheads stored there."

The words washed over Luke in a blur. He couldn't seem to organize his thoughts. He'd gone without a real night's sleep now for several days—he wasn't even sure when the last time was. And when you were tired like this, your sharpness began to blunt.

"What?" he said. It was all he could manage.

"Eight of the warheads were recaptured during the battle. But at least eight others are gone. American military police have captured a man they believe was involved. In effect, they rescued him from a patrol of Turkish airmen who were about to murder him. There were serious casualties on both sides, and it isn't clear who is cooperating with whom. We need information from this person, and quickly. The Turks are demanding his release to them. We assume they will kill him as soon as we comply."

"Okay," Luke said, still not getting it.

"We need you to go there," Susan said. "We need you to take control of the interrogation and, if possible, the entire investigation."

"I don't speak Turkish," Luke said.

"We'll get you a translator."

Luke shook his head. "No good. Interrogations work best when the communication is direct. Let me think about it. I may have someone. When do you want us to go there?"

Susan didn't hesitate. "Now."

Now?

"As soon as you can get back on the plane. We're behind the ball on this, and falling further behind every minute."

Luke felt the exhaustion creeping into his bones. His eyelids were heavy. If he closed them, he might be asleep in seconds.

"Okay," he said. "Make sure they keep that prisoner alive until we get there. I can't question a corpse. And in the meantime, let me make some arrangements. I'll be back in touch in a little while."

He hung up the telephone and looked at the team. They all stared back at him.

"Belgium was never the target. The big airbase in Turkey, Incirlik, was hit this morning. They made off with at least eight nuclear warheads. It looks like an inside job. Our guys captured someone they think was involved, and they want us to go there and head up the investigation. I guess we'll skip that dinner in Brussels."

"I was going to get the snails," Swann said. "You ever have them dipped in melted butter? Man. Better than lobster."

Luke shrugged Swann off. Maybe Luke was overtired, but he felt like this wasn't a great time for wisecracking. He looked at each of his people in turn.

"This is where it gets serious. They're asking us to go into what right now is a war zone. There's a coup attempt happening right now—these things have a nasty habit of turning into civil wars. In the middle of all that, there's the missing nukes."

"I'm in," Ed Newsam said. Luke knew that would be his response without having to ask. Ed was a war machine. This was the kind of responsibility he was paid to take on, and this was also the kind of thing he lived for.

"I'm in," Mark Swann said. No surprise there, either. Swann was not a fighter, but he was Luke's go-to tech guy. He had repeatedly kept Luke and Ed alive in the craziest circumstances.

Luke looked at Mika. She was young, and she was inexperienced. She had never been involved in something like this before. Her eyes were wide with fear.

"What do you think, Mika?" he said. "You can't let these guys decide for you. They're older, and they've both been through the wringer. They know what to expect. You don't have to do this. It's not in your job description. You could potentially help us from here, or go back to Washington and do it from there. You have nothing to prove to me, or to anyone."

Mika shook her head. "It's better for you if I come, isn't it?"

Luke wouldn't lie to her. He nodded. "It is better. Having immediate access to you is better than having to call you. But again—"

"I'll come," she said. "I'll ride with the legends."

Luke almost laughed. Ed and Swann smiled. Neither man probably knew what to make of this tiny young woman just out of school. Luke sure didn't.

"Okay, then there's no rest for the weary. I need you to start pulling down the details about what happened last night, and the background on it. Get us those nukes and how they work. The bad guys have something in mind for those things, or they wouldn't have taken them."

"Okay, Luke. Will do."

Luke looked at the other two. "You guys know the CIA special agent they used to call Big Daddy?"

Ed shrugged. "Maybe."

Swann nodded. "Yeah. I know of him. I thought he was retired. Actually, I thought he got his hands dirty on something, and they pushed him out."

"Yeah," Luke said. "He had the dirtiest hands in the business. But I think we should bring him back in, if he'll do it. Ten years ago, I was on loan to the CIA from Delta. Big Daddy built my cover and inserted me into Iraq. He was my lifeline. Nobody gets to the meat of an interrogation as fast. And nobody alive knows the Middle East like he does."

CHAPTER SIXTEEN

8:57 a.m. Eastern European Time
Santorini Island, Greece

When the telephone rang, Big Daddy jumped.

The phone didn't ring here, not really. Not *that* phone. He glanced at it. It was an old-style wall phone, hanging in his kitchen, a long cord dangling from it. He glanced out the window, at the whitewashed buildings stacked along the rugged cliffs, and beyond that, the deep blue of the Mediterranean. The day was already bright, if just the slightest bit hazy with sea mist.

His real name was Bill Cronin, though people rarely called him that anymore. He was a bear of a man, well over six feet tall, heavyset, with a thick beard that had once been blond, and now was trending toward white.

He was shirtless, wearing only a pair of swimming trunks and flip-flops. His skin was deeply tanned from the searing sun of the Greek islands. He had the look of a man who had worked with his hands for many years—it wasn't far from the truth.

He was cooking a big omelet, with fava beans, onions, peppers, and mushrooms, all of it grown in his own tiny backyard. The eggs were from his neighbor's chickens, which tended to wander all over the neighborhood, and even turn up here at his feet once in a while, pecking at whatever scraps and leftovers they found on his stone floor.

The phone was still ringing. There was no answering machine connected to it, no voice mail. If he let it go, maybe the person would eventually just hang up. It must be a wrong number, anyway. No one had this number.

"Honey," a voice called from the other room. "Are you going to answer that?"

He glanced at a small sign affixed to the stone wall of the kitchen.

Grow old with me, the sign read, *the best is yet to be.*

He picked up the phone, but he didn't speak.

"Big Daddy?" a voice said.

"There's no one here by that name."

The voice changed its mind. "Bill? Is this you?"

"Who may I tell him is calling?"

"Bill, it's Luke Stone. Cut the crap. I know your voice anywhere."

The name echoed out of the past like the sound of an air raid siren. Big Daddy spent much of his time trying to forget everything that had happened. But of course he remembered the face that went with that name, and the person.

Luke Stone, a man who had gone deeper undercover as a Western mujahid than anyone Bill had ever known. He vanished, and Bill had been sure he was dead. When Stone finally resurfaced, he was on the run—he had wiped out a squad of Al Qaeda to rescue an Iraqi doctor and the man's daughters. They were all marked for death. Luke had blown a carefully crafted cover that had taken two years to create to save a family of the Baha'i religious minority from execution. So Bill had gone in himself and gotten them out— what the hell else was he going to do?

Luke Stone was not the first person that Bill Cronin wanted to hear from before nine in the morning.

"How did you get this number?" he said.

"I asked around. You're easier to find than you probably think."

"Why are you calling me?"

"I need you. You might not have heard, but somebody stole nuclear warheads from an airbase in Turkey last night. They escaped, and the trucks they were driving disappeared. It looks like an inside job, seventy miles from the Syrian border."

Big Daddy went numb listening to the details of the heist. He was fifty-nine years old. He had done his time fighting these insane wars. He wasn't that person anymore. He didn't like that person. He didn't like the things that person did. And he didn't like the way his own government had flushed him down the toilet when the things he did went out of fashion.

He liked being the person he was now. He liked waking early and snorkeling in the crystal waters of the Aegean Sea. He liked walking home up the steep hills and buying bread in the local bakery. He liked sitting on his terrace in the evening, drinking wine and watching the sun go down in the west. Neighbors would stop by and join him. They didn't know what he used to do, and they didn't ask. That's how he liked it.

He lived here with a woman. She liked to put up signs everywhere. Some of them were meaningful. Some of them were silly. There was one in the corner. He glanced at it. *If you're waiting for a sign,* it said, *this is it.*

He stared out the window at his terraced vegetable garden as Luke Stone's voice rambled along. Stone seemed to think there was no doubt that Bill would leave here and join him in his mindless quest. Why did he think that?

Big Daddy knew why.

The terrorists weren't really Muslims. That's what had become clear to him during his long years of fighting them, spying on them, infiltrating them, and killing them. They pretended they were Muslims, but really they were nihilists. They were murder junkies—they were addicted to the thrill of killing and dying. They had no long-term plans.

There was not going to be a caliphate—the men who talked about creating one were not interested in the dreary work of governance. They couldn't build systems, or maintain ones that already existed. They couldn't deliver the goods that a society delivers, and they didn't care to. They wanted to loot, and rape and pillage, and move on. They didn't care if they lived or died, and they didn't care if anyone else did. They were having fun. They would kill everyone on Earth if they could. These were the ones who had stolen nuclear weapons. It was an ugly thought.

You couldn't negotiate with people like this. You couldn't reason with them. You could not cajole or threaten them. So at some point, Bill had stopped trying. He had changed his focus to breaking them. He had become very, very good at it.

Stone was done talking. "What do you think, Bill?"

Big Daddy shook his head. He was, quite literally, too old for this.

"No," he said.

"I need to interrogate a Turk," Luke said. "I don't speak Turkish."

"So get someone to translate."

"You know that's no good."

Bill did know. He spoke Arabic. He spoke Turkish. He spoke Farsi. He spoke Chechen. He spoke Russian. He liked to break men in a language they could understand.

"Look," Stone said. "You got a raw deal. I know that. No one drew clear lines for you, then they decided you were out of bounds. Nobody gets that better than me."

"I was tarred and feathered," Bill said. "And run out of town on a rail."

"There's nothing I can do about that," Stone said. "But I've got something real here. It's a mission, and I'm holding it in my hand. Don't tell me you haven't wanted one, because I know you have. Show me a spy who doesn't want a mission, and I'll show you a spy laid out in a coffin."

"Who do you work for now?"

"I work for the President of the United States. I report directly to her. No middlemen."

Mmmm. That was interesting. What would they call it?

A shot at redemption.

"I need a Middle East guy," Stone said. "If you won't do it, they're gonna give me some kid."

"All right," Big Daddy said. "I'm in. I need to clear up a couple of things here, and then I'll be there as soon as I can. But just so you know, I'm on an island. It's pretty far flung."

Stone didn't miss a beat. "I can send an airplane."

Big Daddy nodded. Of course Stone could send a plane. When things happened, they happened fast. "Okay."

After they hung up, he stood quietly in the kitchen. The eggs cooked on, nearly forgotten. After a moment, she came in. She slid in behind him and put her arms around his thick stomach. She rested her head against his back.

She had been very beautiful once, and she was still was, but it was different now. Age changed everything. She was like him, a refugee from the work. She'd had many names over her career, so many that people had come to call her by a code name. It was the name that Big Daddy called her by now, and in fact thought of her as: Q.

They had settled here because it was beautiful, but also because there was nowhere for them in America anymore. You can't fight to the death for thirty years, and go home again. Not to a place where the people mindlessly watch empty entertainment on TV all night, and obsessively take pictures of themselves during the day. Not to a place that rejected you and called you a disgrace to their high ideals.

This was home now.

"What was that call about?" Q said.

He didn't answer her right away. But after a minute, he did. "You know."

"Is it bad?"

He nodded. "Looks that way. I doubt they'd ever call me otherwise."

"Who was it?"

"Luke Stone." The name would be familiar to her.

"Jesus," she said.

He nodded again. "Yeah."

A long moment passed between them. It was nice, just to stand here. Nothing had happened yet. Maybe if he stood here long enough, nothing would happen.

"Are you going to go?" she said.

"I think maybe I will."

He turned to face her. He was nearly a foot taller than she was. She stared up at him now, her deep brown eyes piercing him. When she was young, she was someone they could never put their finger on. She was an enigma, a cipher, here one minute and gone the next. She could look at a person with the utmost sincerity and tell them dangerous lies. She could knowingly send men to their deaths.

She wasn't that person now, if she ever had been. Maybe, unlike him, she had only been doing her job.

"Don't die out there, Big Daddy," she said now.

He laughed, but didn't feel it. His age hung on him like a heavy overcoat, extra weights sewn into the pockets.

"I'm not planning to," he said.

CHAPTER SEVENTEEN

9:45 a.m. Greenwich Mean Time
(4:45 a.m. Eastern Daylight Time)
The Skies over Central Europe

He had swallowed the pill about twenty minutes ago, and it was just starting to hit his bloodstream now.

He could feel the changes happening. His heart rate was up. His vision was sharper. His mind was more alert. Before, he had been asleep on his feet. Now he was awake. He was confident. He was eager for information. These were the same feelings a normal person might get from a strong cup of coffee, only vastly exaggerated.

Dexies. They'd been Luke's friend for a long time.

"The W84 thermonuclear warhead," Mika said, looking closely at her tablet.

Outside the plane, the skies were overcast and gray. There was more turbulence than normal. Luke barely felt it. Inside, his team sat in a group, all eyes on Mika. She had been compiling research since the moment they heard they were going to Turkey.

"It's a small two-stage weapon, meaning that the bomb actually detonates twice. The first stage is a relatively small fission explosion, which causes the much larger fusion explosion in the second stage. I'm sure you've seen this in archival film footage of nuclear explosions—a first detonation when the bomb hits, followed by a gigantic mushroom cloud causing secondary explosion."

Luke nodded. Newsam and Swann did the same.

"These warheads are considered obsolete. They were designed for tactical strikes against the Soviet Union during the Cold War. They offer yields up to one hundred fifty kilotons—for your reference, the Hiroshima bomb was roughly fifteen kilotons."

"In other words," Ed Newsam said, "these bombs are ten times the size of the one that caused the Hiroshima explosion."

Mika nodded. "Yes."

"How many people died at Hiroshima?" Swann said.

"No one is quite sure. The estimate is about a hundred forty thousand in the initial bombing and the three months that followed.

But there is no agreed upon assessment of how many died of cancer, lung diseases, and other ailments in the years after that."

"A million people could die from just one of these bombs," Swann said.

"Oh yeah. And they made it out with eight of them. We don't know what state of repair they're in, but I think we have to assume one or more of them are operational."

"How can they launch the bombs?" Luke said.

Mika shrugged. "Well, I don't know. They need the codes."

"Let's just assume they have, or can get the codes," Luke said. He wasn't ready to share what Susan had told him. He would do it when they absolutely needed to know.

Mika nodded. "Okay. This is the strange thing. If they have the capability to steal or decrypt the nuclear codes, then they've stolen some difficult bombs to use them with. Those warheads are designed to be fitted to a Tomahawk missile variant which was retired at the end of the Cold War. The missiles were supposed to be launched from mobile ground-based platforms that rode around on the backs of tractor-trailer trucks. The trucks can be camouflaged to blend in with a variety of landscapes. The system was intended for limited nuclear skirmishes that were supposed to take place along the European-Soviet border. The idea was wholly imaginary, as even the Pentagon admitted that the confusion caused by a limited nuclear exchange would likely lead to full-scale ballistic missile attacks, and mutually assured destruction within a short time. It was a flawed concept, and as far as we know, the launch platforms, along with the missiles, were all decommissioned and destroyed, certainly by 1992."

"But they kept the warheads around?" Swann said.

Mika shrugged. "Yes."

Ed laughed. "If you know about the military, you know they never destroy everything. The launch platforms are out there. I've been on a lot of battlegrounds in my days, and you wouldn't believe the stuff that pops up. To me, it makes sense why they took the small warheads and left the B61 missiles behind. They don't have airplanes that can carry the B61. But maybe they can launch the small warheads from the ground."

Luke nodded at the truth of that. "In that scenario, they've got the warheads now, and they probably have the missiles and a way to launch them. Another option is that they don't have the missiles or launch pad, or don't even have the codes. Then we could be looking at a dirty bomb. Mika, how likely is that?"

He realized he was putting her on the spot.

"My guess?" she said.

"Your best guess."

She exhaled, as if she'd been holding her breath. "They have the missiles and the launch pads. Maybe they hired a rogue Chinese aerospace firm to reverse-engineer the hardware needed from old specs. Maybe, like Ed says, that hardware is just lying around out there and on sale. But I doubt it's a dirty bomb."

"Reasoning?" Luke said.

She shrugged. "There's a lot of radioactive material in this world that's easier to steal than intact, operational warheads. My data tells me that three entire squads of hardened jihadi fighters went to their deaths to make sure the trucks escaped. Unless they plan to detonate those warheads, then those men were better deployed on battlefields."

Luke nodded. He agreed with her call on this. In a sense, that was the worst news possible. Dirty bombs were bad; 150 kiloton explosions were much, much worse.

But he liked the way she was starting to think. Maybe she'd been nervous on the earlier flight—she seemed calmer now, more relaxed, and more willing to test some ideas on them. That's what he wanted, and needed, from her—someone who was willing to take a flier, someone who was willing to be wrong in order to be right.

"You have IDs on those fighters?" Ed said.

She nodded. "A few have been identified so far, mostly because they had records and fingerprints on file with Interpol or our own government. I'll give you a taste. Alixey Kurchaloy, age thirty-seven, also known as Alix the Chechen. Began his career as a teenager fighting in the First Russian-Chechen war. Implicated in the bombing of a Russian passenger jet in 2001, which killed a hundred forty-seven people. A fixture on battlefields throughout Iraq and Syria since at least 2004. Thought to have masterminded the bombing of a Shiite mosque in Najaf in 2009 during Ramadan, an act which killed ninety-three people. He's a big one.

"Next is Abdullah al-Sistani, age forty-five. Former commander in the Iraqi army under Saddam Hussein. Fought against the United States as a young conscript during Operation Desert Storm, then again during the Iraq War. Taken prisoner and held at Abu Ghraib for eighteen months. Upon release, he went underground and joined Al-Qaeda in Iraq. Pledged allegiance to ISIS in 2013. This guy was probably in charge of the attack—the fact that they sent him on a suicide mission is pretty close to astounding."

Luke raised his hand. That was all they needed. "Okay, so they were willing to sacrifice valuable personnel for this operation. What does that tell you?"

"It tells me that no matter what, they didn't want the operation to fail."

"And if they really can launch the missiles, what type of damage are we talking about?"

She shook her head. "Bad. Devastating. The missiles, assuming they're still operational and in the same working order as when they were built, have a range of up to two thousand miles. As we said before, the warheads can deliver an explosion ten times the size of the Hiroshima bomb. If they deploy the missile launchers in a chaotic war zone, for example in Syria, they'd be hard to spot until it was too late.

"The cities within easy range, and which would likely be completely or mostly destroyed by just one of these bombs, include the following: Damascus, Tel Aviv, Jerusalem, Cairo, Amman, Baghdad, Teheran, Riyadh, Dubai, Beirut, Ankara, Istanbul, Athens, Astrakhan, Sebastopol, and Sarajevo, among many others. To be honest, although I doubt thirty-year-old missiles would be likely to manage it, Moscow, St. Petersburg, Kiev, and even Rome would all be within theoretical range."

They were all looking at Luke now. He found he didn't have much to add.

"We've got to get those warheads back," he said.

CHAPTER EIGHTEEN

12:50 p.m. Eastern European Time
(6:50 a.m. Eastern Daylight Time)
Incirlik Air Base
Adana, Turkey

"You know something, Ahmet," Bill Cronin said in fluent Turkish. "And you want to tell me all about it. Don't you?"

The man chained standing up and facing the wall inside the empty room said nothing. He was blindfolded, but even with the rag obscuring part of his face, it was easy to see that he was bruised and beaten. His mouth was swollen. His face was covered by sweat and some blood, and the back of his white T-shirt was stained with perspiration.

He was secured to the wall with thick chains. His bare feet were also chained around the ankles. All of the damage to this man had been done before Bill even arrived—the Turks knew how to treat their own.

"Go to hell," the man said.

Bill smiled. "Oh yes, Ahmet knows something, all right. And in a few minutes, he's going to tell us what it is."

Bill leaned in close to the man's face. He could smell the sweat on the man, the body odor, and the fear. This was the part that Big Daddy didn't like about himself—he *enjoyed* this. He would lose himself in it, if he wasn't careful.

"I have your work records," he said, his voice just above a whisper. "I've seen photos of your wife and your three... beautiful... children." He let the words linger.

"I know where they live. You don't want me to visit them, do you?"

Bill was here in this dungeon beneath the military base with Luke Stone and his partner Ed. Was this what Stone was hoping for when he called Bill—to unleash this part of him? Bill imagined it was.

The three men stood in a rough triangle around Ahmet, looking at his broad back. In Bill's right hand was an eight-foot bullwhip. To his left was a table with a few photographs on it.

"Strip his shirt off," he said.

Ed walked up to Ahmet, and in his own strong hands, ripped Ahmet's white, sweat- and blood-stained T-shirt apart, revealing Ahmet's tattooed back.

"You ready, Ahmet?"

Ahmet didn't answer. It seemed like he was through talking. He was probably preparing himself for what was sure to be gigantic mental effort. In fact, it was probably going to be a spiritual effort as well. It was going to be a test of endurance. But endurance had its limits, and Bill was just getting warmed up.

He worked his wrist around, getting a sense of the bullwhip, its weight, its motion, and how it would handle. It had been a long time since he'd held one of these. Just holding it raised some odd memories from out of the mists of the past. Good memories, in one sense. Nightmarish, in another.

"I can't tell you how much this takes me back," Bill said to Ahmet. "It just takes me way back to the good old days."

He gave the whip a few practice swings. It howled, it hissed, and then, on the fourth or fifth try, it CRACKED. The sound of it echoed off the walls of the big empty chamber surrounding them. Ahmet knees buckled at the sound of it.

Good boy, Ahmet. Lay down for me. Let's do this the easy way, shall we?

Bill fired the whip across Ahmet's back, bringing a red welt almost instantly to the surface. Immediately, Ahmet fell to his knees. He howled. He began to weep abjectly, his entire body shaking with sobs. Bill had only hit him once so far, and he'd actually pulled it a bit. He was sure it stung, but holy hell. Not this much.

Oh well. He settled in for the effort. It had been a long time since he whipped a man. It was a form of punishment that was long out of favor, but Bill had used it before. The memory was still there in his muscles, along with the knowledge that if this went on long enough, his right arm would gradually become sore from exertion.

He fired another lash with the whip. Then another. Then another. The whip hissed and crackled.

He knew that you could whip a man to death. But of course, that wasn't the plan today. Ahmet was already cowering on the ground, the chains that bound him pulling his body into a strange contorted shape similar to a lost soul burning in the crackling flames of hell. Bill stopped, glanced at Luke and Ed, and shrugged. The man was already broken. It was Break #1, Bill knew. There would have to be others.

"Show him the pictures," he said.

Bill watched as Stone took the photos off the table. He walked over to the man kneeling on the ground and removed his blindfold. Ahmet's eyes were squeezed shut. Luke slapped his face. The man was sniveling and crying.

"Open your eyes!" Bill barked in Turkish.

Ahmet did for a second, just long enough to glance at the photo in Luke's hand. It was a photo of Ahmet's wife. It was a glamour shot, a little bit sexy, with the wife reclining on a couch, fully dressed in tight jeans, a short abaya dress and hijab over her head. Incredibly chaste for the nude beaches in southern France, but flirting with years of hard labor in Saudi Arabia. Bill imagined Ahmet had paid a professional photographer to take that photo.

"We have you," Bill said. "We can have her, too."

"They'll kill me if I tell you anything," Ahmet said.

"Yes," Bill said. "That's true. But better you than your wife and your children. We can protect them."

Stone held the photos of Ahmet's children under his face, a boy and a girl—cute kids. Ahmet barely looked at them before squeezing his eyes shut again. Bill had sympathy for him, he really did. Ahmet was in a bad place. He had run out of options. Ahmet had made some poor choices in the recent past, and now his future looked very grim indeed.

"I'll tell you," he said. "I'll tell you whatever I know."

Ed Newsam raised an eyebrow, and Bill shrugged.

"Four lashes, in case anyone's keeping score," Bill said.

"That was easy," Ed said.

"Yeah," Bill said. "But looks can be deceiving."

He squatted on his haunches and turned his attention to his prisoner again. "So Ahmet, let's do the first thing. Tell me who you've been working for."

"The Kurds," Ahmet said without hesitation. "The Kurdish Peshmerga. They want to—"

Bill punched Ahmet hard across the face. The impact snapped Ahmet's head around and he fell to all fours. Bill looked at his own hand. There was a scrape across his knuckles. As he watched, it started to bleed.

It didn't really hurt, but it did annoy him.

"Liar!" Bill shouted.

It was always the Kurds with these people. That was the first line of defense. The Kurdish minority in the south... every act of sabotage, every explosion, every downtick in the economy, every overcooked dinner... It was the Kurds!

To Americans, the Kurds were that independent-minded, battle-hardened people who just wanted their own country. They were lovable underdogs. To the Turks, they were demons from hell, people who secretly had horns, sub-humans, conniving, manipulating, undermining everything.

When a Turkish prisoner lied, he would start with the Kurds. After that failed, he would move on to the Armenians. Eventually the Armenian thing would collapse—in Bill Cronin's experience, then and only then could you get to the real story, the reason why you came.

He wrapped his big hands around Ahmet's neck. Slowly, he began to apply pressure. It felt good to use his hands this way—they were still strong, they were still huge, like grizzly bear claws.

"The Kurds?" he said.

Ahmet could barely speak. The breath was going out of him. His face turned red, then a shade of purple. His eyes bulged.

"Yes," he gasped. "Yes, the Kurds."

Bill spit in his face. He applied more pressure.

A squeaking sound came from Ahmet's throat—his air passage was totally blocked.

"Big Daddy?" Stone said behind him. "Bill!'

Bill released Ahmet's neck and let the man drop. Ahmet's head bounced off the stone floor. He wheezed alarmingly, trying to suck in oxygen. He was weeping now.

Bill turned and looked up at Stone. "Stone, this is my gig, okay? This is what you called me in for. The first thing you need to know about Turks is they're inveterate liars. They blame everybody but themselves for their problems. We'll get there, but you have to let me work. All right?"

Stone shrugged. "Don't kill him. We clear on that?"

"Clear as a bell."

Bill turned back to Ahmet. The poor man was a puddle on the ground.

"I'm going to ask you one more time," Bill said. "Who do you work for?"

"The Armenians," Ahmet said. "I'm a spy for the Armenian government."

Bill shook his head. He almost laughed. He stood and picked up the bullwhip again. He looked at Luke and Ed.

"We're gonna be here a little while."

Luke paced the halls of a three-story building on the American side of the air base. Ed Newsam and Bill Cronin walked at his sides. Ahmet had spilled the beans and they had a lot to do.

"What will the Turks do with Ahmet?" Luke said.

Bill shrugged. "They'll kill him. But it'll take a couple of weeks."

Luke looked at him.

"You have to understand, and I'm sure you already do. He betrayed them. He was involved in a plot that killed men on this base, and made the entire country look bad. They lost eight nuclear weapons to a bunch of extremists."

Luke shook his head. "Then we're keeping him."

"I never knew you to be soft."

"It's not soft. I might want to question him again later. I can't do that if he's dead."

Bill shook his head. "I don't know, Stone. You're a guest here. You're playing on their turf. I'd recommend against it, but that's up to you."

Luke glanced at him. "Thanks."

He pulled his phone out and speed-dialed a number. Swann answered on the first ring. "Swann."

"Swann, where are you right now?"

"I'm with Mika. We've got a little command center set up on the eighth floor of a hotel... Mika, do you know what the name of this place is?"

There was some cross-talk as they gabbled back and forth. The upshot was they didn't know where they were. That was okay. His people were tired.

"I don't know what this place is. They wanted us off the base because we're civilians and they're expecting another attack. So we're here. It's okay. We came in by chopper. I went down to the lobby for a Coke. They've got the place sandbagged, with concrete barriers out on the street in front of the doors. There's a bunch of middle-aged former black ops guys turned mercenaries standing around with big guns down there, checking their bank balances on their telephones."

"Okay, Swann, never mind all that. We got some intel confirmation that the trucks were en route to Syria. Did you get any satellite imagery?"

"Just letting you know that we're probably safe over here."

"My heart is warmed by that fact," Luke said.

"And I got some satellite imagery, yeah."

"Do you care to share it with me?"

"Sure, if you like. I was able to pinpoint both trucks. I triangulated them using American, Russian, and Israeli spy satellites. They took separate routes out of town, but both circled back and got on the road directly south from here, to the port city of Karatas. I lost them in some cloud cover that came in, but I spotted six ferries or tankers that left early this morning from Karatas, all within two hours of the theft. Three tankers went into the open ocean—I was able to track them down, including their owners. All three are legitimate container vessels playing routine trade routes. Two headed toward Western Europe, Italy and Spain, to be precise, and one headed across the Mediterranean with a next port of call in Algiers. I called those into my people at NSA—Interpol is waiting for the ones that went to Spain and Italy, and will board and search upon their arrival. Algeria is a little trickier. We have that one under surveillance, and the Italian navy is going to intercept before it reaches port."

Luke nodded, pleased. "Okay, good work. The others?"

"Two Turkish passenger and vehicle ferries, which are open to the public and run scheduled routes, and which the Turkish police have already intercepted and searched. Nada."

"And the last one?"

"Those are probably our boys," Swann said. "They left Karatas and made a short crossing to the Syrian port of Jalmeh. The city had been held by the government, but was suddenly overrun by ISIS ten days ago. That fits—if they were planning to sneak nukes into the country, it makes sense to take and hold a port, at least for a little while. The town is under heavy bombardment by the Syrian army and the Russians. From what I could tell, the boat made it into port. I can give you the coordinates of where it's currently docked. I'm monitoring that spot now, and I haven't seen anything loaded onto or off that boat since it got in."

"Awesome, Swann. Keep an eye on it. Any other options?"

"Sure. The other possibility is they brought the bombs into Karatas, and holed up in a warehouse along the docks. It was morning by the time they got there, and they probably want to travel at night. I've taken the liberty of asking our Turkish allies to shut down that port. They wouldn't cooperate, something about being busy right now, so instead we've got choppers from the base flying routes along the waterfront, watching anything that tries to leave, and relaying that information first to the base, then back to me. If they've still got those nukes in Karatas, they can't leave by water or on the road without us seeing them. They could try to drive out again, but the roads are crawling with checkpoints. The Turks are belatedly limiting highway traffic in response to the uprising."

"Beautiful. Nice work. I owe you some drinks for that."

"Twist my arm," Swann said.

"Can you give me Mika?"

"Sure. She's right here."

There was a pause as Swann passed the phone.

Mika's small voice came on the line. "Luke?"

"Mika, hi. Look, I've got some intel I need you to track down. We talked to the prisoner, and he told us a couple of things. This is sensitive stuff, so be careful who you talk to, and make sure Swann has you on an encrypted network, okay?"

"Sure, Luke."

"Okay, here goes. The prisoner claims that a Colonel Hassan Musharaff was behind the infiltration of the base. He said there was an extensive tunnel dug from the city to the base, and Musharaff not only allowed it to happen, but supervised it and covered it up. Get me everything you can on Musharaff. We're going to want to bring him in for questioning, but it may be difficult because he's apparently a guy with protection at high levels. See if you can find out where he is at this moment, and anything that might tie him to the coup attempt. We're going to need some leverage to take him into custody. The Turks will not want to give him to us."

"Okay," she said. "Got it. What else?"

"Just this," Luke said. "Something a little less clear. The prisoner said that a jihadi known as the Phantom, and in some circles by the first name Jamal, was involved in the theft. He either organized it or was actually onsite when it happened, or both. Apparently he's a secretive guy, and he operates in deep cover and under various aliases. I need to know more about him—country of origin, age, combat or terrorism experience, who he's working for. Have we, or has anybody else, had him in custody before?"

"Got it, Luke."

"Okay. Be as thorough as you can, but keep in mind I need that stuff today."

After Luke hung up, he looked at Ed and Bill.

"Swann's got some satellite imagery. He thinks the nukes may have gone by boat to Syria, a port town called Jalmeh."

Bill nodded. "I've been there."

"How is it?"

"A rat hole, filled with scum and villainy. But the weather's not bad this time of year. I think you'll like it."

CHAPTER NINETEEN

8:05 a.m.
The Situation Room
The White House, Washington, DC

The room was out of control.

Susan walked in carrying her coffee, Kat Lopez with her step for step, two Secret Service agents—a woman and a man—one step behind them. Susan had barely slept. The heavy paper cup in her hand was her third dose of java in the past half an hour. Kat looked about as bad as Susan felt—Susan had given her the Lincoln Bedroom to sleep in, and Kat had sent a car to her home for clothes and personal items.

"Order!" Kurt Kimball shouted as Susan came in. "Everybody, let's come to order!" He clapped his big hands. Even that didn't impose quiet right away. The sounds of frantic conversations trailed off instead.

"Order," Kurt said, calmer now. "The President is here."

"What do you have for me, Kurt?" Susan said. She slid into her customary chair. The room was packed. Young aides who were men all looked like they needed shaves. The place was starting to smell like everyone needed a shower. Eyes were tired, and some of them were nearly closed.

"We've got eight stolen nuclear warheads still at large. Luke Stone and his people have been in Adana for a couple of hours. Apparently they hit the ground running."

"Why don't you tell her who's with him?" Haley Lawrence said.

Susan looked quizzically at Kurt. "Who's with him?"

Kurt shrugged and sighed heavily. His body language suggested this was about what he'd expect. "Stone contacted a former CIA agent living in Greece. His name is Bill Cronin, and he was a Middle East operative for close to thirty years until his retirement a few years ago."

"He was drummed out of the Agency," a square-jawed, crew-cutted man in a dress green uniform to Susan's right said. "He didn't retire."

Susan glanced at the man.

"Madam President, I'm General Frank Loomis of the United States Army. I'm a liaison to the Pentagon from JSOC—the Joint Special Operations Command. The Secretary of Defense asked me to attend this meeting."

"Welcome, General."

"Thank you. I know Big Daddy Cronin. He worked with our people in the Middle East many times. Much of that history is Top Secret, but I can say that Cronin and Luke Stone worked together in Iraq when Stone was with Delta Force. Cronin was a good agent. The problem is that over time, he became a little... what? Unhinged, shall we say? That environment will do it to anyone. His methods would make your Luke Stone look like a choirboy."

"In what way?"

"He initiated and oversaw the systematic torture of prisoners at various sites in Iraq, Afghanistan, Pakistan, and Egypt."

"And Luke contacted him?"

Kurt sighed. "Stone did more than contact him. He sent a small jet to the Greek Islands to pick him up. Agent Stone interrogated a prisoner at Incirlik Air Base sometime in the past hour, and despite not having any official reason or clearance to be involved, Bill Cronin participated in that interview."

Susan was careful to make no sign. She had sent Luke over there, and this was what you got when you sent Luke Stone somewhere. Unpleasant surprises tended to pop up. Was it worth the trade-offs? So far, it certainly had been, and in spades.

"Is anyone alleging torture?" Susan said.

"No one is alleging anything," Kurt said. "Stone has apparently declined to release the prisoner back to the Turks. And he has with him a man who has no official position with the United States government, and who appears to have been relieved of his duties because of possible human rights violations."

"Big Daddy Cronin is a burnt-out case," General Loomis said. "He's seen too much, and he's done too much. He has no business being in a war zone, or in a sensitive situation of any kind. He should probably be in a mental hospital."

"That's just dandy," Susan said. She found that she wanted to move past this Big Daddy person. Stone brought him on board—the same Luke Stone who had been right again and again and again. Luke didn't do what the data suggested—he went on instinct, like a wild animal. So far it had worked.

"What else?" she said. "Let's leave personnel issues aside until we can talk with Agent Stone. What about the warheads?"

Kurt nodded. "Amy, can you put up those satellite stills from Mark Swann?"

On the screen, an overhead zoom image of an old, middle-sized freighter appeared. It was followed by several more. In the first image, the ship was at anchor in port, then there were a few of it at sea, and then once again at anchor, this time in a different port. It was docked at what looked like a long concrete wharf, lined with low buildings with green peaked roofs. A couple more images materialized on the screen, these of what might be the same ship, except from a ground-based perspective. The ship might have been red once, now it was a sort of decrepit orange—the color of rusted steel. It had Greek lettering along the bow.

"Agent Stone's systems person is a data analyst from the NSA named Mark Swann. He has traced the trucks to the Turkish port of Karatas. He believes they went from there to the Syrian port of Jalmeh. He sent us these images, of a ship called the *Helena*. He believes, but not with one hundred percent uncertainty, that the stolen warheads were driven onto this ship. The ship made the crossing from Turkey to Syria early this morning. The warheads, if they ever were aboard that ship, may still be."

"Can we send someone to intercept them?" Susan said.

"Difficult," Kurt said. "That port is held by ISIS. The Syrians and the Russians are trying to dislodge them, but they're dug in.

"If you look closely at the port images, you can see there are between a dozen and twenty men on the docks, likely guarding the ship. Those images are only about thirty minutes old. The city, and the port, are surrounded by Syrian government troops, and are under constant bombardment by Russian jets and helicopter gunships. It's basically a siege situation, with thousands of non-combatants caught in the crossfire. Between the ISIS fighters, the Assad troops, and the Russians, that dock is a hard place to reach."

"The ship made it in there," Susan said.

Kurt shrugged. "The ship is flying three flags—a white surrender flag, as well as the flags of the Red Cross and the Red Crescent. It came in camouflaged as an aide ship."

"Madame President," General Loomis said. "We have teams of special operatives, highly trained, well-rested, and fit for service, waiting right now at our embassy in Baghdad. Within an hour, we could present you a plan for getting them on the ground near those docks. The plan would include air cover and possible softening bombardment of the vicinity."

"The Russians are already bombarding the vicinity," Haley Lawrence said. "They control the skies above that port. We'd need to communicate our intentions to them in order to—"

Kurt waved a hand. "I don't think we can talk to the Russians about this. Not right away. These are American nukes. We need to try to get them back before we say a word to anyone. The Turks let them get stolen, but we are hardly blameless. I don't think we want to advertise that we've lost control of our own nuclear weapons."

"Eight, one-hundred-fifty-kiloton warheads," Haley Lawrence was saying. "It doesn't bear thinking about. Maybe we *should* tell the Russians, and have them sink that ship right at the dock. That seems like the—"

"Could *we* just bomb it?" Susan said.

"Dicey," Kurt said. "There's the threat of contamination, for one. A bigger issue is that if we bomb it, that doesn't tell us if the warheads are on board. We're still at square one."

"Within four or five hours from now, we could have the drop teams onsite," the general said, cutting Haley off. "All we have to do is say go. At the very least, they'd be able to determine what's on board that ship, and possibly even take possession of the warheads if they—"

"Kurt," one the young aides said, cutting off the general in turn. "We've got Agent Stone patching through right now from Adana."

Kurt gestured with his head at the strange black speakerphone device in the center of the conference table—it had five or six protuberances that stabilized it. Staffers invariably called it the octopus. "Put him on the speaker system."

A long moment passed. Susan sipped her coffee. She had been living here for less than twenty-four hours, and she'd hardly had a moment to think. Perhaps that was for the best. She didn't like it here. She wanted her house back.

Stone's disembodied voice came from the octopus. "Hello?"

"Agent Stone?" Kurt Kimball said.

"Yes. Kurt? Is Susan there with you?"

"I'm here, Luke," Susan said. "We're all here, but I'm going to save the introductions for another time. What have you got for us?"

"Swann sent you the images of the ship?"

"Yes."

"That's what we've got. Also, hearsay from a prisoner that we're trying to get some verification on. This very much looks like an inside job, which is no surprise, but it also appears to go as high as at least one officer involved in the command of the base. I don't want to divulge too much at this moment, and I want to caution you that we don't have confirmation."

People around the room were silent. "Are you saying that a rogue element in the Turkish military—"

"I'm not saying anything yet," Stone said. "Maybe your people can figure that out. Another person we're interested in, and I have one of my people looking into it right now, is someone known alternately as Jamal or the Phantom. He might have been here when the nukes were stolen, and that's all we know. I've never heard of him, and I've been around the block a few times. It wouldn't hurt to get a bunch more eyes looking for this person."

"Agent Stone," Kurt said, "have you been to the Turkish-controlled side of the base?"

"Negative. They've got it locked down. The only reason we even have the prisoner is because an American military police patrol caught him on our side of the field. Apparently, the Turks were looking for him, beat him pretty bad, and were about to execute him when our guys got there. What does that tell you?"

"They didn't want him talking to anyone?"

"Bingo," Stone said.

"So what are your plans?" Kurt Kimball said.

"Plans? Well, first I'm going to take a little power nap, and then we're going to Syria. It's two p.m. here, and we should have sunset just before five p.m. It's about ninety miles from here to Jalmeh. By helicopter, we can be there in forty-five minutes. We'll go in under cover of darkness, flying low over the water, lights out. I've already got a couple of Night Stalker chopper pilots willing to—"

"Stone, General Frank Loomis of JSOC."

There was a pause. "Yes, hi, General, I'm familiar with your work."

"Son, do you have Bill Cronin with you?"

"Uh… yes, General. I do."

"Do you intend to bring him with you to Syria?"

"I hope not, General. He's a little out of shape."

There was a burst of laughter in the room behind Stone. Susan bit the inside of her mouth so as not to smile. Cronin must be there, listening to this call.

"That was my little joke. Bill has a lot of experience in-country, General. He's fluent in Arabic. He's been to Jalmeh. He doesn't look like much these days, but I think he'll be invaluable on the ground."

"Stone," Loomis said, "under whose authorization are you operating?"

"The President of the United States, sir. That's why I'm in Turkey right now, and that's why I'm calling. To ask my boss for the green light. I believe I have the best team for the job. We can be in and out of there very quickly. If the nukes are on that boat, we'll scuttle it. If they're not on the boat, we'll know they haven't left Turkey."

"And the war criminal Bill Cronin?" the General said. "He's on your team?"

"If you say so, sir."

There was another long pause over the line. Susan watched General Loomis. He was clearly concerned about the man that Luke had brought on. He was also clearly interested in having his own team go in there. His motivation could be as simple as showing his stuff, and making this visit to the Situation Room a regular thing. Or it could be something deeper.

"Madame President?" Stone said. "Obviously this is your decision. What do you want us to do?"

Rare for Stone to ask for permission. If she gave him the green light, whatever happened was no longer his fault. It was hers. You break it, you own it.

So be it.

"You've got eight hours, Agent Stone. I want regular updates on your whereabouts and activities. And if you find the warheads, I want to know that as soon as it's safe for you to tell me."

"Very fair," Stone said. "I'll be in touch."

* * *

"Susan, we've got a problem."

Susan had noticed Kat Lopez slip out of the meeting when her phone rang. Now they were walking back through the West Wing to the Oval Office, their shoes clacking on the marble floor. Two big Secret Service men trailed them.

"Tell me inside."

Once in the Oval Office, Susan shut the door. She didn't need any more problems, but of course there was no end to them. She looked at Kat up and down. Long black hair, pretty face, dark almond eyes, and a tall, voluptuous body hidden inside a blue business suit. Her eyes were tired, though, and were starting to show crow's feet at the edges. Susan also had a hunch she colored her hair to keep it that dark. Kat was young, but getting old before her time.

"Let me have it."

Kat shook her head. "The news is out."

"What news?"

"The stolen nuclear warheads."

"Tell me you're joking," Susan said.

"I wish I could," Kat said. "A Turkish-language tabloid, a scandal sheet, got wind of it sometime in the past couple of hours. A leak from inside the base, I imagine. They went with a short, our-sources-say piece, running it up the flagpole to see who would salute. In no time, it was picked up by a couple of far-left websites associated with the Communist Party in Greece. After that, it spread across Europe. The *National Enquirer* and Drudge were in a race to get it online here—it was neck and neck, and both stories went up about fifteen minutes ago. Our press people are already feeling the heat. We're going to need a response, and quickly. Marybeth Horning has an appearance at Franklin Middle School at ten a.m., and you can bet it's going to be a media circus. Marybeth *hates* nukes, and we need her on our page."

"Cancel it," Susan said without hesitating.

Kat raised an eyebrow. "Cancel the new Vice President's meeting with inner-city schoolchildren? The appearance is in less than an hour."

Susan nodded. "Cancel it. Tell her I'm sorry. We need to circle the wagons. We can't leave her naked out there—the sharks will go into a feeding frenzy. And what's she going to tell them—that she doesn't like nuclear weapons anyway? That'll show 'em. And we'll all look like idiots."

The phone on the desk in the middle of the room began to ring. Susan pressed the speaker phone button.

"Susan, it's Kurt Kimball."

"Hi, Kurt."

"The Russian embassy just called. The ambassador would like to know if there's any truth to the news reports he's seeing about unsecured American nuclear weapons being stolen from an air base in Turkey."

Susan looked at Kat.

"I think I'd like to vomit," she said.

CHAPTER TWENTY

4:40 p.m. Eastern European Time
(10:40 a.m. Eastern Daylight Time)
Incirlik Air Base
Adana, Turkey

Swann seemed to be speaking inside Luke's head.

"Luke, I need to run a test. Turn on a beacon and let me see what I'll be looking at."

Luke stood on the tarmac, in a rough circle with Ed Newsam and Bill Cronin. They all wore flight suits.

Luke was barely listening to Swann. Gunner had just sent him a text message.

Where are you?

Turkey, Luke wrote. *Where are you?*

A moment passed, a little pencil icon indicating that something was being written.

School. What are you doing in Turkey?

Luke smiled. *What else? Eating turkey sandwiches.*

"Luke?" Swann said again. "You gonna give me that beacon?"

"Yeah. Sorry. I was distracted for a minute."

Luke twisted the cylinder in his hand and tossed it about ten feet away. It rolled along the ground. It didn't seem to be doing anything. It could be one of those pneumatic tubes you put your money in at the drive-thru bank teller.

"Might be a little early to see that," Luke said into his helmet microphone.

Nearby, a jet fighter took off and immediately broke the sound barrier. The noise was deafening. The sun was setting toward the west, a dim orange glow. The evening was just coming on, but wasn't there quite yet.

"No, I'm getting a nice green strobe, just to your left. It's blinking every three seconds, very pretty. That'll work fine."

"Luke?" a female voice said. It was remarkable how young the voice was—it sounded almost like a little girl talking.

"Hi, Mika. What have you got for me?"

"Colonel Hassan Musharaff," Mika said. "Sixty-two years old. Three times divorced, seven children. Colonel Musharaff is a lifer in the Turkish Air Force. He joined when he was eighteen. He was an early mover, reaching the rank of Major at the age of thirty-two.

But that's where he stalled. Throughout his career, he's been associated with hard right elements in the Turkish military, as well as with mosques and organizations known to harbor extremist sentiments. He has been vocal in his disdain for the secular nature of Turkish society, and has been especially critical of the Turks sitting on their hands since the Russians seized their islands in the Black Sea. He has also expressed sympathy for the idea of reestablishing a Muslim empire based on Sharia law."

"The caliphate," Luke said. "Which means ISIS."

"Exactly," Mika said. "These views put him at odds with most of the military brass, and the elite of Turkish society. Which is likely why he never attained the rank of general, despite more than forty years of service."

Luke sighed. "How did he manage to stay in the military at all? He's so far out of the loop you'd think they would have shown him the door by now."

"He comes from a wealthy and prominent family. His grandfather was an olive farmer who vastly increased his holdings with land seized during the Armenian genocide. He became one of the largest exporters of olives and olive oil in the country. He developed lucrative side businesses in wine, dates, and specialty foods. The family's Turkish delight candies are still popular all over Europe. So there's that. Also, the colonel's older brother is a government functionary who's held high-level cabinet and adviser posts across three administrations. Musharaff may be a malcontent, but he's an untouchable malcontent."

"Where is he now?" Luke said.

"Nobody knows. He went underground once the uprising started. The rumor is that if he isn't behind it, he is somehow involved."

"Okay," Luke said. "Keep digging, see if you can scare up his location. What about this other guy? The Phantom?"

She hesitated. "Uh… sketchy. There are accounts of someone known as Jamal, or the Phantom, taking part in all kinds of terrorist activities over the past fifteen years. He's here, there, and everywhere. But there's nothing solid. If he's ever been in custody, I can't find it. If he was born and grew up somewhere, there's no record of it. It seems just as likely that there is no such person, and it's a rumor that the jihadis share among themselves. Kind of like the boogeyman, or Santa Claus."

Luke wasn't sure he agreed with her on that. Then again, he once met a Chechen rebel who fought against Russia, and who insisted that in the winter of 1995, there were women guerrillas in the Chechen mountains, dressed all in white to camouflage themselves against the snow. They were expert riflewomen who killed Russian soldiers with a single shot, then disappeared on skis. This was because in their former lives, the women were world-class biathletes from Finland. The Chechen said they were known as the White Tights—so-called because of the skin-tight outfits they wore. It was totally absurd, but people believed in things like this.

"Okay, Mika," he said. "Good job. Thank you. Let me know if you pick up anything more."

"Will do."

Luke glanced around.

Ed Newsam was gearing up for the apocalypse. He had his M79 grenade launcher and six boxes of grenades, four to a box. He had an MP5 machine pistol and two ammo belts looped over his shoulders. He had two Glock nines strapped around his waist. He had a six-inch dagger. He had a pair of spiked brass knuckles, in case it came down to that—Ed would be punching holes in his people's faces.

"What are you gonna do with all that?" Luke said.

Newsam shrugged. "Keep your pale white ass alive."

"Swann, you and Mika should see this guy."

"We do see him."

Luke smiled. He felt loose and ready. He was tired, but he'd caught a couple of winks on a cot in a quiet corner of the airmen's barracks. He ate a banana and a yogurt, and drank a cup of coffee in the mess hall upon wakening. None of that really got him going, but he and Ed had each dropped a Dexie a few minutes ago.

That was going to do the trick.

He gave his men the once-over. Ed looked fine. Ed rarely changed. He was big, broad, and physically imposing, but his body always seemed fluid and relaxed. Luke had seen him slumped in a chair with his feet on a desk. And he'd seen him in the minutes leading up to a firefight with the North Korean military. The look on his face was the same both times—impassive, blank, impossible to read. Maybe he was terrified. Maybe he was bored. It was hard to tell.

"Ed? How you doing, man?"

Now Ed looked at Luke. He flashed a smile—bright white, perfect teeth. "Ready to rock, brother. Of course."

Luke glanced at Bill. Bill looked sick. He was bigger than Luke remembered him—his stomach was rounder, sure, but there was more weight everywhere. Bill had a couple of handguns and a knife. He didn't look like a man who could fight anymore, if fighting was ever his thing. Luke had always thought of Bill's specialty as interrogations.

"Big Daddy?"

"Yeah."

"How you feeling?"

"Ready."

Luke shook his head. Seeing Bill had changed his mind—he didn't want to bring him along. Bill knew the layout of the town, sure, and he was an old Syria hand. He knew the language and the culture, he knew who all the players were, and he knew the map like he knew his own face. But he looked like he was past it.

"Bill, I want to tell you a story."

"Tell away."

"A few months ago, I let an old friend of mine come with Ed and me on an operation. He was my age, but he had let himself go a little bit. I told him I wasn't going to be able to keep him alive on the mission. I told him that, but I didn't really try to talk him out of coming. And that was because I needed him."

"Okay. And the point of this is…"

"He died. He died during the mission, and I watched him die. There was nothing I could do to save him. He was alive one second, and dead the next. You see where I'm going with this?"

Now Bill looked at him. His eyes were hard, in the sense of eyes that had no emotion. They were the eyes of a child who could pull the wings off of houseflies, or of a man who could pull the tongues out of helpless prisoners.

"I do. Yeah."

"I'm not gonna lie to you, Bill. We're probably going to need you down there. But if you die…"

Luke shrugged.

"It's my nickel," Bill said.

"Exactly."

Bill shook his head. "Don't lecture me, Stone. You called me, and I came. What's the old saying—in for a penny, in for a pound. Anyway, I was flying missions when you were in grade school. I think I'll be fine."

Luke smiled. "That's what I like to hear."

He picked up his rucksack, and the other men followed suit. The tiny helicopter was on the pad fifty feet away.

They called it the Little Bird. And sometimes they called it the Flying Egg.

It was the MH-6 helicopter—fast and light, highly maneuverable, the kind of chopper that didn't need room to land. It could come down on small rooftops, and on narrow roadways in crowded neighborhoods. The chopper was beloved by special operations forces. As they walked toward it, the chopper's rotors began to spin.

Luke ducked then and ran to the open passenger hold. The engine revved up, and the blades turned faster and faster as the men climbed over the wooden side-mounted bench and aboard. All around them, night descended.

* * *

The chopper flew low and fast.

The ocean buzzed by below them, maybe fifty feet down, almost close enough to touch. Luke watched its inky darkness from the open doorway. A stiff, cool breeze blew in. He guessed they were moving at over a hundred miles per hour.

He pictured Gunner in his mind. Tow-headed boy, twelve years old, getting bigger all the time, *changing* all the time. A year ago, the kid was in love with zombies. Where did that go? The first twelve years had passed so quickly—in twelve more, Gunner would be a young man of twenty-four.

Luke would be in his early fifties.

Don't waste it, man. Don't waste that time.

"I ain't seen my little girls in a while," Ed Newsam suddenly said. He spoke quietly, but his voice inside Luke's helmet cut through the wind from outside, and the effect was almost enough to make Luke jump out of his seat.

Luke glanced at him—the big man sat back with his MP5 across his lap. His beloved M79 was at his feet.

"Great minds think alike," Luke said.

"Is that what you guys like to do?" Bill Cronin said. "Gas each other up before you drop in?"

"Pretty much," Ed said. "What do you like to do?"

Cronin shrugged. "Pray."

"Gentlemen," another disembodied voice said, "we are approaching target, ETA approximately ten minutes. Not sure how much time you guys have spent in Syria lately, but I've done a little. I can promise you this is gonna be hot."

Luke went to the cockpit—it was barely two steps away. He leaned his head in between the helmeted, flight-suited pilots. Two men were up front, both of them from the U.S. Army 160th Special Operations Aviation Regiment, code name Nightstalkers. Luke and Ed were used to flying with people like this. The 160th SOAR were the Delta Force of helicopter pilots.

Through the bubble windshield, far ahead, there were flashes of light in the darkness. A person might think it was a lightning storm at sea. Luke could tell what it was without thinking about it—firefight. The word didn't even reach his conscious mind. They were flying right toward the middle of it.

He glanced at the chopper commander's nameplate. ALVAREZ.

"You know the plan, Alvarez?"

Alvarez nodded. "Primary landing site is on the upper deck of the freighter. We have the coordinates. If it's too hot, or there are unexpected obstructions on the upper deck, we go to secondary landing site, an old parking lot three hundred meters to the southwest. Failing that, third and final landing site is an open field two miles to the north, northwest. We make the drop, circle around, and if the situation permits, provide air support. If not, we bug out for Turkey."

"Beautiful," Luke said. "Let's do this. Do everything you can for us, but make it home alive, you get me?"

Alvarez's co-pilot smiled. "We always do."

Luke gestured with his head at the flashes of light up ahead. Now he could hear faint rumbles.

"That where we're headed?"

"You bet. Like I said, this place is as hot as it comes."

Luke ducked back and took his seat between Ed and Bill.

"Approximately seven minutes to the destination," Alvarez said. "We should be exposed to incoming fire well before that. Second thoughts? Now's your last chance to jump."

Luke glanced out the door again. Whitecaps whipped up on the surface of the black waves.

Without warning, Mark Swann's voice appeared inside Luke's helmet.

"Luke, you with me?"

"Yeah, Swann. How's it going?"

"Mika and I are here at the hotel. We've got you on real-time satellite with, I think, about ten- or fifteen-second delay. I've got a gossamer drone high above that ship, and I've got a Reaper that I can do a Stinger missile strike with, if it comes to that. If you ID those nukes, I could sink the ship with it, if we want. Then the SEALs can go deal with those nukes after the war is over."

"Okay," Luke said. "How does the theater look?"

"Bad. There's street fighting maybe a quarter of a mile from the docks. Assad's people are in there with a couple of heavy tanks. They're blowing holes in everything. They're shelling the buildings just to the west of where you're headed. There's a helicopter gunship, my guess a Russian Mi-24, circling the battle, putting the heavy guns on rebel positions. Everything's on fire, a lot of tracers flying, the sky is lit up. You're going to be visible in there. There's nowhere to hide."

"How does the boat look?"

"Uh, I counted about twenty fighters there earlier, taking up positions on the docks and on the upper deck of the boat. Maybe a sniper laying prone on the roof of the pilot house. Now, it's hard to tell. There's very little light along the waterfront. I suspect those guys are still there, but are probably pulled back into darkened corners. They don't want that Russian chopper giving them any attention."

"Alvarez, you hearing any of this?" Luke said.

"Loud and clear."

"Thoughts?"

"Continue as planned," Alvarez said.

"You heard the man," Luke said to Swann. "That's good enough for me. Thanks, Swann. Keep in touch. Keep us alive."

"Will do," Swann said.

Luke took a deep breath. It wasn't a full one—the air caught at the top of his lungs. "Ready, boys?"

No one had time to answer. The second he spoke, a jet flew by overhead, the shriek of its engines ripping open the night.

"Bomber!" Alvarez shouted. "Incoming! Right stick! Full speed!"

The chopper banked sharply to the right, flying on Alvarez's instinct alone. Luke, Ed, and Bill tilted crazily to the side of the cabin.

Dark shadows went by, to the left and behind the plane. Bombs were falling. A line of them hit the ocean, marching in toward land, the impact on the water enough to detonate.

Just below them, the darkness lit up in red and orange—a fierce line of flame. A shockwave hit and the chopper shuddered violently.

"What are they launching at?" the co-pilot said.

"It was a miss," Alvarez said. "They don't see us. They're bombing something on land. They released too early."

Luke looked back. Fire burned on the surface of the waves. Far to the left now, a new line of bombs dropped, this time hitting pay dirt. Luke saw what looked like a tall building blow apart, consumed in flame.

"Holy hell," Bill Cronin said.

"ETA three minutes," Alvarez said. "Prepare for disembark."

Luke and Ed scrambled for the side-mounted benches outside the doorways, Luke going left, Ed going right. Luke did a quick check—he had a small rucksack with food and clothing, three guns, a knife, grenades, ten meals-ready-to-eat, and water. He had a flashlight, three strobe beacons. He had night vision goggles on his helmet. Body armor under his flight suit. He was good.

He glanced inside the chopper. "Bill, you're out here with me."

Bill Cronin clambered out onto the bench.

Another jet screamed by overhead.

"Bombs?" Alvarez shouted.

"Not yet," his co-pilot said.

Swann's voice was there again. "Luke, you've got trouble. I think the trailing jet must have spotted you in the glow from those bombs. That big chopper just peeled off from the battle. He's coming out to take a look."

"Jesus. Alvarez?"

"Okay," the pilot said. He didn't sound like it was okay.

"Can we outrun him?" Ed said.

"Maybe, but then we can't put our guns on him, if he's behind us."

"What are your rules of engagement?" Ed said.

"Don't get in a shootout with Russians."

"You don't want to tangle with that guy," Swann said. "I've confirmed his shape with my database—he's an Mi-24, so-called flying tank. The specs are outrageous. He's fast, hard to hurt, and bristling with weaponry."

Luke looked out at the sky. He saw something big out there, with bright lights, getting brighter all the time. It was high in the sky, sweeping the water below with a spotlight.

"We're below him."

"I know," Alvarez said. "Not good. He's gonna have the drop on us. But if we try to get above him, he'll see us do it. We don't have a lot of good options right now."

Luke didn't like it. Alvarez had been brimming with confidence a minute ago. For a split second, he wondered when the last time Americans and Russians had directly engaged in combat. Not for a long time.

"Ed, can you hit him with the M79?"

"I can try."

"Alvarez, we know he's there. He doesn't know we're here. We might have surprise in our favor. Spin this bird around and give Ed a shot at that thing."

"You're going to shoot first at a Russian military helicopter?"

"You have a better idea?"

"No," Alvarez said. "But I think you might be wrong."

"About what?"

"He knows we're here."

Gunfire erupted all around them, like a swarm of killer bees. Luke was exposed on the outside bench—he dove back into the helicopter. Bullets ricocheted inside the cabin. Metal shredded. Glass shattered. Bill Cronin screamed.

"Ah, man," he said. "I'm hit. Jesus!"

The Little Bird pulled up abruptly. It made a steep climb and banked hard to the left. Luke fell over sideways. He clung to the floor, his fingers gripping metal slats. Another burst of gunfire came. THUNK, THUNK, THUNK, it shredded the skin of the chopper. Steam began to release from a severed line.

An alarm in the cockpit began to sound.

BEEP, BEEP, BEEP...

"Okay, we're hit," Alvarez said.

"Swann?" Luke said. This wasn't going anything like the plan. They weren't even near the ship yet. "We've got problems. Can you take that guy out?"

* * *

"Watch the satellite footage," Swann said.

He threw his headset down and pushed out from the desk, as Mika slid in behind him where he was sitting only seconds before. He stood and went to a bank of three computer monitors he had set up on fold-out tables near the wall. He dropped into an office chair with wheels at the bottom.

He had set his hotel room up as a makeshift command center—the electricity was still out in the hotel, so the only light came from the eerie glow of Swann's computer equipment. The detritus of food containers littered the areas around the computers. He and Mika had taken all of their meals here.

Swann took manual control of the MQ-9 Reaper drone that had been on auto pilot, tracking the movement of the Little Bird chopper. He held a joystick controller in one hand and a throttle in the other. He stared intently into the screens in front of him.

He watched the large Russian helicopter gunship, outlined in green below him. Equivalent ground speed: 119. It was moving at a good clip. He spun the Reaper's video camera and looked back at the Little Bird. It had taken a direct hit from the attack copter's machine guns. He brought the camera back and centered it on his prey.

A drop of sweat ran down his forehead and into his eye. He wiped it away.

His hand moved the joystick with a mind of its own. He was not conscious of controlling it. He moved the drone into position, above the gunship and a little behind it. He put the cross hairs onto the body of the chopper, right below where its chopper blades spun, glowing green on the readout. He moved the drone's bottom-mounted machine gun into place. The helicopter moved erratically, and Swann lost it for a second.

But he was patient. He put the crosshairs right back on there.

"I've acquired the target," he said, more to himself than anyone. "Everybody take it easy."

He held his breath.

"Steady… steady…"

He fired one of his Stingers. An instant later, he saw the projectile hit the top of the helicopter gunship, throwing sparks of green light. As he watched, the rotors began to wobble.

"Direct hit," he said to Mika.

"Direct hit," she said into Swann's former headset.

The Russian chopper began to spin crazily. The pilot was trying to regain control—the chopper spun hard left, then spun all the way back again hard right.

Green translucent sparks flew.

Swann watched as the rear of the fuselage cracked, separated, and fell away, taking the tail rotor with it. Now the helicopter spun out of control, arcing in big loopy circles across the sky. It spun nearly due east, headed straight out over the water.

It never regained control. It dropped suddenly, losing 10,000 feet of altitude in a couple of seconds. It slapped hard against the surface of the ocean and exploded.

Swann nearly cheered, then thought better of it. He glanced over at Mika.

"Did you *see* that?"

* * *

"I can't hold it!" Alvarez said. "We gotta land."

The chopper was in a dizzying spin. Luke had been just about to commend Swann for hitting that Russian chopper, but now it didn't matter. He dragged himself to a seat, buckled Bill Cronin in, and then himself. Bill was spitting up dark blood—he'd been hit somewhere deep inside. Ed was already buckled in, eyes closed.

"Ed! What's the matter?"

"I'm dizzy, man."

BEEP, BEEP, BEEP… the cockpit alarm kept sounding.

"We're not going to make the third landing area," Alvarez said.

"So set it down!" Luke said. "Put it anywhere." Bill needed a medic, and if this chopper spun many more times, Luke was going to pass out.

"We're still over the water."

Luke glanced out through the doorway. That was true—they were over water—but not for much longer. The city was coming toward them with frightening speed. The chopper was spinning, but seemingly under Alvarez's control.

"My rudder's going. It's shuddering. I'm about to lose it."

Suddenly, everything seemed to move in slow motion. The chopper, which was spinning before, went into a violent, gyroscopic whirlwind. They came down over the port, passing the docks, the warehouses, and the tall buildings along the waterfront boulevard. Many of the buildings were half-demolished, the sides of them crumbling down in landslides of brick and stone and dust.

"Rudder's gone," Alvarez said, but now it seemed like a dream.

The chopper moved horizontally at fantastic speed, maybe fifty feet above the ground. "Hold it up!" Alvarez shouted.

It dropped with a sickening lurch, three stories in one second. Luke looked out again—they were just above the ground, careening down a pockmarked roadway, a canyon of rubble between two lines of destroyed buildings.

"Here we go," Alvarez said, his voice resigned. "Mayday, mayday."

The chopper hit hard, skidded along the ground for a second, then flipped head over heels. Luke felt it go, all the weight coming down on the cockpit. The pilots' screams were in Luke's headset for a split second, but were cut short. The cockpit windshield collapsed, spraying glass inward.

The chopper rolled, tumbling in darkness. Luke's head slammed against the front of the cabin. He heard a ringing, loud, like church bells on Easter Sunday. Then there was flying dirt and grit all around him.

He closed his eyes and gripped the straps harder than before. His hands were wrenched free, and then he was tumbling in space. His head whipsawed.

Everything went black.

* * *

"Luke? Luke? Stone! Do you read me?"

His eyelids fluttered. For a moment, he couldn't understand what he was seeing. Then he got it—he was hanging upside down. The straps had held him in place. His head felt like it might explode from the pressure.

He looked to his right and left. His neck screamed in pain as he did. Ed hung next to him on one side, Bill on the other. Both of their arms dangled down. Bill was bleeding. The blood ran from inside his shirt, along his throat and then down his face. His visor was smeared with it.

Blood dripped from Bill's fingertips and pooled beneath him.

There was fighting going on very close. He could hear the sound of cannon fire, and the heavy WHUMP as the missiles found their targets. The chopper trembled from the force of the explosions.

He played back the last seconds of the crash in his mind. He pictured the cockpit caving in from the weight of the chopper. The pilots were dead. No one could have survived that. He shook his head. He couldn't think about that now.

"Stone," Luke said. "Here."

"Luke, can you move?" It was Swann. "You have to get out of that chopper. Unfriendlies are on their way to your position."

125

Luke's mouth was dry. He could barely speak. "Who are they?"

"I don't know."

"Then how do you know they're unfriendly?"

"There aren't any friendlies there, Luke. It's ISIS fighting Russians and Syrians."

Luke took a deep breath. "Right."

He reached up to his calf and pulled the tape off the knife strapped there. Quickly, he cut his shoulder straps away. Now he was dangling from the lap belt, all of his weight on his legs. He grabbed the lap belt, worked his legs out, then flipped over right side up and dropped to the ceiling of the up-ended chopper. His impact shook the chopper, and Ed's eyes popped open.

"Good morning, sunshine," Luke said. "You hurt?"

Ed blinked. "Just my feelings."

Ed's voice wasn't inside Luke's helmet.

"Your radio working?" Luke said.

Ed tapped his helmet. "I don't know. Say something."

"Something."

Ed shook his head. "No, it's dead."

"Then you didn't hear Swann," Luke said. "We got trouble. Bad guys coming."

Ed nodded. "So I guess I can't relax here for a while?"

"Upside down like that? You should talk to Don Morris. Could become a new health craze."

Luke handed Ed the knife and began to paw around on the ceiling, looking for their weapons.

"Swann, where are those bad guys?"

"Moving to the crash site on foot, about three blocks away from you. Taking it careful, keeping under cover. Moving without obvious organization."

"ISIS."

"I'd say."

Luke gritted his teeth—it wasn't what he wanted to hear. They could probably surrender to Russians. There'd be a lot of explaining to do, but that was okay. Bill needed medical attention, and Russians could provide it.

"Uh-oh. Bad guys just rendezvoused with a pickup truck. Looks like a heavy gun mounted in the bed. Definitely ISIS."

Luke sighed. This day just kept getting better and better.

"Can you put that Reaper on them?" Luke said.

"Uh, negative, Luke. That's a civilian area. There are residential buildings all around you. I'd be really—"

"Okay. Okay."

Ed flipped out of his lap belt and dropped feet-first to the floor. Luke handed him his M79 grenade launcher. Ed strapped it to his back. They went over and cut Bill down. He came awake as they maneuvered his bulk to the floor. He groaned—it was very nearly a scream. His eyes opened. They rolled for a few seconds, trying to find something to focus on.

He looked at Luke, his face a mask of pain. Bill's voice was barely above a whisper. "Stone, I was cooking eggs when you called."

Luke shook his head. "Yeah. I'm sorry about that. Any idea where you're hit?"

"Everywhere."

Luke kneeled beside him. He removed the man's helmet. Gently, he began to feel under the flight suit. When he found an entry wound, he touched it gingerly. Bill grimaced each time. Luke counted thirteen holes, then stopped counting. "Oh man, Big Daddy."

Bill shook his head. "You know, it's not so bad. It hurts, but I never minded a little pain. I've done a lot of really rotten things in my life, Stone. I've spent years thinking about them. I told myself I was doing this for my country, but you know what the truth is? The truth is I *enjoyed* it."

"Be quiet, old man," Ed said. "This is no time for that kind of—"

Swann's voice squawked inside Luke's helmet. "Luke, you are almost out of time. Whatever you're going to do, you better do it now. They are coming for you."

"Which way?"

"From the east."

"Swann, did you see this bird hit? We were playing dizzy bats at high speed. I was upside down a minute ago. Where are they coming from?"

"You're at one end of a long block. They're coming from the other end. They're going to be turning that corner any second."

"We gotta get out of here," Luke said to the others. "Now."

He scanned out the bay door to his right. There was a ruined building maybe fifty yards across the way. It looked about eight stories, the whole face of it Swiss cheese. It looked like it had a lobby on the ground floor once upon a time—the front doors of it were blown out. The entire building was dark.

"Ed, give me a hand with this guy. If we can make it to that building right there, we might be able to—"

"I'll never make it over there," Bill said.

"Shut up, Bill," Luke said. "We're out of time."

Luke and Ed tried to lift him, but his eyes rolled and he shrieked in pain.

"Oh man, Bill." It was a cascading series of failures, getting worse all the time. Why had Luke called this guy? Because he was a Middle East expert? He was fluent in the lingo? He could break a prisoner in four minutes flat? All of that, but what good was it going to do now?

"Luke!" Swann shouted.

"Give me a couple of guns," Bill said. "And put me in the doorway. I'll take that machine pistol. And the Glock there. Leave me a grenade, too."

"Bill—"

"It's too late, Stone. What else are we going to do? I'll draw their fire. I'll take out as many as I can. You guys finish up."

"Jesus, Bill. It looks like I killed you here. I really didn't mean..."

Big Daddy shook his head. "You didn't kill me. I killed myself years ago."

Ed seemed done with the group therapy. He handed Bill an MP5 and two grenades. He touched Luke on the shoulder. "Let's go, man."

Luke gave Bill his own Glock. "Make them count."

"I always do."

They helped him to the doorway, propped him up, then jumped out of the chopper. Luke glanced at the cockpit—it was totally destroyed, but he could spot the remains of the pilots inside. Their bodies were ruined.

Ed was already running low across open territory toward the wrecked building. Luke followed him, outright sprinting. He passed through the blasted entryway and into the shadows. Ed was kneeling in a corner, checking his weapons. Luke took the corner across from him and crouched. Something moved behind him.

He turned, and three small children stood, still as statues, at the bottom of a crumbling staircase.

Luke waved at them. "Get lost!" he hissed. "Get out of here!"

128

They stared at him with dirty faces and big eyes. They didn't look afraid. They didn't look like anything. Just blank.

Shooting started out on the street. The rat-a-tat of a lone gun, was soon joined by several more.

"Ed, we got kids over here."

Ed glanced over at him. He spotted the kids, and his shoulders sank. He shook his head in frustration.

Ed whispered fiercely at them. "Get! Go on!"

The kids didn't move.

From Luke's vantage point, he could see the chopper lying upside down in the street. It looked like the loser in a demolition derby. Bill was perched in the doorway, firing bursts from the MP5. Luke crept to his right, trying to get an angle on the street. The fighters were moving up the street, leapfrogging, doorway to doorway. On the other side, a handful of them had just gotten the memo—they were on Bill's blind side. They began to run.

"They're moving on him," Luke said. He moved forward to the low wall, his own MP5 out. Then Ed was there with him. He put a hand on Luke's gun. Luke looked at him. Ed shook his head. He lifted his M79 and pointed down the street. The pickup truck was out there, a man in a headscarf at the heavy machine gun in the back.

On the street, the jihadis reached Bill's blind side. Bill fired back into the helicopter. His body shuddered as he was pierced by their bullets. Luke stared, helpless, as his old spymaster died.

"Come on, Big Daddy," Ed whispered. "Pull that pin."

A group of fighters had gathered around the chopper. Luke counted them… eight, nine, ten… maybe as many as a dozen. They climbed inside of the chopper. They inspected it. They scanned the surrounding buildings. They had been sent to investigate, and now they had done so. It was an American helicopter, downed in the battle zone. Even though it shouldn't be here, it was no more confusing than anything else going on. In another minute, the fighters would probably head back to the war.

Then the chopper exploded.

There was a blinding flash of light, then a long, rolling BOOOOOOM. Luke and Ed ducked as flaming shards of metal and shredded chunks of instant human corpses flew in every direction. What was only recently a helicopter was now a flaming ball, lighting up the night. Luke could hear the crackling of the flames.

Just like that, Big Daddy was dead. In a war zone, a human life was like a priceless vase—here and gone. One second, it was in your hands. The next second, it fell to the floor and shattered into a million pieces. There was no way to turn back that clock, not even one second.

"Beautiful," Ed said. He stood and fiddled with his M79. He aimed down the street toward the pickup. "Get ready, white man. It's about to get ugly in here."

Luke scrambled away from the gun. An instant later, Ed fired.

Doonk!

The hollow report of the M79 was all out of proportion to its destructive power. It reminded Luke of a tennis ball being shot out of a serving gun. He watched the trajectory of the grenade, nearly flat, Ed's specialty.

BAM!

It hit the pickup in the front windshield, passed through, and blew out the cab. Light and heat. The doors flew off. The heavy gun was thrown in the air, a fireball beneath it. The shooter's limbs flapped away like birds.

Luke was already up and running for the stairwell. Now the children were moving. He pushed them up the stairs ahead of him. One of them, the smallest boy, was moving too slow, so Luke picked him up and ran with him under his arm like a football. Ed's heavy steps were on the stairs right behind him.

Behind them and below, machine gun fire strafed the ruined lobby.

CHAPTER TWENTY ONE

9:03 p.m. Eastern European Time
(3:03 p.m. Eastern Daylight Time)
Adana, Turkey

"Luke can you give me a strobe, so I can get a look at your location?"

"What if the Russians are up there with you?"

Swann shrugged. He stared into the computer screen, watching the Little Bird and the pickup truck burn. A handful of ISIS fighters were left on the street, hiding in doorways and alleys, firing at the building Luke and Ed were most recently in. They took up positions around that front doorway, but made no attempt to enter the building. They had about one-fifth of the men they'd come with.

"The Russians were doing fast bombing runs. They've got a few choppers out over the water now, looking for the bird I downed. I think the Russians are the least of your worries."

A green light appeared on a rooftop, three quarters of the way back down the block. It blinked every three seconds.

"Okay, I see you."

"How do we look?"

"Well, the bad guys are digging in where you fired from. They don't look like they're in any hurry to come inside, though."

"How far are we from the boat?"

Swann smiled. Of course. These gung-ho lunatics had survived an aerial dogfight, a helicopter crash, and a firefight by the skin of their teeth. Now they were going to go after the original objective.

"You are almost three miles from the boat. It is south and west of you. There's nothing but ugly between you and there. You've got a pitched battle going on half a mile to your south—I don't see any way you can make it through. There are running gunfights damn near all the way to the docks. The Syrians are pushing through with heavy guns. They're taking out entire buildings. God help any people still inside of them."

"We know. We can see it from here."

"I'd say you want to wait that thing out."

Luke didn't respond. The moment dragged on.

"Luke? It's a shit storm. You won't make it through there."

"I heard you the first time, Swann."

Swann shook his head. He glanced up at Mika, who was staring at the screen with wide owl eyes. Mika was undergoing a trial by fire just witnessing this, and her face showed it.

"Luke," Swann said, "we're supposed to report to the Situation Room. I need official status on Bill Cronin and the pilots."

"The pilots died in the crash," Stone said without hesitating. "Cronin died in the shootout. He was wounded, and volunteered to stay behind to draw fire."

"That's confirmed?"

"I saw him die," Luke said. "And the chopper is scuttled. Bill took it with him, wherever he went." A long moment passed. "What do you suggest we do down here?"

Swann shrugged. "I'd say find a dark corner to hole up in. If the battle dies down, or the lines shift, a corridor might open up. Mika and I will keep an eye on it."

"All right. I'm going to sign off. The last thing we'll need is for this battery to die. Just about everything else has gone wrong, so why not that?"

* * *

The hours passed.

Swann sat alone and dozed in the darkened hotel suite. His headset was still on. He had turned off most of his set-up to conserve power. The hotel was still blacked out. From his windows, if he cared to look, he could see the skyline of the city of Adana. There was still sporadic fighting going on out there. He could hear the gunshots, and the rare explosion, from here.

On the monitor in front of him, Stone's green strobe blinked every few seconds. It cast an eerie glow around the room. He minimized the screen—the blinking bothered his eyes. In the next room, he could hear the sound of Mika's gentle snoring. Mika was out of her depth here. That was okay—Swann didn't judge it. She was young. Maybe she would grow into this kind of thing, maybe she wouldn't.

He had called Washington. The conversation hadn't gone well. The aide to the National Security Adviser had been curt, to say the least. Swann had dealt with her before—Amy was her name, and she'd been friendly enough in the past. Well, that made sense. Luke had lobbied for this mission, and it couldn't have gone much worse. One hundred percent SNAFU. Three dead, an engagement with a Russian helicopter, destruction of same, our owned downed chopper in the battle zone. Two operatives stranded on a rooftop in ISIS-held territory. We weren't even supposed to be there. But we went in because there were stolen nukes on a boat at the docks.

Jesus.

"There isn't much hope of keeping this a secret anymore, is there?" Amy had said.

"Secret from who?"

"I don't know. The Russians. The media. The world in general."

Swann shook his head. "Oh. No. I don't see how. The Syrians on the ground and the Russians in the sky have been slicing the ISIS fighters to pieces the past hour. It's only a matter of time before they break through and find our chopper."

She was about to sign off.

"Amy, we need to get those guys off that roof. And we need to recover those bodies."

"I'll let them know."

Now, Swann sat and stared into the darkness. He drifted. Luke and Ed were not far from the port, just a few miles. They could walk that distance in half an hour, if there weren't hundreds of fighters and a wide open killing zone in the way.

He spun his chair around to face the terminal. There had to be a route there—maybe go straight west to the water, steal a boat, and come south. Anything. If they snatched a boat, they could also get out into international waters. Hell, maybe the Syrians had cleared out the ISIS fighters by now, and small children were laying roses along the boulevards. Luke and Ed could dance to the docks.

He pulled the screen up. There was an instant message on his desktop. It was an internal NSA messaging service, encrypted, secure, but used for unclassified communications. It was probably somebody from work. He opened it.

"Swann?"

The user ID was one he didn't recognize.

"Yes."

He waited several seconds while the cursor blinked.

"You sent Stone the wrong way. And people died."

Swann didn't answer. What was this? He'd made a report to Kurt Kimball's aide, somebody at NSA had gotten wind of it, and now they were going to taunt him? There were a lot of jerks in this business, and there was a lot of professional jealousy. Luke Stone stepped on toes—it was what he did. Stone had been winning it his way for a long time, and people out there had been dying to see him and his team taken down a peg.

Don't count us out just yet.

"I know where the warheads are. You don't."

Swann waited.

"Not on the boat."

Okay, enough is enough.

"This is a United States National Security Agency messaging service," Swann typed. "Identify yourself."

"You made a mistake. Meet me in Adana. I will show you the error of your ways."

It was possible, Swann knew. The boat had been his best guess. The trucks had gone to Karatas, right down to the port. But the weather made it impossible to tell if they'd gone on the boat or not. Still, the Turks had Karatas locked down. If the bombs were still there, they weren't going anywhere.

How does this person know about this?

Okay, he would play along. "Are they still in Karatas?" he typed.

The cursor blinked.

"No."

A moment passed.

"Never made it to Karatas. Decoy. I will show you."

"Show me now," Swann typed.

"Can't come there. Not safe. Meet me at the Sabanci Central Mosque. Public place. Easy to reach. Any taxi will take you."

Swann's heart skipped a beat. "When?"

"Now."

Swann stared hard at the screen. He thought about taxis. They were funny things. They kept running, even while bombs dropped and gunmen ran in the streets. Stranger than taxis, of course, was this mystery person who claimed to know where the stolen nukes were.

"How did you access this…" Swann started to type, but a new message appeared.

"Come alone. If I see anybody… a soldier, a cop, anybody… I'm gone."

Swann logged off the service. He could try to hack the guts of it, and find out where those messages had come from. But what would he discover? The person said they were in Adana, and if he managed to find anything, that's probably what it would be—an IP address here in the city, and in all likelihood, on the military base. Watching you, watching me. That was the game they all played. Some American spy agency, or sub-agency of a sub-agency, skunk works, lone wolves, moonlighters, somebody... They'd been monitoring this whole thing as it unfolded, but for whatever reason, they couldn't step into the light.

It was like in his early days at the FBI—one time he provided radio support on a drug house raid, and when the agents went in, they busted half a dozen guys, three of whom were undercover cops from the local police department.

Swann was an intelligence analyst, a desk jock, not really a spy. He knew that about himself. But you know what? He could hack it. He could do this stuff. Being around people like Stone and Ed Newsam helped. But in the end, you either had it in you, or you didn't. Swann had it in him.

He stood and shrugged into his jacket. He went to his bag and pulled out his gun—a matte black Glock nine-millimeter, just like Luke Stone carried. He touched the handle of the front door to the suite.

In the other room, Mika stirred in her sleep and rolled over.

He wouldn't bother her with this. After watching that battle earlier tonight, she seemed like she'd lapsed into shock, and this... meeting, he guessed you'd call it... was way outside standard protocol.

Anyway, he'd probably be back in an hour.

* * *

"Here he comes," a voice said in Jamal's ear.

Jamal stood in the shadows under some trees, just off the grand boulevard that led to the gigantic Sabanci Mosque. With power out in the city, the mosque and the water around it—normally so beautifully lit in green, or gold, or red—was lit instead by burning torches. That was beautiful in its own way, and reminded Jamal of the time of Muhammad.

He glanced back at the sprawling complex with its great dome and six tall minarets, reaching to the sky. He wondered what the Prophet might think of a place like this—traditionally designed, but totally modern, and built in 1998.

The man named Swann approached. Jamal knew him on sight—tall and thin, with stovepipe legs and long hair pulled back in a ponytail. He wore jeans and funny checkerboard sneakers, and a leather jacket. He wore expensive black square-framed eyeglasses on his face. He looked nothing like a military man or a special operative. He looked like a man who had never been in a fistfight.

Jamal stepped out into the walkway.

"Swann."

Swann turned to him. They stood about ten feet apart. The nearest torch burned perhaps thirty feet away, and it was dark here. Swann's face flickered orange in the flames. His eyes showed confusion, then recognition. Then they returned to confusion.

"How are you, my friend?" Jamal said.

"You?" Swann said.

Jamal nodded. "Yeah. Me."

"Okay," Swann said. "You want to talk?"

Jamal shook his head, as if to lament the awkward position in which he found himself. "I'm afraid not."

Swann glanced to his right and his left, as though he might run. Instead, he pulled a gun from inside his jacket. Jamal made no move. A tiny projectile flew from Swann's left. It was barely visible, and it made a sound just at the edge of Jamal's hearing.

Sssssssspppp.

Jamal stepped quickly, closing the distance between them in one second. A small black dart was lodged in Swann's long neck. It was administering a drug that would hit the man's bloodstream instantly. Swann's eyes fluttered. His gun dropped from his open hand and clattered on the pavement.

Jamal hugged him as his body went limp, then slowly lowered him to the ground.

"Got him," Jamal said into the microphone concealed inside his collar.

Within seconds, two large men emerged from the shadows on the other side of the walkway. One pulled the dart from Swann's neck, as the other removed Swann's glasses and pulled a black canvas bag over the thin man's head. He cinched it tight around Swann's neck. He dropped Swann's glasses onto the ground.

One man took Swann by the arms, the other by the legs. They nodded, hoisted him into the air, then walked away with him, back into the small knot of trees from which they'd emerged. In almost no time, it was if Swann had never been here at all. The only evidence of him was the black eyeglasses lying on the paving stones.

Jamal crunched them under his boot as he walked away into the night.

CHAPTER TWENTY TWO

6:13 p.m. (12:13 a.m. Eastern European Time)
The Situation Room
The White House, Washington, DC

"Come to order, please. Order, everyone!"

The room was packed. Coffee cups, empty food trays, and discarded sandwich wraps littered the conference table. Staffers huddled with decision makers, gabbling, pointing at data, swiping through screens.

The sharp clap of Kurt Kimball's hands broke through the noise.

Yet another break, followed by yet another call to order. Susan had reached her limit—Kurt's thunderous hand claps had her at the end of her rope. The hours kept slipping by, and things kept getting worse. Susan's advisers, and their staffs, didn't seem to have any answers. The situation was slipping out of control.

"Okay, Kurt," Susan said. "Sum it up for us, if you can."

Kurt raised his eyebrows.

"This is what we know. Agent Stone's helicopter was intercepted by a Russian helicopter gunship over the ocean near the port of Jalmeh in western Syria. The port is where we believe the stolen nuclear weapons are docked, aboard the Greek freighter the *Helena*. We believe the Russian helicopter was lending air support to Syrian army tank and infantry units trying to dislodge ISIS fighters from the port."

Kurt took a breath. "The fight was a mismatch. Agent Stone's helicopter was shot down and crashed a few miles away, within a densely populated residential zone of the city. The Russian helicopter was then shot down by a drone circling the area, piloted by Stone's team member Mark Swann, who gave us the report. The Russian chopper went into the sea about a mile west of the port. Preliminary reports we've intercepted are that there were no survivors."

"Do we know who fired first?" General Loomis said.

Kurt shook his head. "We don't, but it hardly matters. Three hours ago, we were in direct conflict with a Russian military helicopter. We are in a very dangerous situation. We didn't communicate the presence of our helicopter, or the reason for its presence. But by now, since the news of the nuclear theft has been leaked worldwide, I'm sure the Russians are well aware of why we were there."

"What is the status of our helicopter and its personnel?" Haley Lawrence said.

Kurt cleared his throat. "The helicopter pilots, Captain Wayne Alvarez and Lieutenant Ian Rogers, both died in the crash. The helicopter itself has been destroyed. It was scuttled by Bill Cronin, who died in a firefight with ISIS ground forces after the crash."

"Bill Cronin is dead?" General Loomis said.

Kurt nodded. "Mmm-hmmm."

Loomis shook his head.

"Where is Agent Stone?" Susan said.

"Agent Stone and Agent Newsam are alive as of the last report. They survived the firefight with ISIS troops, and intend to make their way to the docks to investigate the *Helena*. Communication with them is limited, and the area is a live war zone. Whether they reach the *Helena* or not, I'm not sure we have many options as to how to extract them again. General, if you have any ideas, I think we'd love to hear them."

Loomis scowled. "I told you people last night that I had drop teams ready to go. But you went with Stone instead, an aging cowboy who operates without oversight, and we see how that worked out. We can still turn the situation around, but it will take a change in tactics. You guys wanted to use a scalpel. Now it's time to go with a hammer."

Loomis looked around the table. His eyes flashed anger. Clearly he was one of these military people who thought civilians had no idea what they were doing. He turned his hot eyes on Susan, but she was having none of it. She returned all the heat he gave her, and more.

"Please enlighten us, General. We've never neutralized a threat before."

He shook his head. "This is what I suggest. We bomb that ship, and sink it right there at the dock. The warheads are not activated, as far as we know, and will easily withstand a bombardment with the kind of conventional weapons needed to sink a small freighter. If ISIS wants those bombs, they can send divers down to bring them up from thirty feet of water."

And if the bombs aren't even there?" Haley Lawrence said.

"Simple," said the general. "The Turks have Karatas in lockdown. We take over for them, put about a thousand troops on the street, and search every warehouse, freighter, ferry, and truck in the entire city. It'll take a couple of weeks, but if we cut the road out, and shut down the port…"

Kurt shook his head. "We'll need the cooperation of the Turks. They're currently putting down an insurrection, and I'm not sure we're going to get agreement from them to put our troops in their streets."

Loomis frowned. "We don't need their cooperation. We don't need their permission. They are Turkey. We are the United States of America."

"What if they are activated?" Susan said.

"Excuse me?" the general said.

"The warheads," she said. "The terrorists stole them for a reason. Presumably it wasn't to decorate their homes with. What if they somehow activated the warheads, and we drop bombs on them?"

"I'm not a physicist," the general said. "These are two-stage weapons. My understanding is it takes a lot of energy to detonate the first stage. Even if it happened, what do we lose? A town called Jalmeh? Which is infected with ISIS? I'd call that an inoculation."

Susan shook her head. "There's no way I'm going to—"

Kurt Kimball pointed at his aide. "Amy, we need an objective ruling on this, and fast. Get us an expert on the phone—someone from McDonnell Douglas, from Stanford, hell, even someone from the Pentagon." He stared hard at the general, then slowly turned to look at Susan.

"We won't bomb it if there's one chance in a billion of an explosion, or even a leak. In the meantime, I think we need to have a talk with the Russian president. I'd leave it to the Secretary of State, but we are teetering very close to something bad here. When the Syrians or the Russians find our downed helicopter, they're going to have even more questions than they already do."

"It's after midnight in Moscow," the aide Amy said. "I doubt we'll be able to schedule until tomorrow morning."

Kurt looked at her now. "Well, give him a try. He might surprise us. Stolen nukes on your doorstep is the type of thing that keeps people up at night."

* * *

Susan had lied to her husband.

139

She felt like a piece of saltwater taffy from when she was a kid—being pulled farther and farther apart, becoming a long, droopy skinny string. She had been serious for a long time. She had been chaste for a long time. She had been alone for a long time.

Pierre was on the west coast. When the going got tough here in Washington, Pierre had decided to run and hide.

She was trying all the different ways she could rationalize this to herself. None of them fit quite right.

She sat in the White House family dining room, at the small round table. The lights were dimmed, and candles burned in the centerpiece. The doors were closed, one Secret Service right outside, listening in on this conversation through an earpiece. The room was mic'ed. Of course it was. Everywhere in her life, she was never more than a few steps from the Secret Service, and never out of their earshot. She wished, for once, she could be.

Just across from her, and to her left, sat Tommy Zales, the Hollywood actor. They were eating a dinner of chicken, pasta with marinara sauce, and broccoli rabe. The chef had been going all out these past couple of days—the food was garlicky, tomatoey, impossibly good. The chicken melted on your tongue. The food reminded her of the meals she and Pierre used to enjoy together in the Belmont section of the Bronx—the old Italian neighborhood where once upon a time, a capella singers serenaded passersby on street corners.

There was a bottle of red wine on the table—sulfite free, organic Cabernet Sauvignon, which Tommy had brought with him. Susan had a few sips—she was on the job, after all. Tommy had already polished off half of it.

He was a handsome man. That was natural—Hollywood dealt in perfection, and physically, he was pretty close to it. His face had the angular lines and perfect right-left symmetry that she remembered artistic directors of magazines lusting over. He had a great body, well-muscled and defined in a tailored dinner jacket and slacks that showed off the reverse triangle of his broad shoulders tapering to his narrow waist. His head was slightly too large for his body—again, she knew all the tricks, and she knew big heads meant star power. His eyes were pale blue, like the waters of the Caribbean. His teeth were blindingly white and even. He was beautiful to look at.

And he was young. Thirty-three years old. With his three-day growth of beard, he looked like a man, but one who had left adolescence ten minutes ago.

She couldn't believe she was doing this. The Secret Service knew he was here—they were the ones who had cleared him to come in. It was going to be impossible to keep it under wraps. But it wasn't like she had done anything…

Yet.

"It seems pretty stressful, being President," he said. "Is it?"

She shrugged. "It can be. Some days are worse than others."

"Why do you do it?"

"I don't know. It kind of fell into my lap."

He nodded, and his face darkened, then pinched in sympathy. "Yeah, I guess so. That was rough. There's been a lot of terrorism, hasn't there?"

"There has. Yes."

She thought about it for a moment. Truer words were never spoken. There had been a lot of terrorism. Way too much. She was learning that Tommy Zales was an idiot savant of current events.

But with Tommy, the darkness never lasted long. She was learning that, too. Suddenly, his winning smile returned. "You know, I played the President once."

She nearly laughed. "Did you?" When he first arrived, she thought it might be better if he didn't speak at all. But now she was starting to have fun. His smile was infectious. Maybe it was him. Maybe it was the wine.

"Oh, yeah. Don't you remember? It was called *45th.* I'm the new President, and I'm aboard Air Force One. I'm on a trip to South America, but we get shot down by rebels over the mountains of Colombia. Now I have to survive, just me and a sexy female Secret Service agent, who are the only ones that lived through the crash."

"I do remember that," Susan said. "Did you shoot it in Colombia?"

"Nah. We did it in Canada. Tax breaks and all that." He shrugged. "Hey, British Columbia."

He sounded disappointed. Susan felt disappointed for him.

"Sure."

A long moment passed between them. The smile was back.

"I want to tell you something," he said.

"Hit me."

"Susan, you are so beautiful. I've always wanted to tell you this. And don't take it the wrong way. But when I was a kid, thirteen, fourteen, I was in love with you. You were the most beautiful thing I had ever seen."

She smiled. She was a lot older than he was. It was okay. Who really cared? "*Sports Illustrated* Swimsuit Issue, right?"

He nodded. "Oh yeah."

This time, she did laugh.

Just then, the door to the dining room opened. The Secret Service man outside the door poked his head inside. "Madam President? I've just been informed that they have the President of Russia on standby. He is awaiting your call."

Susan smiled. "Uh… I have to take this. They told me he wasn't going to be ready this soon."

Tommy shrugged. "Can he wait?"

"Unfortunately, no. Nuclear weapons, the Red Army, all that. Mutual Assured Destruction. You know how it is. Look, don't get up. And don't run away. Stay right there, enjoy your dinner, and I'll be back as soon as I can."

She glanced back one last time as she went out the door. Tommy Zales was pouring himself another glass of wine.

* * *

It turned out that Putin had been awake.

The Russians were on high alert and waiting for the call. They'd made it clear to Kurt's aide that they had expected it a little sooner.

Susan walked to the elevator with Kat Lopez.

"He speaks English, but maybe not as well as he'd like," Kat said. "In all likelihood, he will choose to speak through an interpreter. When it's his turn to talk, he often makes long drawn-out speeches with barely a pause, and the person he's speaking with has to wait to hear the entire translation. He is likely to be sarcastic towards you. Without directly saying it's because you're a woman, he has been openly dismissive of your leadership. On Russian TV, he routinely refers to you as the Fashion Model."

Susan nodded. "I guess I knew that. Maybe I'll start referring to him as the KGB Agent."

She took a deep breath to steady herself. Susan was nervous. Five sips of red wine made it a little better, but the feeling was still there. She hated these calls.

She didn't mind talking to world leaders who were on the same page as her. Olga Aker, the Prime Minister of Sweden, had been a world champion skier when she was young, and afterwards spent several years as a ski fashion model, mostly in the

Scandinavian countries, but also in France, Austria, Italy, and Switzerland. Susan loved Olga. They talked nearly every week.

Susan also had a friendly relationship with the Prime Minister of England, and cordial working relationships with the heads of twenty other countries.

Putin? She'd had one five-minute conversation with him in the past six months. It was a weakness of hers. She didn't want to talk to Putin, so she didn't reach out to him. He made her uncomfortable, and it was easy to put him out of her mind. With no open dialogue, difficult calls like this one became even harder.

Somewhere deep inside, Susan lacked confidence. She suspected that people like Putin were the real hardball power players in the world, and she wasn't up to dealing with them. Maybe it was because she had stumbled into the Presidency, while he had been working toward it, and gradually amassing power in a cutthroat environment, his entire life. Maybe it was just because he was a man, and an aggressive one at that. She didn't know. One day, when she had some time to navel-gaze, she might figure it out. But that wasn't going to happen now.

As the elevator dropped through the earth to the Situation Room, she could feel her body beginning to tremble.

Kurt Kimball was ready as they entered. Kurt was always ready. He was the definition of tireless. He was the poster boy for it. He worked long days, often seven days a week, but it seemed to have no effect on him. It wasn't that he got tired and somehow bulled his way through it. He never seemed tired at all. He was a great big bald-headed wall of endurance.

He stood at the front of the Room, with his pointer.

"Ready, Susan?"

There were only about ten people in the Room. Kurt and his aides, Haley Lawrence and a couple of aides, General Loomis and one aide, Susan and Kat. Even so, all eyes were on her. Not only would she have to talk to Vladimir Putin on the phone, she would have to do it in front of an audience.

That part used to bother her, but really didn't anymore. Being President was like visiting the proctologist every single day of your life. And the proctologist worked at a teaching hospital, so the gallery was full each time he examined you—everybody was in your business.

She sat down at the head of the table. The red phone of legend was in front of her—the direct line to the Kremlin. It really was red.

143

And it was heavy, and old. They had rebuilt the entire White House, but decided to keep the same telephone.

"Couldn't they have made it a princess phone, or something just a little bit fun? I mean, look at this thing. Where did they even find one of these, in their grandmother's cellar?"

"Susan?"

She nodded. "Yes, I'm ready."

"Okay," Kurt said. "Before we make the call, here's the one-minute data dump on Putin."

Several photos of Vladimir Putin appeared on the screen behind Kurt. Here he was a young man, somewhere with snow on the ground, and he wore a heavy overcoat and a tall furry hat. Here he was maybe thirty years old, in a uniform jacket and a dark dress shirt with a tie, a badge pinned to the breast of the jacket—the up-and-coming KGB spymaster. Here he was, shirtless, virile, fly-fishing in a mountain river. And here, as the late middle-aged leader of his country on a dais at a state event.

He was not smiling in a single photo.

"You know the drill on Putin. Sixty-five years old. As the modern era goes, about as hard a case as you'll come across. Raised and came of age during the time of the Soviet Union. An exceptional student and athlete as a child. Joined the KGB right out of university. A consummate and ruthless political player. Got his first break in politics as an aide to the mayor of St. Petersburg. By the time Boris Yeltsin became President, Putin was an aide and close confidante to Yeltsin, and, some say, encouraged Yeltsin's alcoholism.

"Putin is a complete autocrat. As far as we can tell, he has total authority to take whatever actions he deems necessary—the rest of the Russian government exists to rubber stamp and carry out his directives. But don't confuse him with a madman like Hitler or Mussolini. He rules with an iron hand at home, but on the world stage he treads lightly and carries a big stick. He positions his pieces and makes a bold move only when his opponents have no good counter-moves."

Kimball paused.

"Under Putin's rule, the Russians have crushed the Chechen rebellion, demolished the Georgians in a war over South Ossetia and Abkhazia, encouraged left-wing resistance to the government of Ukraine, and annexed the Crimean peninsula from Ukraine. They have intervened in the Syrian Civil War, and are systematically annihilating all opposition to the Assad regime, including ISIS and al-Nusra Front, but also including what we consider legitimate resistance, like the Free Syrian Army. Two months ago, the Russians annexed three Turkish-held islands in the Black Sea, which has ramped up tensions between those two countries. This has probably contributed to the current unrest in Turkey—the President there is seen as weak in the face of Russian aggression."

Susan stared at the red phone. It loomed there on the table, large and menacing. This was the person she was about to call to explain how the US had misplaced some nuclear weapons?

But Kurt wasn't done.

"Finally, at Putin's order, Russia has developed the largest and most dangerous nuclear missile ever devised—the RS-28 Sarmat, also known as the Satan 2. It can deliver a fifty-megaton blast— roughly fourteen hundred times the size of the Hiroshima and Nagasaki bombs combined. A single successful strike from the Satan 2 would wipe out an area the size of Texas. Five such bombs could kill all life on the East Coast from Washington, DC, north to the Canadian border. Moreover, the Satan 2 can fly six times the speed of sound, and employs advanced stealth technology to beat radar and missile defense systems."

"He sounds like a very nice man," Susan said. "Shall we talk to him?"

The room was quiet.

"Amy, what time is it in Moscow?"

Amy consulted her tablet. "It's after five in the morning."

"The man never sleeps," Kurt said.

Susan took a deep breath. She had that nervous feeling, butterflies fluttering in her stomach, as if she were going on stage. That was fine. She had been on stage many, many times. Normally, she was there to whip up the crowd. Today, she was going to… what? Convince Vladimir Putin that these missing warheads were no problem?

"Okay," she said. "Are we ready?"

"The line is open," an aide said. "We can put you on anytime."

Susan nodded. "Now is good."

"Your speaker is on," Kurt said. "All other phones are muted."

She picked up the receiver to the red telephone. The handset was big and attached to the phone by a spiral cord. It made her hand seem small, like an Alice in Wonderland telephone. She held the handset to the side of her head.

"The President of the United States is on the line," a male voice said.

"Hold one moment for the President of the Russian Federation," came another voice.

Susan looked at Kurt. He was standing with a remote telephone to his ear. All around the room, people were holding remote phones.

Several seconds passed.

"Hello? This is Vladimir Putin."

"Mr. President," Susan said. "This is Susan Hopkins. It is a pleasure to speak with you. Thank you for receiving my call so late at night."

"Madam President," Putin said. "My English... You will forgive me if I speak through my trusted interpreter Vasil."

"Of course."

Putin began to talk. After a few phrases, Vasil jumped in. Vasil had a deep, gravelly voice, which at the same time was clipped and cultured. He spoke slowly, and enunciated each word carefully, as if his very life depended on the perfect pronunciation and total understanding by the person listening to him. Maybe it did.

"It has come to our attention that nuclear weapons belonging to the United States have been stolen from a military base in Turkey, and have yet to be recovered. Many things about this situation concern us. For one, it is clear that the weapons were not safeguarded properly, and were in fact left in the custody of the Turkish regime, who have demonstrated again and again that they are unreliable and faithless partners in the most elementary endeavors, never mind in matters of utmost importance."

Susan nearly spoke, but Putin was still going, and Vasil plunged on.

"For another, we learned of this security breach, not from the United States government itself, but from news media reports in countries throughout the world. The reports began in what are considered the most ridiculous and least dependable news sources, and the coverage from country to country and outlet to outlet has been inconsistent and conflicting. We have no way of knowing what the real truth is, because we have not, until this moment, received any contact from the United States."

Susan looked at Kurt and shook her head. She waited a beat. Putin was still talking. This wasn't a conversation. It was a lecture. It was the scolding of a wayward child.

"For yet another, it is our deep concern that the warheads have fallen into the hands of Muslim extremists, who are active very near our borders, who have attacked our friend Syria, and who are an existential threat to the people of Russia. Indeed, these elements have sworn to destroy Russia, if only their loving and benevolent god will permit it."

"Mr. President?" Susan said. "Mr. President."

"One moment, please," Vasil said. "Please, I will finish."

Vasil himself took a deep breath. Susan could feel the man's anxiety. On the one hand, Putin could launch into this tirade, but to Susan, it sounded like a wall of gibberish. Vasil actually had to say the words that she would understand, the words that would likely anger her.

"Finally, there is the little matter of a provocation that occurred in Syrian territory during the past several hours. A Russian military helicopter lending aid to the Syrian army in that country's fight against these same Muslim extremists, was shot down and destroyed, either by an American military helicopter or a robot drone. Six crewmen were aboard our helicopter, all of whom lost their lives. Each man had loved ones who are now bereft. Between them, these men leave eight children behind."

Susan began. "Mr. President, I would like to—"

"Considering the sensitive nature of the airspace above Syria," Vasil said, "and the very real danger of this type of encounter taking place, the Russian military is scrupulous in submitting flight plans to the American military command. This courtesy, however, is not reciprocated."

"May I speak?" Susan said.

"Of course."

"Mr. President, to assuage your fears, I would like to inform you that the weapons in question cannot be detonated. They are warheads designed to be used with a legacy missile system, which was decommissioned and destroyed more than twenty years ago. Without the proper system to launch them, and the missiles to deliver them, the warheads cannot reach the velocity, and therefore the energy on impact, needed to detonate them. Further, the warheads cannot even be made operational without the correct codes to activate them."

Putin barked out a sentence in response.

"If they cannot be used, Madam, then why would someone steal them?"

"In all likelihood, to scrape the radioactive material from them, either for use in a small-scale dirty bomb–type weapon, or as part of an attempt to secure the material for an ongoing nuclear weapons development program."

It was a missile all its own. The only country in the region with those aspirations that didn't already have the bomb was Russia's friend Iran.

"Weapons development program? Come now."

Susan decided to run with that concept. "The warheads have built-in fail-safes, booby traps if you will, that make it nearly impossible to access the core of the weapon. The only actors that would have the resources or the facilities to work with these weapons are nation states. A ragtag terror group would be more likely to disperse a cloud of uranium in their own faces."

Putin began to say something.

"Need I remind you, Mr. President," Susan said, "that the most lax country in the world when it comes to safeguarding nuclear materials, and weapons of all kinds, is Russia. I won't even touch upon the Chernobyl disaster and its implications."

Putin was in the middle of talking, but Susan kept going. He wasn't going to do the man thing and just talk over her, not if she could help it. He might be the great dictator in his own country, but Susan didn't live there. He'd had his say. It was her turn.

"Thousands of Soviet-era weapons are on the market in Third World countries, particularly in Africa. My country routinely buys these weapons and destroys them to keep them out of the hands of the same terrorist groups you abhor so much. Nuclear facilities throughout the former Soviet Union were left open and unguarded for years, and as you know, a significant amount of radioactive material has gone missing from these facilities. Your country has proven very reluctant to share the exact details of how much material is missing, or where it might have gone."

Now there was silence.

"Further," Susan said, "Russia is a well-known sponsor of state terrorism. The Assad regime in Syria, as well as the Iranian regime, have used poison gas on their own subjects over a period of decades, right up to the present moment. Where do these countries obtain their chemical weapons, sir?"

There was a long pause over the line. It went on and on. Had they hung up? It sounded like open space. Far away, there seemed to be a whistling sound, like the winter wind howling across the Great Plains at night.

"Hello?" Susan said.

"President Putin has just left the chamber," Vasil said. "He would like you to know something further. Should the missing weapons be used in an attack on Russia, any Russian territory, or against Russian citizens in any way, we will consider it an unprovoked act of nuclear war by the United States against Russia. And we shall respond in kind."

"Is that all?" Susan said.

"No, there is one more thing. President Putin wishes you a good evening, Madam President," Vasil said. "He enjoyed speaking with you."

"Thank you, Vasil. Please give the President my regards."

Susan hung up the phone. She looked around the room. Ten people were hanging up their own telephones. Kurt Kimball made a slicing motion across his throat to someone in the back of the room.

Susan sat back and put her hands on top of her head.

"I think he's starting to warm up to me," she said.

CHAPTER TWENTY THREE

October 22
4:22 a.m. Mediterranean Time
(10:22 p.m. Eastern Daylight Time—October 21)
Jalmeh, Syria

The radio was dead.

That was okay. Swann wasn't answering anyway. Luke had never known Swann to go to sleep on a job, but he supposed it was possible he had dozed off.

He and Ed were approaching the waterfront. Sitting tight until morning wasn't in either of their DNA. They had hugged the ruined buildings, racing in and out of the shadows, communicating through hand signals and eye movements. They had barely spoken the entire time. One was the left hand, one was the right hand, and they knew exactly what the other one was doing.

Now, they were in a narrow stairwell, dark as pitch. They moved through it silently, night vision goggles on, weapons ready. At the top of the stairs was a doorway. The flimsy door moved in the breeze, opening and closing, creaking, and sometimes slamming hard against the doorjamb. That was good.

Ed was first. He pushed the door open the smallest crack, and held it there for a moment. Through the tiny sliver, Luke saw two men on the rooftop. They stood at the parapet, rifles on their shoulders, watching the harbor below them.

Luke could shoot them both from here, but it would make too much noise. Ed pushed the door wide, and Luke dashed through it. He darted around the edge of the small outbuilding formed by the stairwell. It was made of slapped together cement. He crouched there, perfectly still.

In a moment, he glanced around the corner. The guards were chatting quietly, laughing about something. One of them lit up a cigarette. Luke reached to his calf and slipped the knife away from the tape holding it to his leg. Just around the corner, the door creaked again, and suddenly Ed appeared.

Ed pointed behind them and around the outbuilding. He was going to go the other way. Luke nodded. Luke held up his knife to show Ed, as if to say, "You're going to need one of these."

Ed shook his head.

Luke shrugged.

Ed went around the back. Luke crept to the edge. He glanced around the corner. Thirty yards to those men. Probably five or six seconds with these boots and this gear on. Okay. As he watched, Ed appeared, coming from the other direction.

The big man walked toward the guards. Now they spotted him. Ed had his hands in the air. One of the men said something in Arabic.

Luke burst around the edge, knife in hand. One second. His heavy footfalls crunched on the gravel roof. Three seconds, four.

The men heard him, turned to look.

Ed attacked, grabbing his man by the head, twisting his head viciously to the right.

Luke hit his man chest high. He plunged his knife hard into the man's breastplate. It punched through. He clamped a hand over the man's mouth, feeling the bristles of the jihadi's beard. He stabbed again, and again, in and out, fast, like the piston of a machine. The man struggled and squirmed, but Luke kept jabbing.

The man's arms fell to his sides. His eyes were still open, and he was alive. Luke tilted his head up, hand still crushing his mouth, and swiped the serrated blade across the man's throat. A jet of blood pulsed out. Done.

Luke kept the man's mouth covered until he was gone.

He glanced at Ed. Ed was still twisting the other man's head. He wrenched it with hard, jerking motions, his teeth gritted from the effort. Finally he got the sound he wanted—an audible SNAP.

"Ain't like in the movies," Ed whispered.

They sat against the parapet for a moment, divvying up the men's weapons. They both had AK-47s and extra magazines for them. They each had cheap pistols that Ed and Luke discarded. Neither of these guys were booby-trapped or wearing suicide vests. They weren't in the martyr game—they had expected to live another day.

Luke looked through cracks in the masonry. Three boats were moored below them, across the wharf. The one they wanted—the *Helena*—was the largest one, in the middle. Luke put the night vision on them. He spotted two men on the upper decks of each of the other boats, more guards. Half a dozen men congregated on the dock at the entry to the *Helena*.

"I'll come in from the left," Luke said. "See that warehouse loading dock?"

"I see it," Ed said.

"We'll triangulate our fire. I'll be right behind there. When you see me show up, give me thirty seconds, then blow that boat on the left. Put it right between those two guys and send them to see Allah. Drop down and reload. I'll give you covering fire. They'll draw to me. When they do, you pop up and take out the boat on the right. With a little luck, I'll have taken out half those guys in the front by that time. Then we finish up the leftovers."

Ed nodded. "Beautiful."

"Okay, brother," Luke said. "See you on the ground."

As he went down the stairs in the dark, he had a moment when Bill Cronin's face flashed in front of him. Luke had killed him, it was that simple. He couldn't say that Bill was a decent man and hadn't deserved it—Bill had deserved it in spades, if anyone did—but it wouldn't have happened. Luke called him, brought him on this job, and now Bill was dead. It was an ugly, ugly reality. A lot of people had died on missions with Luke Stone. He should come with a warning label—could be hazardous to your health.

He shook those thoughts away. It was time to focus. He moved down an alleyway, silent as a ghost. When he came out, he was right where he wanted to be. He slid along the walls to the warehouse dock. He raised a hand for two seconds, then disappeared.

He crouched, checked the MP5. Fully loaded. Full auto.

A moment passed. Then he heard the sound.

Doonk!

A second later: GA-BANG!

Light flashed and the sound wave hit him. He popped up, the explosion ahead and to his left. A man was on top of that boat, walking in circles, engulfed in fire. The upper deck of the boat collapsed onto the bottom. The men in front of the *Helena* were pointing and shouting, but not running or taking cover.

Luke gave them a burst from the gun. It bucked in his hands as he sprayed them. The sound was loud, an ugly blat of automatic fire. Two, maybe three went down.

Luke ducked and hit the ground. He crawled like a worm away from where he had just been. Bullets whined off the dock above his head, ricocheted. The wooden side of the building began to collapse, shredded by machine gun fire. Chunks of it rained down around him.

Doonk! The hollow M70 sound came again.

Luke smiled as he kissed the dirt.

GAA-BOOOM! Bigger than before. Ed must have hit a gas tank or some kind of weapon storage. Someone was shrieking.

Luke crept to the edge of the platform. Three men were still in front of the *Helena*, crouched, firing at the rooftop now. Clowns. These were the guys the entire civilized world was worried about?

Luke popped up again and dropped two of them with another spray from the MP5. The third one escaped back up the gangplank to the *Helena*.

Now Luke ran for the boat. He reached the plank in seconds. Three men squirmed on the ground in front of the boat. He paused, and finished each of them with a blast from the gun. No sense having one of them jump up and follow him inside.

Two others were already shredded, their bottom halves separated from the top. They weren't going anywhere. All around him, the two boats burned, quickly becoming infernos. The opening of the *Helena* was a gaping black maw. For a second, Luke considered waiting for Ed. But it wouldn't do—they had the initiative right now, and the longer it took to get inside, the more time that last guy, and whoever else was still here, would have to regroup. Luke wanted them in disarray and on the run.

He dropped the night vision over his eyes and ran up the plank.

He passed into a wide hallway, half expecting to take a bullet in the first second. He hugged the wall, moving low and fast, head on a swivel. There was a heavy door across the hall from him. He went to it, yanked it open, and ducked back behind it.

He scanned the inside. The boat was a car and truck ferry. There were two tractor trailers parked inside the holding bay, side by side. In front of them was the man who had run inside. The man glowed green. His hands were in the air. In one hand he held a white handkerchief.

"I give up!" he shouted in a thick English accent. "My name is Nigel Sayles, and I surrender." He was panting like a dog that was too hot.

Luke drew a bead on him and moved slowly into the chamber. His eyes were everywhere at once. "Get on the ground."

The guy was crying now. "I'm nineteen years old. I come from Manchester. This was all a terrible mistake."

"On the ground, I said."

This was exactly how they did it. Set a decoy in front of you, get your attention, then the sniper hits you.

"I didn't mean it!" the kid screamed.

Luke shot him. He dropped his aim and popped him with a short burst in the lower leg, breaking the bones in his calf, knocking off a chunk of meat from there. Then he ran to the kid, grabbed him by the collar, and dragged him back into the shadows between the two trucks. The kid shrieked in pain and terror.

Luke put the muzzle to his head.

"Who else is here?"

"Don't shoot! Please don't shoot!"

Luke jabbed him with the gun. "Listen, kid! I don't give a damn where you're from, you ISIS scum. I'll kill you right now. Who else is here?"

"No one!"

He jabbed him again. "Who else is here? Three seconds before I pull this trigger... One... Two..."

"No one! You killed the last lot of them. I swear to God."

The kid was sniveling now, holding his shattered leg. "Oh my God. I'm shot."

Luke was breathing heavily.

"If you so much as move, I will come back here and blow your brains out."

Luke went around to the back of the trailers. The trailers were beat to hell, strafed and pockmarked with gunfire. The doors were locked with heavy padlocks. He shot them off in turn. The kid screamed again each time he did. Luke threw open the doors of the first truck.

"What the—?"

The inside of the trailer glowed green in the night vision. It was empty. Just a big empty truck. He went to the other truck, threw that one open as well. The same thing—nothing.

"What's in it?" a voice said.

He turned and a huge man with broad shoulders stood in the wide doorway. A man carrying an AK-47, with a battle helmet on his head, and night vision goggles.

Ed.

"Nothing," Luke said. "There's nothing here."

"We gotta go," Ed said. "The boat's on fire."

* * *

"Ow! Ow, that hurts!"

Luke dragged the kid by his good ankle along the dusty ground. To the east, light was coming into the sky.

154

Behind them, all three boats were a raging inferno now. The two flanking boats had set the *Helena* aflame. There was a stiff breeze off the water—embers were flying across and alighting on the warehouses across the wharf. The air was dry as a bone. The whole neighborhood could go up in a few minutes.

Ed had looted some more weapons from the dead men near the gangplank to the *Helena*. He carried a stack of rifles and pistols in various states of neglect.

"Who are you guys, man? You don't know how to maintain your weapons? Do you know how to do anything? We capped your whole squad without taking a scratch. All your boys are dead back there."

The kid didn't answer. He was crying, his teeth clenched. He grabbed at his ripped out calf. Luke dragged him into a space between buildings and dropped his leg. The kid rolled in agony on the ground.

"Please don't kill me," he said.

Luke shook his head. "Shut up. I'll kill you just for talking."

Ed dropped his stack of guns nearby.

They were protected on three sides in this little alcove. The only opening was from the water, and there didn't seem to be anything out there. A highly-trained sniper at 2,000 yards, barely visible from here in a tiny rowboat, rolling on the sea—well, that seemed a little far-fetched. Those guys liked stability.

Still, they couldn't stay here forever.

"What do you think, Ed?"

"I don't know what we're gonna do with this punk, man."

Luke glanced down at the kid. He was on his side now, rolling just slightly. At least he wasn't talking anymore. "Let's let that sit for a minute. I'm talking about the bombs. They weren't on the boat. Where are they?"

Ed leaned against the edge of the alcove, AK-47 hanging by his side, scanning the wharf in either direction. Luke looked past his big shoulders. To the right, the flames were three stories high. Black smoke erupted from the center of them.

Ed shrugged. "Simple enough. It was misdirection. You'd do the same. They made us think they were going one way, and they went the other way instead. Maybe they're back in the port city in Turkey. Maybe they never left the base."

"The bombs left the base," the kid said.

"Shut up, punk. I'm about to put my gun in your mouth."

"They sent the bombs to Russia."

Luke squatted down next to the kid. He pawed through the pile of guns that Ed had dropped, picked out an old Ruger pistol that looked pretty clean. He popped the magazine out—fully loaded. He checked the barrel. It seemed okay. He slid the mag back in and drove it home. The gun probably wouldn't blow up in his hand.

He pressed it to the kid's temple. "What's your name again?"

"Nigel. Nigel Say—"

"Stop right there. Nigel is good enough. So tell me, Nigel. You seem to have zero useful combat experience or training, and you don't have much fight in you anyway. You're just a decoy and obviously an expendable. Why would a nobody like you know something like that?"

"I'm in a great deal of pain," Nigel said. "I'm going to need medical attention."

Ed laughed.

Luke smiled and shook his head. "Nigel, you don't need medical attention. You're not even alive unless I say you are. You died in that firefight back there. Do you understand what I'm telling you? My friend and I need information. The possibility that you might have some is the only reason you're breathing right now."

Nigel stared into Luke's eyes. Nigel's face was crimped with pain. Nigel had jumped into the deep end of the pool without ever learning to swim.

"People talk," he said. "They're not supposed to, but they do."

"Rumors," Ed said.

"Rumors, yes. But rumors coming straight from the top."

"And why would they send the warheads to Russia?" Luke said. "Last I checked, ISIS hates Russia."

The kid nodded crazily. "Oh, they do. They do. And that's why. They're going to sneak the missiles into Russia, and launch them at Russia from inside the country. Who can the bloody Russians attack after that? They got bombed from inside their own territory. It's genius, man. It's brilliant."

"How do they plan to get them in there?"

Nigel shook his head. "I don't know the details. I'm sorry. That's all I have."

Luke stood. He had to admit it made a certain amount of sense. If it was true, that was a problem. They had gone the wrong way. It was a bad call on Swann's part, but there was more to it than that. Trudy was gone, they had a neophyte doing intel, and Luke was distracted by Becca's health. Swann and Ed were on loan from other jobs. This team was not the well-oiled machine it used to be.

Now he and Ed were in Syria, shot down by the Russians, in running firefights with ISIS, out of communication with Swann, and with no clear way back out again. Luke shook his head. Maybe he should have turned this job down.

"Hey, man," Ed said. "Look what we have here."

Out on the wharf, a tall black van had pulled up. The windows were blacked. There were three satellite dishes on its roof. Across the side, the white letters TV were spray painted in characters four feet high.

"The news has arrived," Luke said. "Well, at least we can get a call out. Ed, give me a hand with this guy, will you?"

"Wait! No, just leave me here."

Luke shook his head. "Can't leave you with the guns. You're the enemy, remember? What if you started shooting at us? That wouldn't do, would it?"

They each grabbed Nigel under an arm and dragged him out into the road. He screamed in pain the whole time. They dropped him in the dust near the van. By now, two men had emerged from inside.

One of them had long hair and wore jeans, sneakers, and a T-shirt with a heavy black equipment vest over it. Like the truck, the vest had the big white letters TV written in masking tape on the front and back. He looked like he was in his early thirties. He had a video camera on his shoulder, and a boom mike contraption in his hand. The other was a handsome guy in his twenties, wearing khaki pants and a dark blue windbreaker.

He smiled.

"Hello, what's going on here?" He sounded like an American. "Look at that fire! Is that your handiwork?"

"TV," Luke said. "Who are you guys with?"

"We're independent, but we work for everybody. We're just about the only westerners on the ground down here. CNN and FOX don't like their people getting killed. Those guys tend to report the war from someplace nice."

"We need to call Washington, DC," Luke said. "Can you do that?"

The guy looked at Luke and Ed. He glanced at the shivering wreck on the ground at their feet.

"You guys Special Forces? Navy SEALs?"

Luke nodded. "Something like that."

"They send you in here to look for the missing American?"

Luke stared at the guy. "I don't know anything about a missing American."

He might have stared a little too hard, because the reporter put his hands up.

"Hey, I just figured American commandos in ISIS-held territory... you know. We heard a couple of choppers got shot down last night. We've been out scrounging around for them this morning. And we found you instead. I just figured maybe you guys were looking for him. You're probably not going to find him. ISIS has him, but they wouldn't bring him here. They've just about lost their grip on this town."

"Who is he?"

"I don't know. An American spy. Bobby, what's that guy's name?"

Bobby the cameraman checked a small handheld device pinned to his vest. He sighed as he scrolled through some web pages.

"Name? Uh... let me see."

Then he found it.

He looked up.

"His name is Mark Swann."

CHAPTER TWENTY FOUR

1:05 a.m.
The White House Residence, Washington, DC

The phone was ringing.

Susan nearly jumped out of skin. She had been dreaming, one of many dreams she'd had about flying recently. Just flying, not in an airplane, or on a magic carpet, just herself as though she were a superhero. She had been flying close to a mountain, scraping the knuckles of her right hand along the edge of it.

It was dark in the room. She was sprawled across the king bed by herself. By the time she'd gotten back from her call with Putin, Tommy Zales had moved on to greener pastures. It was probably for the best. She'd been crazy to invite him here.

Would you really have slept with him?

"I don't know the answer to that. But I do know that I'm lonely. And it doesn't hurt that he's good-looking."

She looked at the phone. It had gone silent. A red light on it was blinking. It wasn't even that late. She'd only been asleep for an hour.

Abruptly, it started ringing again. She picked up the receiver.

"Hi."

"Susan, it's Kurt. Did I wake you?"

"What do you think?"

"We've got a new problem."

"No surprise there."

"Will you meet me in the Oval Office?"

"Of course. What else am I doing right now?"

Slowly, she got dressed. Within a few minutes, she was prowling the darkened colonnade, headed to the West Wing. Two Secret Service kept a respectful distance behind her. When she entered the office, Kurt Kimball and Kat Lopez were in the sitting area, waiting for her. They were wearing the same clothes she'd seen them in hours ago. Kurt had a dark five o'clock shadow growing across his face. For a second, she imagined him, as bald as he was, with a thick beard. Kind of like a reverse Chia pet.

Kat's eyes had black half-circles beneath them.

"Why are you two still here? Don't you have homes?"

"Susan, I'll get right to the point," Kurt said. "A video has been released online within the past hour. We need you to watch it."

Susan sat in one of the high-backed chairs. Kurt had a laptop computer on the coffee table. He turned it around to face her and pressed play.

The video was shot outside. It showed what looked like the ruins of a large building. Steel girders leaned diagonally, near shredded masonry. In the foreground, a man with long blond hair wore an orange jumpsuit. He was on his knees, and his arms were tied behind his back. Looming behind him on piles of rubble were five men wearing black hoods. Four of the men brandished rifles. The fifth held a large scythe or scimitar, similar to a machete. Behind the men, there was a black flag with white lettering in Arabic.

"Oh my God, is that—"

"Yes, the data analyst from Agent Stone's team. Swann."

"My name is Mark Swann," the man in the video said. He squinted at something off-screen, as though he was reading from a prepared statement.

"I work for the National Security Agency of the United States. In other words, I am a spy for the Crusaders. I am in league with the Jews, the Satanists, the apostates, and the enemies of Allah wherever I find them. We spread false histories. We fill the people's heads with lies. My efforts have directly resulted in the deaths of many thousands of innocent women and children, believers all across the Islamic world."

Swann's voice seemed to hitch in his throat, and his eyes watered.

"I have been condemned to death by the defenders of the true faith. I cannot dispute this ruling, for it is"—he hesitated, stumbled over the words—"fair and just. I regret the life I have led, which has brought me to this dismal end. I regret the actions I have taken which have hurt so many. I am abject in my remorse, and I go to this fate urging others not to follow my path."

Now Swann clearly was crying. He looked straight at the camera.

"I love you, Mom."

The screen went black.

Susan was quiet for a long moment. "What do we do?"

Kurt shook his head. "There's not much we *can* do. We've never successfully rescued a prisoner held by ISIS. There's often a lapse in time between when these first videos are made, and when the death sentence is carried out, but… we don't have the people on the ground. We have analysts matching the data in that video against previous videos and known places where ISIS holds prisoners. If we can determine a location, there may be a chance. It's a race against time, but one that so far has always proven futile."

"Do we know where Stone is?" Susan said.

"We don't. Still missing inside Syria. About all we have right now is Stone's intel person, Mika Dolan. She's very young, and apparently is having what I would call, for lack of a better term, a nervous breakdown."

"Where is she?"

"She's in a hotel room in Adana. She was with Swann last night, and has no idea what happened to him. Fighting ramped back up in Turkey early this morning. Adana is one of the hot spots. She is terrified. My aide Amy is in touch with her, and believes that she is no longer capable of functioning independently, and is probably a liability in the field. I think we need to extract her from the hotel, get her back to the military base, and bring her home."

Susan nodded. "Okay. We can do that at least. Get her out of there."

CHAPTER TWENTY FIVE

7:30 a.m. Eastern European Time
(1:30 a.m. Eastern Daylight Time)
Adana, Turkey

Her mind was racing. It flitted from one thing to the next like a butterfly, but never landed anywhere for more than a few seconds.

"Yes, I'm almost packed," Mika said into her phone mic. "I don't even care. If I forget something, I'll leave it behind. I just need to get out of here, somewhere safe."

She was stuffing her clothes into a suitcase. They fit fine before, but now she couldn't close the damn thing. She didn't have time to fold everything just so. She had to get out of here.

She didn't want to be a spy anymore. She didn't want to be law enforcement officer. If she made it back to the United States, she didn't know if she would ever go back to her job at the FBI. They had put her on loan to Luke Stone? What did that even mean?

Three men had died in Syria. That helicopter crash... Swann had shot down another helicopter. Now Swann was gone, kidnapped. He had been here in the room when she went to sleep last night. And when she woke up, he was gone. Just... gone. Of course she knew what had happened to him. She had seen the video—half the world had seen it by now.

They were going to kill him.

"Mika, you can't leave anything behind," Amy said into her ear. "Do you understand me? You have to breathe deeply, try to calm down, and pack everything up. You have to take it all with you. You are handling classified materials. There may be evidence on Swann's computer equipment. The analysts are going to want to—"

"I can't do it!" Mika screamed. "I can't do it, Amy. I have to get out of here."

Everything about this hotel suite was malevolent now. There were killers lurking behind every corner, inside of every shadow. Every single light in the suite was on, and it was broad daylight outside.

"Mika! Get hold of yourself. There are some elementary things that you have to do. If you can't do them... I can't help you. You're going to lose your job."

Amy was crazy. Mika realized that now. She always spoke in that serious tone of voice. Everything was just so important. She was over there, safe and sound in Washington, DC. She was an aide to the National Security Adviser. She worked at the White House, ate in nice restaurants, took a car service home to her place in Georgetown every night. She lived inside a bubble.

"Lose my job? Lose my job? Do you really think I care about that? I'm going to lose my life. They're going to kill me, Amy. They're going to kill Swann, and they're going to kill me."

Amy sighed, and in her sigh, Mika heard the devastating performance report in its entirety. Agent was loaned to the Secret Service Special Response Team for a classified overseas assignment. Agent failed to perform tasks as assigned. Agent failed to meet responsibilities in a stressful environment. Agent was repatriated before operation was completed. Recommendation: Termination of Employment.

"Okay," Amy said. "Listen to me. All non-combat flights are grounded at this moment, including helicopter flights. All right? So you can't go back to the base the way you came. We're sending an armored car for you. There will be a motorcade of three cars—the other two will have armed American contractors in them, providing security."

"Why are the flights grounded?" Mika said.

"There are rebel anti-aircraft guns in the vicinity."

Mika froze. This was never going to end. "How am I going to get home?"

"You're going to wait on the base until the guns have been cleared from the area, then you're going to get on the next flight to Germany. From there, you'll catch a connection home."

Now Mika sighed. Okay. A sudden realization hit her. There was something going on. Some mystical force was at work, trapping her in place. It was out of her hands. Maybe the force would let her go, or maybe it would kill her. But there was nothing she could do about it. She was helpless, and for some reason, being helpless made her feel a little better.

"Okay," she said.

"I can send contractors up to your room to escort you down and help carry everything, but I need you to pack up all everything before they get there. They're not going to have classified clearance, and we can't have them sorting through classified materials."

"Fine," Mika said. "Don't worry. I'll pack everything. I'll wait for their knock."

"Good girl," Amy said. "That's my girl. Fifteen minutes, all right?"

Mika nodded. "Got it."

Now she felt more placid. She took her time, packing in an orderly fashion. She closed Swann's computer—since she had found his instant message exchange, she'd been afraid to touch it. His other computers were already closed, and it was a simple matter to put them in their cases. She managed to close her suitcase and gather her equipment together.

A heavy knock came at the door.

She went to it and opened it without thinking, expecting two big military men to come bustling in.

A woman stood there. She had long curly dark hair and blue eyes. Mika couldn't tell any more about her than that. She wore a hijab over her head, and a veil over her face that obscured everything but her eyes. A conservative black abaya wrap covered her entire body to her wrists and her ankles. The abaya had an elaborate multi-colored print across the front.

"Mika?"

Mika almost couldn't answer. Was it an assassin? "Yes," she said, resigned to her fate. It didn't even occur to her to slam the door. "I'm Mika."

"I'm a friend of Luke Stone," the woman said. "When you see him, give him this for me, will you?"

Despite the clothes, the woman's voice was that of an American. She held a black hard drive in her outstretched hand. Mika took it absently.

"What is it?"

The woman seemed to smile, but there was no humor in it. The eyes watched Mika. "It's something he'll want to see. It's encrypted. So when he needs to open it, ask him if he remembers his old friend's number. Okay?"

"Ask him if…"

"Yes. Does he remember his old friend's number?"

"His old friend's number," Mika repeated.

The woman nodded. "Good. Please remember that. What do you want to ask him?"

"If he remembers his old friend's number," Mika said automatically.

"That's right. Does he remember his old friend's number. It's very important."

Down the hall, the elevator made a tone, suggesting it was on its way. The woman turned, and glanced at it.

"Gotta go," she said.

An instant later, she was gone. To Mika, it seemed almost if she had evaporated, but really what she had done was leave the other way and enter the stairwell. A moment later, a warm tone sounded and the elevator opened. Two big American men came out of it, dressed neck to toes in combat fatigues, Oakley sunglasses perched on their crew-cut heads.

"Mika!" one of them said. "We just came from the air base. It's a little hot between here and there today. Ready for the ride of your life?"

CHAPTER TWENTY SIX

7:40 a.m. Mediterranean Time
(1:40 a.m. Eastern Daylight Time)
Jalmeh, Syria

"They took the man's glasses away," Ed Newsam said.

Luke and Ed had just watched Mark Swann, arms tied and in an orange jumpsuit, tell his mom that he loved her. The reporter held a small tablet computer in front of them as the screen went dark.

Luke stared at the black screen a moment. The reporter was no longer smiling. Behind him the boats continued to burn. As Luke watched, a new ball of black and red flame erupted from the third boat in line. The *Helena* was collapsing into the water.

How did it happen?

Last he knew, Swann was safe inside a hotel that was guarded like a fortress.

"They took his glasses away," Ed said again. "How's the man supposed to see?"

Ed's eyes went to that bulging crazy place that Luke had seen before. His nostrils flared. His mouth pursed. His entire body was electric with rage. Without another word, he turned and stalked toward the skinny Brit lying in a ball on the ground.

"Ed," Luke said.

He was there in five steps. He bent over the kid. "You!" he said. "You're gonna tell me. How's my brother supposed to see?"

"Please," the kid Nigel said.

"NO."

With his left hand, Ed grabbed the kid by his collar and yanked him off the ground. With his right, he punched the kid in the head. It was a devastating shot. The kid's head bounced in the air.

Ed reared back and did it again. This time in the face. It was the hardest punch that Luke had ever seen.

Teeth flew. The kid's mouth was instantly bloodied.

"Please," he said, his voice a hoarse lisp now. "I didn't do it."

"Nah, man. You didn't do anything. You didn't do this, you didn't do that. Why you fucking here if you ain't doing anything?"

He hit him again.

Luke started walking toward them, taking his time.

Ed hit him again.

The kid was not trying to protect himself.

Ed pulled a pistol from his side holster. He smacked the kid in the side of the head with it. Then he pressed it to the kid's head.

"Ed!" Luke said.

From the corner of his eye, Luke saw the long-haired cameraman. He had the camera mounted on his shoulder. He stared into the viewfinder. He was filming this.

Luke turned to him. "Put that camera down!"

The cameraman moved away from him, but kept filming. "It's a summary execution, man. I've seen this before. He's about to kill that guy."

"I said put that camera down!"

The reporter tried to step between them. "Hey! Hey, it's freedom of the press."

Luke pushed the guy aside, took three steps, and grabbed the cameraman by the hair. He swung the guy around in a big arc, then let go. The guy stumbled away. Luke followed him, pulled the camera down off his shoulder, and smashed it on the ground. The he stomped on it.

"This isn't America, you idiots. There's no freedom here."

He turned around and now the reporter had a gun out. He was pointing it at Ed. "Hey!" he shouted. "Hey, don't you shoot that guy!"

Luke walked over. In one move, he punched the guy in the face and pulled his gun away. The reporter fell to the ground. He sat on his ass and put a hand to his cheek.

"Don't make me hurt you," Luke said.

His gun was a revolver—a six-shooter, stupid gun to take into a war zone. Luke opened the cylinder and dumped the bullets on the ground. Then he threw the thing away. He turned back to Ed.

Ed hadn't moved. He still had the barrel pressed to the kid's temple.

"I'm gonna do it, man. I'm gonna kill this ISIS punk in cold blood right now."

The kid's eyes were squeezed tight.

"Please," he said, blood streaming down his jaw. "I know where they took him. I know where they took him. It's the same place. They always use the same place."

Luke walked over. "Ed. Wait a minute. Just one minute. Then you can blow his brains out. I don't care. But what is he saying?"

Nigel's chin was red with blood. His neck was red. His mouth hung open. Great thick bursts of blood poured from it. There were black spaces where his front teeth used to be. "I know where they took him." Blood flowed down. It pattered onto the dusty ground and mingled with the dirt.

"Nigel, do you have any idea how badly we're going to hurt you if we find out you're lying? We killed all your friends. They'll be the ones who got off easy."

"I'm not lying. I know where it is. I know where they do the confession videos. I know where they do the executions. That wrecked building in the video. It was the headquarters. It got bombed, I think by the Americans—now they kill people there. You bomb us, we kill you. That's the message."

"Nigel..." Luke said. "This man is about to kill you."

"I'm not lying. I know exactly where that video was shot. Look. I'm smart. I watch what's happening. I know the places where Abu al-Baghdadi hides. I watch where his motorcade goes. I know which ones are the body doubles. I've been there. I've seen everything."

"Where is all this?"

"Al-Raqqa, the capital of the caliphate."

Ed dropped him on the ground. He put his big boot on Nigel's head and pressed. "Say the word caliphate again."

The kid's eyes squeezed shut. "Aaaaannnhhhh!"

"Say caliphate. Say it! I'll crush your skull."

"Please—"

"There ain't no caliphate, you punk. There's never gonna be a caliphate."

Luke looked at the reporter. He was still sitting on the ground, staring into space. He moved his jaw around, adjusting himself to the feeling of soreness. That thing was going to swell up in a little while.

"You. How far is al-Raqqa from here?"

"Two hundred miles. Maybe two twenty."

"How long does it take to get there?"

"On the ground?"

"Yes."

"Oh, man. What's the old saying? You can't get there from here. The siege of Aleppo is in the way. It's a freak show. Assad and the Russians are bombing all the time. Almost nothing can get in or out. People in there are starving. If you somehow slip through, you'll pass through government-held territory, rebel-held territory, contested territory, then into wide open desert. The highway is a killing zone out there. You'll see Raqqa in the distance. It's the only thing for miles. There's nowhere to hide. You will never make it."

"You've been there?" Luke said.

The guy nodded. "We're the press, man. You see those big letters *TV* all over the truck? It's magic. People think twice before killing us. Don't ask me why. They kill everybody else without hesitating."

Luke looked at the news truck, and really saw it for the first time. It was a *Mad Max*–style contraption, the black windows covered with steel grates. It was tall. It had a high suspension and heavy-duty knobbed tires.

"What is that thing?"

"The truck? It's an old ambulance from Paris. We gutted it, swapped out the medical stuff, and put communications stuff in. Plus a couple of cots suspended from the walls. The tires are triple-steel-reinforced run-flats—there's a lot of junk lying around on the roads, and most of it is sharp. Those tires go over anything. We also dropped in a bare bones three-hundred-horsepower engine. Easy to maintain—just add water. It's a beast."

"How fast does it go?"

"I've pinned it at one eighty kilometers per hour. That's as high as the speedometer goes. What's that, about one ten? But you can't maintain that speed. We just use a burst of power for fast getaways."

He looked at Luke. Then the reality hit him. "Hey, no way, man. No. You can't take the truck away."

Luke shook his head. "I'm not taking it away. You're coming with us."

* * *

"Hold for the President of the United States."

It took half an hour to get through on the reporter's satellite phone. They were already on the road, Luke in the shotgun seat. The cameraman was at the wheel. He was quietly seething about his camera—he said it cost him five thousand dollars.

"Don't worry," Luke had told him. "Your Uncle Sam will pay for it."

"We're Canadian."

Luke sighed and shook his head. "I don't care what you are," he said. "Put your foot on the gas. Never mind the brake."

Now Luke was holding the phone, watching the ruined buildings pass outside his window. The sky was pale blue and wide open. The ground was tan and brown. Everything man-made was bombed out. Everything was crumbling.

Luke felt very little about the devastation. He'd been in war zones before, many times. Things got broken, and this was what broken looked like. The only thing he did feel was a sense of time urgency. Swann was out there, being held by remorseless animals. Swann was a talented man. Maybe there were things he could tell them, or do for them, that might buy him a few extra hours. Luke hoped so.

Please let me get there.

Luke didn't know of anyone who had been rescued from ISIS. But he and Ed, if they got inside that city… and they hit as hard as they could… and they caught a few breaks… maybe.

A voice came on the phone.

"Hello?" She sounded small and far away.

"Susan, how are you?"

"I'm okay. How are you?"

"Terrible. But Ed and I are alive and we're still operational."

"*Where* are you?"

"We're in Syria. I'm calling to make a report. We reached the wharf where the boat the *Helena* was docked. There were no warheads. There were two tractor trailers in the hold—both were damaged in a way that was consistent with a gun battle. Both were empty. We encountered ISIS fighters at the dock, and the boat was destroyed in the ensuing firefight. But there was nothing on board."

She was saying something, but her voice cut out for a moment. A few seconds of static, then she faded back in. Luke didn't ask her to repeat herself.

"Next point," he said. "We captured an ISIS fighter at the scene. He told us that the *Helena* was a decoy. The warheads stayed in Turkey. He believes they are en route to Russia. Repeat… warheads en route to Russia. His claims the plan is to launch the warheads at Russian cities from inside Russia. That way, what? Nobody will know who did it, I guess."

"Do you believe him?" a male voice said. Luke couldn't tell who was who. He glanced down at the crumpled form of Nigel, curled into a ball on the floor of the truck, holding a small towel to his mouth, his lower leg in a splint that Ed had made for him. He was about as pathetic a soldier as you'd expect to see in a war zone.

"I don't know what I believe," Luke said. "But I think it's worth pursuing."

"Okay," the male voice said. "We'll look into it." Luke suspected the voice belonged to Kurt Kimball.

"Kurt?"

"Yes."

"This isn't something you look into," Luke said. "What you do is the following. You pull in about a hundred analysts, FBI, NSA, CIA, large municipal police departments, wherever you can scare them up on a moment's notice. Have them go back through as much satellite data as is available over the past two days—both before and after the theft. The warheads must have been switched to different trucks, and probably big ones. If those trucks are headed to Russia, there's really only a couple of ways they can go. There used to be a direct Black Sea ferry between Turkey and Russia—"

"Trabzon to Sochi," Kurt said. "It's been closed since the Russian incursion on the Turkish islands."

Luke nodded. "Good. Then the trucks either have to go on a private craft—which means that someone has to commandeer such a craft and land it at a Russian dock, with Russian inspectors. Or they have to travel through Georgia and cross into Russia at the Georgian-Russian border."

"Considering the tensions between Georgia and Russia in recent years..." Kurt began.

"That's right," Luke said. "A tall order. So analyze the satellite data, and isolate any large trucks—tractor-trailers, delivery trucks, construction vehicles—that have crossed into Georgia. Narrow it to the most likely suspects from there. See if the Georgians will cooperate with security footage. If they won't, then have the Russians interdict at the border. They have skin in this game."

There was a long silence over the phone.

"It's a good idea," Kurt said finally.

"It's not an idea, Kurt. It's how you do it. So do it, okay?"

Luke stared at the phone in his hand. He had just given an order to the President's National Security Adviser, probably in front of twenty people. Those were tired people. It was still the middle of the night there. And Luke was... who exactly?

"Hello?" he said.

"Luke," Susan said. "We are negotiating your surrender with the Syrian government. They will transfer you to the Turkish border, where you can catch a helicopter back to Incirlik."

"Uh, negative, Susan. We have another mission here before we can leave."

"What mission?"

"I'd prefer not to discuss it over this connection."

"Luke, your current mission has been a disaster. We are trying to defuse an international incident with Russia on this end. We lost three men. They lost six. We can't have direct combat with the Russians, Luke."

"Then I suggest you find those nukes," Luke said. "They're on their way to Russia, if what I hear is right. I think I mentioned that, didn't I?"

"Agent Stone," Susan said. "I know what you're planning to do. And I'm ordering you to turn around and return to the base in Turkey."

"I need to speak with Mika Dolan," Luke said. "Is she okay?"

"She's fine, yes. Very upset, but okay, and being transferred to the Incirlik Air Base as we speak. Which is where I'd like you to go."

"Can someone get a message to her? Please ask her to call me at this number."

"Stone!" Susan said. "You're not listening to me. I went out on a limb to send you in there. It was a mistake. We are in a very tense situation. I realize that Mark Swann was your friend. Believe me when I say we are expending every resource available to—"

"Mark Swann *is* my friend," Luke said. "Present tense."

"Stone," Kurt Kimball said. "The President of the United States has just given you a direct order. You can't—"

Luke looked at the telephone again. It was a simple one. Big numbers on the keypad. Green button for call. Red button for hang up.

He pressed the red button.

"Damn satellites," he said. "I lost the call."

CHAPTER TWENTY SEVEN

8:15 a.m. Eastern European Time
(2:15 a.m. Eastern Daylight Time)
Incirlik Air Base
Adana, Turkey

Mika was alive.

It was all that mattered. She sat cross-legged on the floor in a far corner of a half empty office, her belongings piled around her. There were no windows in this office. Windows would be hard because the office was several stories underground. It was inside what had appeared to be a squat building on the American side of the Incirlik Air Base. The building was indeed squat when observed from above ground—below ground, it was ten stories tall.

At the other side of the office, people in military uniforms sat at computer terminals, or paced around, yelling into telephones. The country was in crisis, and the base was under attack. These people seemed to be doing something important about it, or thought they were.

Mika shivered. The drive here had been something out of a nightmare. They had traveled at high-speed in a three-SUV convoy, racing past angry mobs of people running in the streets. Flames and smoke rose from a dozen fires on the horizon. The security contractors leaned out the windows and fired indiscriminately whenever traffic slowed down. They drove on sidewalks. They drove through the middle of a deserted open air café, scattering chairs and tables everywhere

Mika didn't mind what they did. Anything to get here, where it was safe.

She didn't know if she was going to lose her job. She wouldn't mind if she did. She might even quit. It didn't matter. She was Mika Dolan, and she was alive.

She remembered how she used to take long walks on the beach with her dad. She enjoyed that. If she made it home alive, she would do that again. Maybe that's all she would ever do.

A man in tan battle fatigues approached her. He was young and smiling.

"Mika Dolan?"

"Yes. Is my plane ready?"

The smile faded somewhat. "What plane is that?"

"I'm supposed to be evacuated."

"Oh. Yeah. That. No one is being evacuated at the present time. Everything non-combat-related is grounded. Believe me, you wouldn't want to be on a plane taking off from here right now. I've been sent to let you know that people are trying to reach you. You have a call from Amy Pooler, aide to the President's National Security Adviser. She told me to relay to you that you should call Agent Luke Stone immediately. I have the phone number for you."

Inside her jacket pocket, Mika felt the weight of the hard drive the mysterious woman had given her. She hadn't told anyone about it. It occurred to her now what an obvious breach of security protocol that was—a stranger had given her a small black box, and she had carried it onto the base. It certainly looked like an external hard drive, but...

"Why didn't Amy call me directly?" she said.

"You're using a satellite phone, and you're too far underground for the signal to reach. You have to go upstairs to make or receive calls. Better if you go outside."

Outside? She didn't like the sound of that.

The man handed her a slip of yellow paper. "That's the number," he said. "Please give Agent Stone a call."

"Okay," she said.

After he left, she sat still for several moments. Certain feelings washed over her. Sure, there was the job thing. But she was young, and she graduated from MIT. She had been heavily recruited by private industry coming out of school. She would get another job. She had thought she wanted to go into real spy work, but if this was how it went... they could keep it.

The problem was Swann. She liked Swann. He was funny. She liked Luke and Ed, too. And so far she had failed them. Swann's life was in danger.

Who was she kidding? There was a good chance he was already dead.

All the same, she couldn't just sit here, waiting for a plane to take her away. She couldn't abandon them. It wasn't how she'd been raised. Sure, her job was on the line, and she didn't really care about that. This wasn't about the FBI job. It was about honoring a commitment. She had come on this operation, and she had been thrown for a loop. But she should try to finish it out the best she could.

She could quit the job, or keep it, when she got home.

She stood on numb legs, and looked for the elevator to the surface.

CHAPTER TWENTY EIGHT

8:31 a.m. Eastern European Time
(2:31 a.m. Eastern Daylight Time)
Deep Underground
Ankara, Turkey

"They have broken through the perimeter," a voice announced. "The guards have all fled or been killed."

Ismet Batur, the President of Turkey, sat waiting to meet the men who had come to depose him.

He was inside a bunker left over from the Cold War.

When tensions were at their highest, the government had built these sites, where the ruling class and the heads of the military would retreat in the event of a nuclear war. The shafts were so deep it was believed that no radioactivity could ever penetrate to the bottom levels.

At one time, the tunnels down here were extensive. They connected bunkers in various parts of the city. There were living areas, command centers, gymnasiums, even a prison. There were farm areas where produce could be grown under artificial light. Millions of gallons of water were stored for such an eventuality.

The system had fallen into disrepair over the years, but was gradually being rebuilt. Not fast enough for Batur's tastes, however.

He lit a cigarette. He inhaled deeply and exhaled a cloud of smoke. He was not a nervous man, but he had to admit the current state of affairs had left him very nervous indeed. An aide had offered him a pistol a little while ago—the implication being to shoot himself instead of being captured. Batur had declined the generous offer.

"Keep the gun," he told the aide. "You may need it yourself."

He sat inside a rounded chamber in a chair that 1960s designers would have thought of as space age. Just across from him was a large flat-screen, rounded to conform to the wall to which it was fastened. The screen was off, at his request. He had tired of watching bad news.

There were perhaps twenty men remaining in the cavern around him. They were agitated, and very alert. They had drawn their weapons and were watching the elevators. There were four elevators in an alcove, two facing two across a narrow hall. It seemed that when those doors opened, the men here could kill anyone emerging from there.

It seemed pointless to Batur. There were two stairwells—almost certainly enemies were making their way down those as well. It was possible that this small group of guards could hold this chamber for quite some time—maybe even for hours. But eventually the opponent would take it.

Perhaps that was what made people hate Batur—he saw the writing on the wall, and became resigned to the outcome instantly.

"Should we disable the elevators?" a guard said.

Batur shook his head. "Let him them come. It is inevitable. And lower your weapons. We are surrendering."

Within moments, he saw that it was a foolish decision. The first wave of soldiers to arrive arrested his men and bound their wrists. Then the elevators returned to the surface. When the next wave of soldiers entered, they came with the man himself.

The tall mustachioed colonel in the Turkish Air Force dress uniform walked directly to the President and stood over him.

"Musharaff," President Batur said. "I suppose I knew it was you."

"And I knew it was you," Colonel Musharaff said. "I knew it was you who oversaw the dismantling of our great military. I knew it was you who let the swindlers and the speculators run amok and prey on the common people. I knew it was you who stood by while the Russians stole our land. And I knew it was you who must be deposed if we are to restore our country to greatness."

"Very impressive speech," Batur said. "Also very unfortunate. You will never hold the country for long. Your advantage was surprise, but the surprise is over. Perhaps forty-eight hours from now, order will be restored and you will lose your grip on power."

Musharaff nodded. "Yes. Very likely. But forty-eight hours will be more than enough to make the Russians feel the sting from stirring up a wasp's nest."

Batur stared at him.

"You are weak," Musharaff said. "The Russian aggression must be avenged. You won't do it, so I will do it in your stead. The people demand it. The Turkish military demands it. Our history demands it."

Batur shook his head. He knew Musharaff was insane, but he hadn't really considered how dangerous he was.

"A direct attack on the Russians will bring almost certain doom," he said.

Musharaff smiled.

"On the contrary. A direct attack on the Russians will force the Americans to our defense."

CHAPTER TWENTY NINE

8:42 a.m. Mediterranean Time
(2:42 a.m. Eastern Daylight Time)
Outskirts of Aleppo, Syria

Russian bombers roared overhead.

Luke covered his ears as the sound split open the sky. A moment later, the bombs hit, maybe twenty miles behind him. The blasts were muffled at this distance, but the ground still trembled, shaking the news truck. The Russians were bombing the city of Aleppo to smithereens.

Luke sat on the roof of the truck, staring into a pair of high-powered binoculars, scanning the distance ahead. The road was choked with traffic—thousands of people on foot, streaming down the highway like a Biblical exodus, carrying their meager belongings, their children and animals in tow. Mingled in with the people were dozens of cars and trucks. Everyone was trying to leave the city. But there was a Syrian army checkpoint up there, and it was a slow go passing through it.

"Ed, what are we going to do, man?"

Ed stood on the road, gazing at the same checkpoint with a different pair of binoculars. "I don't know. At the rate this is going, it could be another hour before we reach the checkpoint. If they're being thorough, then they're going to find our friend Nigel. He's gonna be hard to explain."

Luke shook his head in frustration. He stood and paced back and forth across the roof of the truck. The giant white letters TV had also been painted on the roof—these guys weren't taking any chances. He walked across the letters.

There had to be a way. Every minute they were stuck here brought Swann another minute closer to death.

"Hey, Stone?" one of the Canadians, the reporter, yelled. His name was Chris. He appeared on the road next to the truck, holding the satellite phone.

"You have a call."

Luke made a hand gesture, indicating to toss it up. Chris flipped it to him, and he snagged it in mid-air. It was probably Washington. Maybe they had a lead on Swann. Maybe they had found him. Luke felt a tickle of nervous dread in his stomach.

"The battery is running down," Chris said. "So please don't stay on there all day."

"Stone."

"Luke, it's Mika."

"Mika, I'm glad you called. Are you okay?"

"I'm fine. I was a little shaken up, but I'm okay now. They took me to the military base. They're going to start evacuating people as soon as the flights are cleared."

"Good," Luke said. He wasn't sure if that was good or not. Mika's acumen hadn't exactly set Luke's world on fire so far, but he was still better off with her here than on a plane back to the States. "Before you leave, we need your help."

"That's why I called. Just before I left the hotel, a woman came to my room. She was dressed as a Muslim, very conservatively, but I could tell by her voice she was American. She gave me a hard drive. She said she was a friend of yours."

"A friend of mine?" Luke said. "I don't have any friends in Turkey. What did she look like?"

"I don't know. Her face was covered. She was thin and had dark curly hair."

"What's on the drive?"

"I don't know that either. It's encrypted. She said to ask you if you remember your good friend's number."

"Do I remember my good friend's number?"

"Yes."

Ed was listening. He looked up at Luke. "Trudy?"

Luke shrugged. "In Turkey? In the middle of a coup d'etat? Somehow I doubt it, but okay."

"Do you know her phone number?"

"Sure."

Ed shrugged. "So try it."

"Are you at a computer right now?" Luke said into the phone.

"Yes."

"Okay, so put in this number." Luke gave Mika Trudy's ten-digit phone number, which he knew by heart. He waited.

"No good," Mika said.

"How many digits is the code?"

"It doesn't show you," Mika said. "That's up to you to decide."

"So try the seven digits, without the area code. If that doesn't work, try the final four digits. If that doesn't work, try the number of her street address—231."

180

Another few minutes passed. "Mika?"

"None of that is working."

"Okay, let me think about it a minute. In the meantime, this is what I need from you. We found the boat here in Syria. There were no weapons on board. We captured an ISIS fighter, and he told us the warheads were sent to Russia. He claims that they're going to launch the missiles at Russia, from inside Russia. I told the President and her National Security Adviser about this—they didn't seem impressed. I want you to find out what they're doing about it, if anything. If nothing, I need you to scare up a tech person there at the base, see if you can retrieve satellite data from the past couple of days, and find some likely suspects on the roads in Turkey, and a route for those trucks into Russia."

Her answer surprised him. "I don't have to do that."

His shoulders slumped. "You don't have to—"

"No. I spent my first six months on the job studying Russia and her former Republics. The most direct overland route from Turkey to Russia is through Georgia. It's really the only way to do it, and that border has been tight since the Russian-Georgian war. It's practically closed. The hassles getting through the crossings aren't worth the trip. I can't imagine anyone trying to sneak stolen nuclear warheads through there."

"What if they paid off the guards?" Luke said.

"Not a chance," Mika's tiny voice said. "There are thousands of troops massed at the border, and the guards pull apart everything that comes through as a matter of policy. On the ground level, there are too many people watching to try to pay someone off. You could try someone higher, I imagine. But what mid-level Russian military functionary is going to let bombs into the country so that ISIS can attack Russia? Those guys hate ISIS. There isn't enough money on Earth to justify that payoff. If Kurt Kimball wasn't excited about that theory, there's your reason. It's impossible."

Luke stood on top of the truck without moving. He thought about the kid Nigel that had caught at the boat. Just some stupid kid who ran away from home. He probably thought he was doing something romantic. Someone had told him the trucks were going to Russia, so in his mind, they were. This was the same kid who thought he knew where Swann was being kept. Jesus.

The warheads were gone. Bill Cronin and two chopper pilots were dead. Swann was kidnapped by ISIS. This operation couldn't have gone any worse.

Half a mile away, at the checkpoint, some kind of commotion was going on. People were running, scattering.

"You seeing this?" Ed said, his eyes planted against his binoculars.

"Yes. What is it, can you tell?"

"Not yet," Ed said.

"Okay, Mika," Luke said. "I see your point. But please don't dismiss this out of hand. Just do what I ask, all right?"

Her voice was cold. "All right, Luke."

"Before you look for the weapons, though, I want you to use the satellite data to help us look for Swann. Specifically, look for anything—a truck, a plane, a car, a helicopter, anything at all—that went from Adana to al-Raqqa in the past eight hours. And please don't tell me it's impossible. I can't hear that right now. Instead, tell me how it is possible, who did it most recently, and where they parked when they arrived. Okay?"

"Is that where you're going?" she said.

"Yes."

"It's the ISIS stronghold."

"Yes, I know," he said.

"The Russians bomb it every day. I've heard that there are Spetsnaz troops on the ground there, trying to assassinate Abu Bakr al-Baghdadi and the other leaders of ISIS. It's a shooting gallery is what I'm trying to say."

"This whole country is a shooting gallery," Luke said.

As if to prove his point, the sound of gunshots came from the checkpoint. Suddenly, an explosion rattled the ground. The small building at the checkpoint blew apart. Everywhere, people started to run. The crowds flowed off the road and into the fields at either side. People flung themselves to the ground and covered their heads.

"Someone just blew themselves up," Ed said. "Looks like they took a few checkpoint personnel with them."

Another, larger explosion rattled the day. Thick smoke rose. Luke could make out fire on the horizon.

"Mika, I have to go."

Luke slid down the windshield to the ground. He landed with a jolt on the dusty highway. Ed was already jumping into the truck. Luke was one second behind him.

He slid into the passenger seat. Chris was in the driver's seat.

"Let's go, man," Luke said. "That's our cue."

Chris's eyes were wide. "Our cue to do what?"

Luke pointed at the suddenly empty highway in front of them. In the distance, flames reached for the sky. Black smoke billowed. "Go through the checkpoint! What are you waiting for? Can't you see? The road is open."

Luke reached for the dashboard siren and turned it on.

"Hit it. This is news up ahead."

The former ambulance took off, siren howling, straight for the burning checkpoint.

CHAPTER THIRTY

3:15 a.m.
The Situation Room
The White House, Washington, DC

"Hold for the President of the Russian Federation."

Susan held the big red phone to her cheek and rolled her eyes. She was beyond tired now. She looked at the other people in the Room—a dozen left. She, Kurt, Kat Lopez, and Haley Lawrence had cooked up the idea to call Putin back. Susan didn't know if it was a good one or not.

It was hard to make decisions at this level of exhaustion.

His voice came on the line. Nothing formal this time—he wasn't even going to bother. "Yes, hello, Missus."

Susan shook her head and almost laughed. "Hi, Vlad."

"You will forgive me, but my trusted interpreter Vasil is still with me."

"Of course," she said.

Putin started talking in Russian again, not waiting for her to say a word. In a moment, Vasil caught up with the gist.

"Six months with no call, now two calls in six hours. They will say we are lovers. I will be the next…"

In the background, Putin conferred with someone else, a gruff masculine voice. There was a momentary back-and-forth in Russian, a debate about something. Then Putin was back.

"Tommy Zales," he said. He didn't need Vasil for that one.

Susan felt a blush creep up her neck. In case she needed a reminder that people were always watching—and she supposed she did need one—this was it. She thought of Pierre, just a fleeting wisp of anxiety—when would he find out?

"Vladimir, I'm calling to share some information with you."

She let Vasil begin translating, then she plunged on ahead of him. He was good at catching up, and she didn't want his boss taking advantage of any pause.

"We have intelligence to suggest that the stolen warheads are going to be smuggled into Russia."

Putin made a sound with his mouth—a child's sound of disbelief, very nearly what Susan used to think of as a Bronx cheer. Then he began speaking.

"Why darling," Vasil said. "Would we steal your obsolete nuclear warheads, or sponsor such an activity? We have more warheads than we need, and ones in good working order."

"I'm not saying you stole them," Susan said. "I'm saying that terrorists, possibly ISIS, may be planning to smuggle the warheads into Russia, then launch them at Russia from within your own country. I'm suggesting that you double and triple security at your overland border crossings—anything within a few days' drive of Turkey. The warheads may be coming your way."

"I want to tell you something," Vasil said. "I want to be very clear. We already monitor our border crossings effectively, and we will quadruple our efforts. But this does not mean we will be successful. These are your weapons. And ISIS is your bastard love child with the Sunni extremist states of Saudi Arabia and Pakistan."

Susan began to speak but was cut off.

"Please don't pretend otherwise, dear one. We know how ISIS began, and from where their funding emerged. We know men like al-Baghdadi were held in your Camp Bucca prison, and we know what kinds of psychology experiments were carried out there. We understand the methods of your CIA very well. Now you have put very dangerous weapons in the hands of very dangerous people. If they manage to use them, we will hold you responsible. Of course."

"Vladimir—"

"If a single Russian city is attacked, we will return fire. What choice do we have? To see our loved ones annihilated, while we stand idly by? I don't think so. But we will be measured in our response. If Volgograd is hit, we will take Boston. If Saint Petersburg goes, so goes New York. Moscow? We take Washington, DC. Does that sound like a pleasure to you? I can tell you I take no joy in it. But it is the most fair and balanced remedy I can think of."

"Vladimir, you can't do that. We have—"

"Yes, I know. You have a missile defense system that will respond automatically to any attack on a major American city. I suggest you take that system offline for the duration of the crisis. We didn't lose these warheads, lovely lady. We didn't empower these terrorists. I am certain that history will absolve us of any responsibility for the unfortunate consequences of your actions."

"Vladimir—"

"As always, it has been my pleasure to discuss world affairs with someone as serious and well-informed as yourself."

The phone went dead.

Susan looked around the table at the faces gathered there. The Russian President had just hung up on her. "It gets better and better with that guy, doesn't it?"

"Susan," Kurt Kimball began. He had black rings around his eyes. His skull was starting to appear hollowed out. Was she hallucinating this? She needed sleep.

"Kurt, how long would we need to bring our missile defense system offline, as he suggests?"

"I don't suggest you do that," Haley Lawrence said. "It would leave us exposed."

Kurt shook his head. "Our defense system is incredibly robust. Bringing it offline would be an incremental process that would take years to complete. It doesn't matter anyway. He was lying when he said their response would be measured. They have a missile defense system similar to ours. Its capabilities have degraded quite a bit since the Soviet Union collapsed, but that just means it's more likely to launch in the event of an attack, not less so. The finer the calibration, the more subtle the response. I believe that one nuclear warhead detonating anywhere in Russia will result in the launch of hundreds of missiles within minutes."

"So if ISIS launches a missile at them, or more than one..."

"Right, then they launch at us in response..."

"And that trips our own..."

"Yes," Kurt said. "And that means game over."

Susan sighed heavily.

"We need to get those warheads back."

CHAPTER THIRTY ONE

12:40 p.m. Moscow Time (4:40 a.m. Eastern Daylight Time)
The Main Centre for Missile Attack Warning
Timonovo, Russia

They had done it to him again.

Yuri Grachev, thirty years old, walked briskly through the hallways of the missile attack warning center, on his way to the large situation room. His footsteps echoed along the empty corridor.

Yuri was the senior aide and personal assistant to the Russian Defense Minister. Six months ago, when the United States had been briefly toppled in a coup d'etat, the Minister's black nuclear suitcase, his *Cheget,* had been handcuffed to Yuri's right wrist for more than forty-eight hours.

Now, in the past fifteen minutes, it had appeared there once again. He supposed he had done such a good job carrying it the last time, he might as well repeat the performance.

He hated the *Cheget.* It was old and heavy, with a battered leather cover over the steel case proper. The handcuff bit into his wrist and left a mark there. As he recalled, the weight of the case should soon cause his arm to ache all the way down from the shoulder to the tips of his fingers. Inside the case were the codes and mechanisms to launch missile strikes against the West.

As before, Yuri didn't want this horrible thing attached to him. He wanted to go home to his wife and young son. But unlike last time, he didn't feel like he might cry or crumble in the face of crisis. He was stronger now, more resilient. He stood tall, with the impassive face of a trusted government official. Something serious was happening. He would do his best to meet the challenge of it.

Just ahead, a wide automatic door slid open. He passed through the doorway and into the swirling chaos of the command center's main room. The chatter of voices hit Yuri like a wall as he entered.

Two hundred people filled the space. There were at least forty workstations, some of them with two or three people sitting at five computer screens. On the big board up front, there were twenty different television and computer screens.

Screens showed digital maps of Russia, Georgia, Ukraine, Turkey, and the wider Middle East. Live video streams showed activity at the border crossings between Russia and Georgia. Satellite imagery keyed in on movement along Turkish highways.

A series of screens showed location maps of American nuclear capabilities and missile sites spread out across the United States, Asia, and Europe.

Two of the screens currently showed President Putin standing near a podium and surrounded by aides and bodyguards. He was about to go on the air. As he approached the microphone, the voices in the command center began to die down.

"My countrymen," Putin began, and the command center went dead silent. "And our many friends abroad."

All eyes were now on the screens where Putin appeared. Yuri scanned the room. Putin's face was now on half the computer terminals in the command center.

"I come before you today to share difficult news. Little more than one hour ago, I hung up the telephone with the President of the United States. She has informed me that during the current unrest in Turkey, the Americans have lost control of at least eight nuclear warheads positioned on a military base there."

A loud gasp went around the command center, two hundred people speaking as one. Conversations broke out, but were instantly hushed by other people in the crowd.

"The Fashion Model in Chief believes these warheads have fallen into the hands of Islamic extremists, terrorists of which we have long and bitter experience. She can make no assurances that the weapons will not be detonated or launched. Indeed, she impressed upon me the notion that it is her belief, and the belief of her intelligence networks, that the terrorists intend to launch the weapons against the Russian Federation."

The talking was louder this time, excitement veering toward panic. Yuri felt his heart begin to beat harder and faster. A strange thought began to come over him—the thing at the end of his wrist was alive, and it was actually its heartbeat that he felt hammering against his chest.

"Shut up!" a three-star general near the front of room shouted. "Shut up, I said."

"Each of the warheads stolen," Putin said, "have a destructive power equal to ten times the Hiroshima blast. In other words, each warhead has the potential to kill at least a million and a half people in the initial explosion alone."

"Oh God," someone in the room said.

"We will leave for another time the recklessness with which these weapons were deployed. We will leave for another time speculation about how the weapons fell into the hands of the terrorists, or about the decades-long relationship the powers in Washington have enjoyed with these same terrorist forces. All of that is for another time. Now is the time for action."

On the screens, Putin paused, giving the world a steel-eyed glare. To Yuri, the gaze seemed like one of resolve, but resolve in the face of another emotion. Was it fear?

"I have instructed our defense forces, including missile defense, to assume the highest states of readiness. Our intelligence services are now scouring satellite and surveillance data to do what the United States cannot or will not—namely, find these weapons before they are launched."

He took a breath. "In the meantime, I am issuing an ultimatum to the individuals responsible for this theft. We know who you are. We know what countries you come from, and where your loved ones live. It is now just before one o'clock pm in Moscow. You have four hours to surrender the weapons, along with furnishing evidence and all assurances that the weapons you surrender are the only ones that were taken.

"At exactly five p.m., if no weapons have been surrendered, we will launch simultaneous and devastating attacks against the state sponsors of terror in the Middle East. Targets will include major cities in Turkey, Saudi Arabia, Pakistan, Afghanistan, Kuwait, the United Arab Emirates, and Israel. At our discretion, we will not limit ourselves to these targets. We are warning these countries in advance so they can take the necessary actions to retrieve the missing weapons and save the lives of their people. Once it begins, our onslaught will be swift, terrible, and impossible to defend against. We will reduce your countries to ruins."

No one in the command center said a word. Yuri glanced around, and spotted moisture in the eyes of several people. Near him, a woman in a military dress uniform choked back a deep sob. She closed her eyes as the tears began to roll down her cheeks.

"To my countrymen, please know that we don't take this action lightly. We will not stand aside and allow millions of our loved ones to perish in an attack that is as avoidable as it is calculated. Thank you."

At the end of Yuri Grachev's arm, the monstrous living thing, its heart already beating, came awake and began to breathe.

CHAPTER THIRTY TWO

5:05 a.m.
The White House Residence, Washington, DC

Susan was drifting, alone on the king-sized bed.

Thoughts came to her, thoughts that made no sense, and that was okay. A dream was beginning. She was playing a large cello—an instrument she had not so much as touched, never mind played, in her life. She sat on a stool in a wide open field, and a beautiful hard rain was falling. It was a bright morning, and she was playing the cello in the rain.

Sleep! Blessed sleep. She needed more of it.

The phone was ringing.

She resisted it for a long moment. They had to leave her alone. A person couldn't live without sleep. A person couldn't make decisions without sleep. Whatever was happening now, it had to wait.

But the phone was implacable. It was not going to stop ringing. It was not going to go away.

She opened her eyes. The room was dark. The tall shades were pulled, but there wasn't even any light in the sky behind them. She glanced at the clock.

Jesus. Thirty minutes. She had closed her eyes thirty minutes ago.

She picked up the telephone.

"Kurt?"

"Susan."

"I need sleep, Kurt. You need sleep. People need sleep. This is crazy."

"Putin went on Russian television fifteen minutes ago," Kurt said. "It was live, and was picked up worldwide. He confirmed the fact of the stolen warheads to the wider public. And he gave the terrorists four hours to surrender them. After that, he's going to start a bombing campaign. He's going to attack Middle Eastern countries he referred to as state sponsors of terror. Saudi Arabia, Turkey, Pakistan, Israel—"

"He never said a word about that on the phone," Susan said. She shook her head to clear the fog. She was honestly confused. "He said if they were bombed, they would respond in kind."

"Yes, I know. I suppose he changed his mind."

Susan was silent. She rubbed her eyes. It never ended.

It was never going to end.

Kurt went on. "Immediately after his remarks, the airwaves went berserk. ECHELON, all the listening stations, Fairbanks, Menwith Hill in England, Misawa Air Force Base in Japan, everything we have. The data is coming in fast and furious. Every country he threatened is going to a war footing. Iran and China are doing so as well. Nigeria will begin massing troops on the Somali border within the next hour.

"The Indians and Pakistanis are already testing their missile launch sequences. They both suspect the other will use the confusion for a preemptive strike. There is a real danger of a nuclear exchange between the two of them, regardless of what the Russians or the terrorists do. Meanwhile, the Russians have immediately stepped up their bombing of al-Raqqa. It appears to be intended to soften ISIS defenses in preparation for a full-on assault by Spetsnaz commandos."

Susan could not find her voice. There didn't seem to be a reasonable response to the things Kurt was saying. Kurt droned on, being Kurt, doing what Kurt did. Susan wondered if on some level he wasn't enjoying this.

"The phones are ringing off the hook," he said. "The State Department is looking for guidance from us. There are protests beginning outside at least twenty of our embassies, across Europe, Asia, and the Middle East. We expect more of them, and we anticipate that some will turn violent. Meanwhile, here in the States, looting has already started in a dozen cities."

What do you want me to do?

She almost said it. She was one person, and these were forces that one person could not stop. She wanted to tell him that, she really did. Instead, she held her tongue. She just let Kurt keep talking.

"I've been in touch with Haley Lawrence and the Chairman of the Joint Chiefs of Staff. The Pentagon wants to elevate Strategic Air Command and NORAD from DEFCON level 4, where we have been for the past two months, straight to DEFCON level 2, bypassing level 3. All other branches will elevate from DEFCON 4 to DEFCON 3 and await further orders. Both Haley and I agreed with the Chairman on this."

"Can you describe DEFCON 2 in English, please?"

"DEFCON 2," Kurt said, his voice taking on the tone he used when reading from a page in front of him. "Second highest readiness level—the next step to nuclear war. Armed forces ready to deploy and engage in six hours or less."

There was a pause over the line.

"Susan?"

"Yes."

"The Cheyenne Mountain Complex outside Colorado Springs is the most secure nuclear bunker we have. It can withstand a near direct hit by a thirty-megaton warhead. The valve system there is the most advanced in terms of filtering radiological contaminants from the outside air. It will take Air Force One approximately two and a half hours to reach the complex, and the plane can land right at the base."

"What are you saying, Kurt?"

"There's still time to make it there. Your family on the west coast can be there in one hour from now. If we wait until an emergency arises…"

In Susan's mind, she saw a long narrow corridor deep underground. She was moving down it, two Secret Service men ahead of her, one trailing behind. They were a couple minutes late to a press conference, and were walking fast.

Suddenly the steel door in front of them blew inward. The first Secret Service agent in line died instantly. Basically, he evaporated. The next turned to come back up the corridor. As he did, he burst into flames.

After that, everything went black.

"Yeah, Kurt, because that worked so smashingly well the last time."

"This is different," Kurt said. "The site is secure. It's swept for bombs or other security breaches every two days. It is at the highest state of readiness at all times. There is an advanced command center there, recently updated. The electronics and life support systems can withstand a direct hit from an electromagnetic pulse weapon. It's also a sprawling complex, larger, more modern, and more comfortable than Site R in Pennsylvania. Site R is obviously closer, but is older, smaller, and less able to withstand attack. With Mount Weather no longer operational, Site R will be the only option available to you if you wait until—"

"I'm not doing it," Susan said. "I'm not going underground like a rat. I'm not going to go on TV and tell the American people to remain calm because all is well while I'm at the bottom of a mine shaft. We can run the show from the Situation Room right here."

"Susan, the Situation Room is designed for convenience first and foremost, security a distant second. In the event of a nuclear war with Russia, there isn't going to be a Situation Room."

"Kurt, my point is that there isn't going to be a nuclear war. It's not going to happen because we're going to do our jobs and stop it from happening."

"Events are moving very fast," Kurt said. "I'm afraid it might be too late for that."

CHAPTER THIRTY THREE

11:20 a.m. Mediterranean Time
(5:20 a.m. Eastern Daylight Time)
al-Raqqa, Syria

The men behind him were chanting.

"*Allahu akbar! Allahu akbar! Allahu akbar!*"

Swann knew enough Arabic to understand what they were saying.

God is great!

Swann had been forced to his knees on the ground amidst some ruined cinderblock. A destroyed building loomed above their heads. Everything was vague and uncertain, a mass of colors and shapes. They had taken his glasses and he couldn't see very well without them. It didn't matter anyway—he didn't want to see anymore. And they had beaten him so badly that his eyes could hardly open.

He was done. He recognized that. They were going to kill him. There was nothing he could do—his arms were tied behind his back. He couldn't see. He was too weak to run. He didn't even care. The thought of death didn't bother him anymore. He had reconciled to it quickly. Everything had been stripped away—all his desires, all his ambitions, his former life, the adventures he'd had—it was all tattered and torn and faded to nothing now, almost like it had never existed. Soon it would all be gone.

Gone.

He just didn't want them to slit his throat, not while he was awake. And he didn't want them to cut his head off.

He couldn't bear the thought of that. He had seen so many heads in the short time he had been here. They held them right up to Swann's face so he could see them better—so he could soak up the blank looks in the half-open eyes of the dead men, their mouths hanging open. The faces looked hypnotized, as if you could snap your fingers and they would wake up again.

These people were animals. They were barbarians. They carried severed human heads around casually, like they were bowling balls. They made piles of stones, like people in the United States did along hiking trails. But then these maniacs placed the heads on top of the piles.

194

Please. Please leave something for my mother.

The sharp rubble was biting through the knees of his orange jumpsuit. It hurt. But that didn't matter, either. It wouldn't be long now.

Planes were coming. That was another fact of life here—the constant bombing runs. The sound got louder and louder as the planes approached. Soon it was a shriek so loud it drowned out everything. Swann couldn't cover his ears. He screamed, but he didn't seem to make a sound.

WHUMP.

WHUMP.

WHUMP.

The ground trembled as the bombs hit. Somewhere nearby, not here.

As the quiet slowly returned, he heard another sound, a sound that was still going from before.

"Allahu akbar! Allahu akbar!"

The executioner leaned down next to Swann's ear. His face was covered with a black mask. Swann had not seen the man's face, but he knew the voice—he spoke with a British accent.

"Why did you come here, Mark?"

Swann shook his head. "I didn't come here. I came to Turkey. You brought me here."

The man held the knife in front of Swann's face, very close to his eyes.

"Your eyes are useless to you. Perhaps I should take them."

Swann closed them shut, as if the eyelids alone could protect them. He didn't want to cry this time—he had promised himself that he wouldn't. He didn't want to beg. He didn't want to hear the sound of weakness in his own voice. He wanted to go out strong.

"Please."

"You are a Crusader spy, yes?"

Swann nodded. There was no sense fighting it. They knew who he was.

"Yes."

"What did you learn? What information did you pass on?"

"Nothing. I didn't have time."

He was lying. There was a tiny space inside him where he could still do that. He had learned something. The man who contacted him, the man who kidnapped him... Swann knew this man.

"Then what use are you?" the executioner said. "What use are you to us? What use are you to anyone?"

Swann started crying. It just hurt so bad. His face hurt. His body hurt—they had beaten him across his torso with their rifles butts. But mostly it hurt inside. He was going to die for no reason. He was helpless before their cruelty.

How did they become this way? Who were these people? What response could there be to such wanton and mindless savagery?

"I don't know," he said. "I don't know anything."

"Mark Swann, you are an admitted Crusader spy. You have been sentenced to death before God, and in accordance with the laws of this sacred land. I now carry out this sentence by the power vested in me by the Islamic State."

The men shouted now, their chant growing louder and louder and louder.

"*ALLAHU AKBAR! ALLAHU AKBAR! ALLAHU AKBAR!*"

"Please!" Swann screamed.

His chest heaved. He hung his head. There was nothing left.

The executioner placed a gun to his head. That was good. It was a relief. They were just going to shoot him. It would be over in one second.

He was going to die. Right now. He tried to breathe. He felt his bladder release. It didn't matter.

There must be some—

The gun moved the slightest amount as the man pulled the trigger.

Clack!

Swann dropped to the ground. He lay there, gasping. Behind and above him, the men were laughing now. Swann had pissed himself, and they thought that was funny. He didn't care.

It was a mock execution. He was alive. He lay on the hard ground, tears streaming from his eyes.

"Cheer up, Mark Swann," the executioner said. "Your time will come soon."

CHAPTER THIRTY FOUR

11:45 a.m. Mediterranean Time
(5:45 a.m. Eastern Daylight Time)
A desert highway
Syria

The sun was riding high now. It was getting hot.

"I found a systems analyst here," Mika said. "He created a program that is running every possible combination of the ten digits in Trudy Wellington's phone number, and using each one to try and log in. So far nothing has worked."

Luke stood outside the truck, held the phone to his ear, and scanned the empty highway. It was twenty miles to al-Raqqa. They were close. As he watched, Russian bombers streaked across the sky and dropped their loads on the city. They veered off to the east, moving fast, trailed by anti-aircraft fire that never seemed to find its target.

The ISIS stronghold, being bombed to dust. If Nigel was right, then Swann was in there somewhere.

"Luke," Mika said. "Do you think there's going to be a war?"

"There is a war. We're right in the middle of it."

"I mean a nuclear war."

He shook his head. "I don't know. I hope not."

"There are fallout shelters here on the base. They're moving supplies down to them, preparing them for use. They told me that if I can't get a flight out, I'll be expected to go into a shelter by early this afternoon."

"Are you afraid?" Luke said.

"Yes."

In his mind, Luke caught a fleeting glimpse of Becca and Gunner. Where were they? Were they afraid? He had this satellite phone—he should try to call them. Even if it was just to say goodbye...

"Keep running those numbers," he said. "It'll take your mind off your troubles."

"Okay, Luke."

In the shimmering distance, Luke saw what he had been looking for all this time. A convoy was coming. He couldn't tell what it was yet. Hopefully something good.

"Mika? I have to go."

He hung up the phone and ducked his head inside the TV truck. Just behind the door was an MP5 submachine gun. Next to it, the Canadian newsmen sat, their backs against the interior wall, their faces stricken.

Just past them, Nigel the British terrorist lay on his side. His face was bruised and misshapen from Ed hitting him. His eyes were black. His mouth was swollen like an overripe fruit.

"We got one," Luke told the Canadians. "Be quiet, stay low, and you'll be okay."

They stared at him. They didn't move.

"Low," Luke said. "On the floor."

Grudgingly, they lowered themselves to the bottom of the truck.

Luke nodded. "Good."

He looked at Nigel.

"Nigel, if I hear a peep out of you, you're the first one to die. Okay?"

Nigel nodded.

Luke took a deep breath. He felt his heart skip a beat. This was going to be interesting.

He stepped out into the roadway and away from the truck. He glanced back at it. The front left tire was off and lying in the road in front of it. The van itself was up on a jack. There was obviously something wrong with it—it was disabled. And this was no place to break down, out in the desert, in the middle of ISIS country.

He glanced out into the sandy scrubland by the side of the road. Nothing out that way, as far as the eye could see. Just empty desert, starting to bake in the searing heat of the day.

He held a white handkerchief high and waved it. He wore the heavy black vest of the cameraman, the big white letters TV emblazoned across the front and the back.

On the road, the convoy rolled to a stop. The first vehicle was an ancient pickup truck with two men in the cab. Behind it was a beat up black Mercedes sedan—looked like there were four guys in there, two in the front, two in the back.

Behind that was pay dirt. Last in line, a large heavy-duty pickup with an M-60 machine gun mounted in the back. A big strong guy in a black hood and mask, a T-shirt, and combat fatigues stood up in the truck bed, manning the gun. He had another man with him, his assistant, who was there to feed the ammunition belt.

Bingo! Luke wanted that gun.

There was one guy in the cab of that truck—the driver.

Luke did a quick calculation. Nine men.

A man climbed out of the passenger seat of the first truck. He wore the same get-up as all these clowns. Black mask and hood, black shirt with ammo vest over it, combat fatigue pants and boots. He carried a new-looking AK-47. Luke waved the surrender flag at him as he approached.

"Americans?" the man said. He had a vague European accent. Dutch? Swedish? What was it with these all these Europeans joining ISIS?

Luke shook his head. "Canadians. We're the TV news."

The man shook his head. "You shouldn't be here. You'll be killed."

Luke stepped closer. "We're trying to get to Raqqa to cover all the bombing. Looks like the Russians are going wild over there. We were going to film the civilian casualties, but our truck died."

The man glanced around. Something about this story wasn't convincing him.

"You are alone?"

"My partner is in the truck. He's not feeling well."

The man gestured with his head. "Bring him out. I want to see him."

Luke hesitated. This conversation had already gone on way too long.

Ed?

The telltale sound came as if Luke had conjured it with his thoughts.

Doonk!

From way off to the left, in the barren desert scrubland, a grenade screamed in on a nearly flat trajectory. Luke could swear it made a sizzling sound just before it hit.

Ssszzzzzzz… BOOOOOM.

It ripped into the side of the Mercedes sedan. The car blew outward in a hundred shattered fragments—metal, glass, flying limbs of the car's occupants. Almost instantly, the gas tank blew, sending a fireball into the sky.

Luke stepped up to the man in front of him. In the same motion as the step, a knife appeared in Luke's hand. He swiped the blade across the man's neck, nearly ear to ear. Blood jetted from both sides. The man's eyes went wide in surprise. He dropped his AK-47 as his hands went to his throat, trying to close the gap there, trying to put all the blood back in.

199

Luke bent and picked up the man's gun.

He ran for the front of the pickup truck. The driver was climbing out. Luke raised the gun and shot him. The man did a crazy death dance and fell to the roadway.

In the rear truck, the gunner sighted on Luke. Luke dove to the ground in front of the first pickup. He crawled in the dirt below the truck's grille.

An instant later, the big M60 opened up, an ugly blat of gunfire, heavy rounds destroying the pickup. The windshield shattered. The tires popped and went flat. Bullets punched holes in the metal. Steam rose from under the hood.

Luke couldn't stay here. If he did, he was going to die. The shooter probably couldn't see him through the flames and smoke from the burning car, but it didn't matter. Those rounds were going to find him sooner or later.

Another burst of machine gun fire came from his left.

Ed had popped up from his cover. He ran across the sand, firing his MP5. He was too exposed out there.

Luke jumped up. In the pickup bed, the gunner was turning his machine gun to face Ed. Luke let him have it with a blast from the AK. The man jittered and jived, but didn't go down—he was wearing a flak jacket.

Luke ran toward him.

Suddenly the truck started going backwards. The driver was backing it away from the carnage, trying to escape, trying to buy his gunner time.

The M-60 was pointing halfway between Luke and Ed. No good. No target. The big man fiddled with his big gun. He was doomed.

His feeder jumped out of the truck bed, fell to the roadway, got up, and started running.

Luke sprayed the windshield with gunfire. The glass sprayed inward and the driver died at the wheel. The truck rolled backwards under its own momentum.

It slowed to a stop.

Ed stepped onto the roadway now, walking fast, coming in from the left. Luke came in from the front. They hosed the big gunner with machine gun fire. He steadied himself on the M-60 mount, stumbled, then fell off the back and onto the road.

The guy was huge. He was superhuman. He was still alive and trying to crawl.

Ed was closer than Luke. He stepped up to his man, pulled a pistol, and shot him once in the head.

BANG.

Luke walked over, breathing hard. He patted the truck.

"This is all I wanted for Christmas."

Ed smiled. "That gun's a beauty."

Luke couldn't help but smile himself. "Oh yeah."

Guns, man. They brought a smile to people's faces. He looked over the side of the truck bed. Piled on the floor were about a dozen ammo belts.

"All gassed up, too."

They stood for a minute. Luke could feel his heart slowing down. Across the road from them, out in the desert, the man who had been the machine gun feeder was running away. He was running toward al-Raqqa in the distance. That was going to be a long run. Even so, the man was a loose end.

"What do you want to do about that guy?" Luke said.

The M79 was strapped to Ed's back. He brought it around, opened the chamber, and carefully loaded a grenade.

You know," he said, "I've been thinking about this hard drive Mika is trying to open. What was the original question? Do you remember your friend's number, right? The question didn't actually ask for the number. It asked if you remember it."

Luke thought about it. "I'd have to ask Mika again, but I think so, yeah."

Ed walked out into the roadway. He looked both ways. There was nothing coming for miles and miles.

Luke pulled a small pair of binoculars from inside his vest.

For a moment, Ed watched the man running across the desert. Then he raised the M79. He fired, this time on a high-arcing trajectory, like a quarterback throwing a bomb to the end zone.

Doonk!

He looked back at Luke. "Well, you remember the number, don't you?"

"Sure. I already gave it to Mika."

"That's my point," Ed said.

Luke held the binoculars to his eyes. Out in the shimmering desert, he found the running man. He watched the man for a few seconds. Suddenly, there was an explosion out there, right where the man was a second before. What had been the man flew apart like a cheap doll right before Luke's eyes.

"Got him."

He looked at Ed.

"You were saying?"

Ed came walking back from the road. "You remember the number. And the question is whether or not you remember the number."

"Yeah."

Ed shrugged. "In that case, the answer, and maybe the password, is *yes*."

CHAPTER THIRTY FIVE

6:55 a.m.
The Situation Room
The White House, Washington, DC

"Susan, you're being very foolish."

It was Pierre, talking into her ear while the Situation Room filled up.

The room was already packed, and more people were coming in all the time. The Chairman of the Joint Chiefs was here, and he traveled with an entourage of aides and assistants. Kurt Kimball was at the front, standing in his customary place before the computer screens, his muscular arms folded, and chatting seriously with his aide Amy.

Susan stood near the doorway, wedged against the wall. Pierre and the girls were already at Cheyenne Mountain, and for that Susan was glad. They had taken one of the company planes from Los Angeles, leaving during what to them was the middle of the night. They had landed fifteen minutes ago.

"Pierre…"

"Susan, I don't pretend to understand you. But know this: no one will blame you for going where it's safe, and no one will praise you if you stay in Washington and get yourself killed. You can't help the American people if you're not alive."

"It's too soon," Susan said. "We can fix this."

"You can just as easily fix it on the plane. Or fix it here."

She shook her head. "I don't agree. I think we need to be here, committed, in the game. If I get on that plane, I'll feel like I'm running away. My staff will be scattered, and the whole thing will slip out of my hands."

"Susan, it's already slipped out of your hands."

She didn't respond to that. She wouldn't. They were growing apart, she and Pierre, more and more all the time. They had been for years, but the events of the past six months had accelerated it. It almost felt like a wedge had been driven between them, and now it was prying their relationship open, cracking it asunder.

"Okay," he said. "I didn't mean that."

"It's all right if you did," she said.

"I didn't. But at least agree to this. If your advisers tell you that it's time to go, listen to them. I love you. Your daughters love you. Okay? If nothing else, if you won't do it for yourself, come here for us."

"Okay," she said. She could do that, she supposed.

But not right now.

Kat Lopez walked into the room and made a beeline for Susan.

"Honey, I've gotta go," Susan said.

"Okay, knock 'em dead. I love you."

"I love you, too."

Kat looked reasonably fresh, like she had found a couple hours sleep somewhere. She had changed into a gray pinstriped suit, which was form-fitting and showed off her curves. Her make up had been reapplied. She looked a lot more human than Susan felt. Even so, her face was completely serious.

"Susan."

"Hi, Kat. How are you feeling?"

Kat nodded. "I'm okay. Listen, I want to give you the update. There's a lot."

Susan sighed. "Let's hear it. I'll do my best."

"Okay, first order. The Vice President has been moved to Site R. She arrived there in the past half an hour. The Secretary of State, the Secretary of the Treasury, and the Secretary of Education are being taken to secure and semi-secure sites as we speak. The Senate Majority Leader and President Pro Tempore—"

"Ed Graves," Susan said.

"Yes. He's also at Site R."

"Is that okay?"

Kat nodded. "It's the best we can do. Karen White is on her way to Cheyenne Mountain. So Marybeth Horning will be at Site R with Senator Graves, and you'll be out at Cheyenne with the Speaker. If either place gets hit, you and Marybeth will always be top dogs in the line of succession."

"I'm not going to Cheyenne," Susan said.

Kat stopped. She glanced around the room.

"You know Kurt, Haley, and I drew straws for the job of talking to you about this, right? I drew the short straw. You're being unreasonable, and there isn't a lot of time. The plane is gassed and ready to go. The helicopter is on the pad. I've already scheduled a press conference for twelve noon eastern time, at Cheyenne. Please don't fight me."

"Kat…"

Susan shook her head. How had this gone so wrong? One moment they were looking for stolen nukes, the next moment Vladimir Putin was announcing that the world was about to end. It really seemed to have happened that way.

"Susan, please. I'm making all the necessary arrangements to get you out of here. We are moving quickly. If it comes to it, the Secret Service is going to drag you onto that plane kicking and screaming. Please don't make me do that."

"Are you coming?" Susan said.

Kat rolled her eyes. "Of course. I want to live, don't I?"

CLAP, CLAP, CLAP.

Susan was startled by the telltale sound of Kurt Kimball calling the room to order. She was overtired, not thinking straight, moving in slow motion. She glanced at Kurt, and when she turned to look at Kat again, Kat was already gone.

"Madam President, we're ready," Kurt said.

Susan noted that he had changed to addressing her formally. She liked it better when he called her Susan. She slid into her customary seat at the head of the conference table.

"Order, everyone. Quiet, please."

Behind Kurt, maps began to appear on the video screens. A map of the vastness of Russia, with red and blue dots for missile silos. A map of the Middle East. A close-up map of Turkey, and one of Syria. A map showing the border between India and Pakistan.

"Madam President, you know General Robert Coates, Chairman of the Joint Chiefs of Staff, don't you?"

Susan nodded. The general was a broad man in his sixties. He wore his dress green uniform, his chest covered with his many medals and commendations. His flattop haircut was white. His face was as sharp and chiseled as the face of a cliff.

"General, good to see you."

The general nodded in return. "Madam President. I wish the circumstances were kinder."

"As do I," Susan said.

"I want to move through this as rapidly as possible," Kurt said. "Everyone here is at least familiar with the broad outlines of what has happened. Since President Putin made his announcement just over two hours ago, we've been dealing with a blizzard of data. It's difficult to keep up with all of it, so I'm going to share with you a few salient points, then we'll hear from General Coates.

205

"Military readiness is at levels I've never seen, all over the globe. The Russians have ramped up their bombing runs on ISIS at al-Raqqa, in what appears to be an attempt to collapse the Islamic State regime once and for all. Indications are that as many as seven hundred Spetsnaz paratroopers are boarding flights bound for al-Raqqa."

"Al-Raqqa is where we believe Agent Luke Stone was heading, wasn't it?" Susan said.

Kurt shrugged his shoulders and gently shook his head. "I don't know where Agent Stone was headed. If he's still alive, and he goes to al-Raqqa, he will be very lucky to survive there. The bombardment is becoming intense. In any event, Agent Stone's whereabouts are the least of our worries right now."

A hand raised in the crowd. "Kurt?"

"Please let me finish," Kurt said. "I don't want to get bogged down in the small stuff. We can assume the Russians hope they're going to find the missing warheads in al-Raqqa. Whether they will or not is anyone's guess, but I doubt it. Meanwhile, we've been picking up chatter from inside the Russian strategic command. More than one hundred missile silos across the Russian heartland and the far reaches of Siberia are reporting combat readiness. These include launch silos for nuclear-equipped intercontinental ballistic missiles targeting the United States."

Kurt paused, letting that sink in.

"I'll repeat that. As far as we can tell, Russian nuclear silos are combat ready."

"What the hell are they doing?" Susan said.

Kurt's shoulders slumped. "I think it's easy enough to understand, if you unpack it. We've had years of low trust and zero trust between our two countries. Our nuclear capabilities are more robust than theirs, and our missile defense system is more modern. They believe we lost those stolen warheads on purpose, and that we're encouraging Islamic terrorists to launch a nuclear attack against them. They know we're listening, so they're rattling the sabers for our benefit."

He looked around the room. "That's what I hope is happening. The danger is what if that's not it? Putin told us one thing when we talked to him on the phone last night, then told the world something different an hour later. Given the disparity between our capabilities and theirs, what if they think their only hope is to launch first? What if his four-hour ultimatum was a cover for a preemptive strike to take place well before then?"

Susan didn't like to hear that kind of talk coming from Kurt. Kurt was most often a voice of reason, and not one to raise unnecessary alarms.

"General?" Kurt said.

General Coates was conferring with one of his aides. He looked up when Kurt said his name. Then he turned and looked directly at Susan.

"Madam President, I came here to offer what I think might be a solution to a dangerous state of affairs. It isn't for the faint of heart, and I'd invite you to hear me out completely before you judge it."

"Okay, General," Susan said. "Say your piece."

The aide handed the general a slim volume in a plastic ring binder. It had a glassy plastic cover on it. The general held it up.

"Last year, we commissioned a study. This is its summary. In the most basic terms, the study is a comparison of Russian and American conventional and nuclear capabilities across a range of possible scenarios and theaters of combat. What the study confirmed again and again is that the dominance we enjoy over the Russians has diminishing returns. Despite our superiority, and the likelihood of an eventual victory in almost any limited conventional war scenario, if nuclear weapons come into play our advantages quickly dissipate. A tit for tat nuclear exchange would be a disaster for them and a disaster for us in equal measure."

He raised a finger. "That's true in every circumstance but one. A massive preemptive first strike on the Russian mainland, with simultaneous launches from our ballistic missile silos as well as our nuclear equipped submarines and destroyers, would overwhelm their aging missile defense system. It would likely result in the destruction of between eighty and ninety percent of their offensive capability, and lay waste to the vast majority of their civilian, military and communications infrastructure. Whatever response they managed to mount would be decentralized, badly damaged and uncoordinated. And our own missile shield would bat down much of what they sent our way."

Susan stared at the general. Was this a joke?

"Follow up bombing runs from the Strategic Air Command would likely finish off what remained of their conventional weaponry, and any nukes we missed in the first go round."

"Do you have a casualty assessment?" Kurt said.

The general nodded. "We do." An aide handed him a piece of paper. He slid a pair of reading glasses to the tip of his nose.

"We estimate more than a hundred million Russian casualties in the initial bombardments. On our side, between ten and twenty million."

Susan sat back.

Kurt was staring at her.

"Susan? Thoughts?"

It took her a moment to find her voice.

"I don't even know where to begin," she said. "How about this: has everyone here gone insane? General, how can you even bring this plan to me? The policy of the United States for the past seventy years has been that we do not engage in nuclear first strikes. I'm not going to be the one to break that policy. I'm not going to be the one who orders the mass murder of tens of millions of people. I'm not even going to consider this idea."

"I think you're being very foolish," the general said.

"You know what?" Susan said. "You're the second man who's told me that in the past twenty minutes. And that's how I know I'm onto something."

She looked around the room. Dozens of blank faces stared back at her. These were the best and brightest, weren't they? What was going on inside their minds? Maybe they'd like to share.

"Does anyone have any other ideas?" she said. "If so, I'm all ears."

CHAPTER THIRTY SIX

"The answer is yes," Mika said. "A three-letter password, all lowercase, y-e-s."

Luke shook his head. He wasn't sure he was in the mood for humorous passwords from Trudy Wellington, if it really had been her.

They were parked in an alleyway between two squat utility buildings on the edge of the city. This was not going to be a good place to park for much longer. They were driving a machine-gun-mounted Toyota pickup truck that practically screamed ISIS. Meanwhile, the skies were filled with super-fast Russian bombers, Tupolev TU-60s, shrieking over the city and reducing it to dust.

The ISIS air defenses, such as they had been, were gone now. The Russians were bombing with impunity. The ground shook constantly from the impacts—it was like one long, never-ending earthquake.

Luke stood in the alleyway with the phone. He was dressed in clothes taken from the ISIS fighters on the highway—black mask and hood, flak vest, combat fatigues. Ed and Nigel sat in the bed of the pickup, dressed in the same way as Luke.

Luke and Ed had cut the Canadian reporters loose. The two men had reattached their tire at warp speed, turned the news truck around, and hightailed it back toward civilization.

"What did you find on there?" Luke said.

"Two files," Mika said. "The first is a dossier on a man named Mustafa Zarqawi, also known as Jamal, also known as the Phantom, along with a dozen other aliases. Thirty-seven-year-old Pakistani national, four years in the Pakistani army, with combat experience along the Kashmir border with India, including high-altitude combat.

"After four years in the army proper, he joined an elite paratrooper unit. Listed as killed in action during an attempted clearing action against the Taliban in northwestern Pakistan. Reappeared an unknown time later as an agent of the Pakistani intelligence agency, the ISI."

209

"Okay, Mika," Luke said. "This guy is probably one of the planners of the nuclear theft. But how is this helping me? I'm under Russian bombardment at this moment."

"Luke, I'm doing the best I can, okay? I'm above ground right now so I can talk to you, and I'm supposed to be in the bomb shelter. We are under missile attack from outside the base. The rumor right now is that the flight wing is loading the B-61 nuclear warheads—the kind that didn't get stolen—on bombers as we speak. They are preparing for a nuclear war and I'm stuck here with no way out. So can I please finish?"

Luke almost smiled. He stared up at the sky—maybe the heavens would help him. But the only thing up there was Russians.

"Please," he said. "Continue."

"Here's where it gets interesting. There are redacted CIA and NSA memos concerning this guy. If what I can make out is true, he's been an American intelligence asset for at least the past ten years, possibly a double or triple agent working for several agencies and countries at once. There is a Paris address for him. There are also bank transfers to a numbered account in something called Royal Heritage Bank, located in Grand Cayman."

Luke stared at the phone. "Did I hear that right?"

"Yes," she said. "Royal Heritage Bank is controlled by a Ukrainian sometime CIA agent. Various American intelligence agencies find it convenient to—"

"I know."

Could that be right? This thing was an American intelligence operation? Why would they do it? Why would they bring the world to the brink of nuclear war? Because they didn't think it would happen this way? Because they thought Russia would get hit with small tactical nukes and strike back at ISIS? Because they made a terrible miscalculation?

He let that sink in for a long moment.

But how would Trudy know about this? It was a softball question, and the answer hit him immediately: Don.

No. Not Don, but his friends, the ones who were still out in the world, the ones who were protecting Trudy, keeping her free and alive.

"Luke?"

"Yes."

"I've got more."

"What is it?"

"The second file. It's basically a series of maps to the Pankisi Gorge in Georgia, with possible vehicle routes highlighted leaving Adana, traveling overland across Turkey, and crossing the border into Georgia. I suppose I should have thought of that."

Luke was still processing the idea of the Phantom being an American agent.

A Russian bomber streaked overhead, blotting out the sun, much too close. This truck was going to be a target as soon as they finished taking down the buildings. The Russians were doing something quintessentially Russian—scorching the earth, destroying absolutely everything.

He looked at the pickup again. They'd better get moving—try to find Swann before this town didn't exist anymore.

"Thought of what?" he said.

"Pankisi Gorge in Georgia is a remote area in the mountains, and home to people of Chechen ethnicity. Over the years, the Georgian government has allowed Islamic extremists to recruit there, and use the area as a safe haven. There's a very good chance that's where the warheads went."

"Our prisoner said the warheads went to Russia."

"I'm going to guess that your prisoner is confused. Georgia used to be part of the Soviet Union. He probably thinks it still is. Does he seem that bright to you?"

Luke looked at Nigel in the truck bed with Ed. He was doped to the gills on painkillers from the Canadian news truck's first aid kit. He looked a wreck, but he was chatting with Ed about something as if they were in a pub back in Manchester. Sports, probably.

What the hell was he doing here?

"I don't know," Luke said.

"There is a location in Pankisi Gorge pinned on the map. I can give you those coordinates."

"Mika? I'm about six hundred miles from Pankisi Gorge."

"Yes?"

"Call your contacts in Washington. Give them the coordinates."

"Okay, Luke. I'll call them right now."

Luke hung up. He walked back to the pickup truck. Nigel and Ed watched him as he came.

"All right, Nigel," he said. "Where did you say they hold those prisoners?"

Nigel's voice had become strangely childlike from the missing teeth and the swelling. He made the lisping, spitting sound of a child with a very fat face.

"Very close. Ten blocks from here. They used to do the executions in the desert south of town. So it was just easier to keep them right here."

Luke gestured at the big M-60 machine gun.

"You ever feed one of these?"

"Yes. Of course."

Luke nodded. "Good. We need you. I'll drive. You'll feed the gun while Ed acts as shooter. If you do anything stupid, Ed will kill you without hesitating, or I will. I'm sure you already know this."

Nigel shook his head. "No. You can't ask me to do that. I won't have a hand in killing my own people."

"These aren't your people, man," Ed said. "Your people are in England."

"These aren't anybody's people," Luke said. "They're a bunch of lunatics. You joined them because you were bored playing video games in your mom's spare bedroom, and you thought it would be exciting, an adventure. Believe me, Nigel, I've seen guys like you before. You don't belong here. You're lucky you stayed alive this long."

Luke pulled a gun from his shoulder holster, a black Glock. He pointed it nonchalantly at Nigel's head. "At this point, your life has come down to two choices. You can help us rescue our friend, or I can kill you right now. I've lost count how many people I've killed in the past twenty-four hours. One more won't mean anything."

Nigel stared down the barrel of the gun.

"Since you put it that way…"

Luke looked at Ed. "You ready, man?"

Ed was chewing on a toothpick he had gotten from somewhere. "Born ready."

"Then let's do this."

* * *

It was snowing Russians.

Luke drove slowly through the streets, picking his way around piles of rubble and giant impact craters. To the west, just outside the city, he could see Russian paratroopers falling out of airplanes. Mostly the remaining buildings blocked his view, but at intersections, he would look over there and spot them. The sky was thick with them, like a dense flock of blackbirds.

Already, he could hear the gun battles starting on that side of town.

He'd better get this done.

The front windshield of the truck was shattered, just gone. So was the window between the cab and the truck bed. Nigel kneeled behind Luke's head, giving him the directions.

"Okay, left up ahead. The building will be halfway down the street, on your right. It's a low brick building with a small staircase, maybe three steps. The prisoners are held in the basement."

Luke saw it up ahead, maybe a hundred yards away. The building was sandbagged, and half a dozen fighters stood outside with AK-47s, staring at the sky to the west, watching the Russians come down.

"Ed?"

"Got it," Ed said. "How you want to play it?"

"Why don't I just pull right up?"

"Sounds fine." There was a sound of a brief scuffle as Ed pulled Nigel away from the window. "Get up here, man. Get ready to feed me."

Luke waited a few seconds, eyes on that building. The road wasn't terrible here. It was a straight run right to the doorstep.

"Ready?" he said.

"Oh yeah."

He stomped on the gas and the truck peeled out in the sand. It tore free and moved like a shot, building speed as it headed toward the building.

On either side, wrecked buildings zipped past.

The fighters, distracted by the Russians, didn't seem to notice Luke's truck right away. But then they did.

They scattered, pointing, just as Ed's gun opened up above Luke's head. It was a loud, ugly blat of automatic fire, combined with the Christmas jingle of spent shells falling to the pickup bed.

DUH-DUH-DUH-DUH-DUH-DUH.

Ed didn't release the trigger for anything.

An ISIS fighter shredded to pieces. Another. Another. They died with their guns on their shoulders.

One man managed to pull a pistol. He crouched behind the sandbags and aimed for the cab.

Luke accelerated.

A gunshot whined off the hood.

The truck went up over the sandbags, crashed into the man, and ran right over him. A body flew over the top of the cab and rolled down off the hood—Nigel. The truck came down the other side of the bags then ground to a halt.

Luke reached to the passenger side floor—his MP5 was there. As he ducked, his window shattered in on top of him. Someone out there was still alive, and firing. He crawled out the passenger side and onto the ground.

A second later, Ed vaulted over the side and crouched on the ground next to him.

"What happened to Nigel?"

"I don't know. He just flew away. I guess he forgot to hold on."

Gunfire pelted the truck from the street side. Behind Luke and Ed, the front doors to the building were shattered and wide open.

"We gotta get inside," Luke said. "You ready?"

"Ready."

Luke waited half a beat. "Go!"

He popped up and fired across the street at the shooters, give them full automatic. One got hit and went down. The others ducked behind the burnt-out shell of a car. Ed jumped up and ran for the doorway.

Luke dropped again. He popped out the spent magazine and let it fall to the ground. He slammed a fresh one in. From the doorway, Ed was firing now.

Luke got up and ran. He burst through the doors and dove for the floor. He rolled into a corner, turned back to the doors, and was ready to shoot from the ground.

Ed ducked back as gunfire strafed the entryway.

Then they were both up and moving down the corridor. There was a stairwell to the left. They checked it—nothing.

Maybe those guys outside were the last ones left in here.

"Here we go," Luke said.

They bounded down the stairs. This was the part Luke always hated—trapped in a stairwell, nowhere to go when the shooting started. But there was no one here.

They exited the stairs and came out into another hallway. And that's when they heard the screams. Bloodcurdling shrieks echoing back to them.

They pressed their backs to the wall and moved along, slowly now, quietly. The lights in the hall were out, but there was an open doorway up ahead. The outlines of it almost seemed to glow. The screaming was coming from there.

They approached it. Neither man said a word.

People were screaming inside that room. People were moaning. More than one person was in physical or psychic agony.

Luke dashed across to the right side of the doorway. Ed pressed himself against the left. Luke held up a fist and Ed nodded.

Luke held up one finger.

Two...

Three.

They burst through the doorway, Ed first, Luke half a step behind.

It was a slaughterhouse. All around the room, prisoners in orange jumpsuits were chained to the walls. There were at least forty of them.

Two men in black masks were moving from prisoner to prisoner, stabbing them in the torso, and sawing at their necks with a serrated blade. They were moving systematically, from left to right, killing the prisoners before the Russians could rescue them. At least a dozen prisoners were already dead, headless, bled out. The floor was awash in their blood. To the right, the living prisoners did whatever came naturally to them—they screamed, cried, scrabbled to the end of their chains, sat in shock, curled into the fetal position.

Luke and Ed pulled their pistols. They walked silently to the men in the black masks. At the moment, they were sawing the head off a prisoner who was already dead. One man held the head by the hair, while the other sawed away. They were so intent on what they were doing that they paid no attention to the killers coming up behind them.

Ed didn't say a word. He turned his gun around and clocked the man with the knife in the back of the head. The man staggered, tried to stand up, and Ed hit him again. Then again. The man slid sideways to the floor.

His partner looked up. There was no fear in his eyes—only surprise.

Luke punched him in the face. When the man fell backwards, Luke kicked him in the head. One, twice, three times. Both of the guards rolled on the stone floor, gripping their heads, half awake, in pain.

"You believe this?" Ed asked. He gestured at the carnage around them. He was standing over the prone guards.

"I'll believe anything at this point," Luke said.

All around them, the able-bodied prisoners struggled to their feet. They came and stood above the two murderous guards. The prisoners were barefoot, gaunt, with haunted eyes. First there were four, then six, then a dozen. One took his own thick chain, kneeled behind the first guard, and wrapped it around the man's throat. The guard's eyes went wide with fear.

The prisoner looked up at Luke and Ed, his eyes darting from one to the other.

"Please do," Ed said. "I left him alive for you. We're not taking prisoners today."

The prisoners moved in, holding the guard's arms and legs down, one man to each limb. They did the same to the other guard. A prisoner picked up the discarded serrated knife. Soon the guards were lost, hidden behind a wall of prisoners. Sounds emerged from that crowd, the sounds of two men dying slowly.

Luke went into the center of the room. He took a deep breath and called out two words, hoping against hope for an answer.

"Mark Swann?" he said. "Is Mark Swann here?"

A long moment passed.

Then a skinny man off to the right, sitting slumped against the wall with his head dropped to his chest, raised a hand. He looked up, saw Luke and Ed there, but didn't seem to register them. He didn't seem to register anything.

"Here. I'm Mark Swann."

CHAPTER THIRTY SEVEN

7:45 a.m.
The Situation Room
The White House, Washington, DC

"There's nothing we can do about Pankisi Gorge," General Robert Coates, the Chairman of the Joint Chiefs of Staff said. "If the warheads are there, it doesn't matter. There's no way we can get there."

Susan looked at Kurt, who was standing at the front. His eyes looked empty, numb, like a man trying to direct traffic at the Indy 500.

"Kurt?" she said.

He shook his head. "We'd have to send planes. At this point, anything we put in the sky in that region is liable to get shot down. Or worse, the Russians will think we've launched an attack."

"Can we contact the Russians and let them know? Maybe they can take them out."

Kurt looked at his aide Amy. She shook her head.

"We've been trying to contact Russian strategic command all morning. Communications are down. They are observing radio silence, and they are not answering our calls."

"Okay," General Coates said. He raised his voice. "I want to tell you all something. It's an announcement of sorts."

The entire room turned his way.

"In the past five minutes, I have informed all Pentagon staff that we are moving to DEFCON 1," he said.

Susan stared at him. Her mouth was agape. She realized this and closed it with an audible snap, her teeth clacking together. The general had gotten up and left the room a few minutes ago. She had assumed he had gone to the men's room. The United States had never gone to DEFCON 1, and this man had sneaked out of the room to do it.

"Full readiness stance across all sectors and all services," the general went on. "With no contact from the Russians, we have to assume that nuclear war is imminent. My next order will be to initiate massive and devastating first strikes from which the enemy cannot recover."

"General, stand down," Susan said. "Please."

He shook his head. "It's too late for that. I've also called for the immediate evacuation of this facility, which should have already begun." He closed the ledger in front of him. His aides were packing up their things. "All essential staff should make their way to Cheyenne Mountain Complex by whatever means still available. I wish you all Godspeed."

"General, this is treason. I am the commander-in-chief of the armed forces of the United States."

He shook his head. "Not anymore."

Susan jumped up. She was hardly aware of what she was saying. "You can be shot for this, General. And I promise you, when everything is said and done, I will see to it that you are. I'll even do it myself."

The general stood and stared at Susan. He pointed a finger at her. "You are a very silly woman. There is no time left for your dithering. I pray that it hasn't cost us our lives, and the future of our country."

He and his aides moved toward the doorway.

"General—"

"Good day, Ms. Hopkins. Feel free to spend it however you wish."

Ten seconds later, Coates and his entire entourage were gone.

The Situation Room was dead quiet now. No one moved. Blank faces and big eyes turned their gaze to Susan.

Kat Lopez was standing nearby.

"Kat," Susan said. "Call upstairs and alert the Secret Service. I'm the President of the United States, and I'm in command. I want General Coates and his entire staff arrested before they leave the building."

* * *

"I've got them," the tall man said into his radio. "Moving through the main hall."

His name was Chuck Berg.

He was thirty-eight years old, and had been in the Secret Service for more than twelve years. Six months ago, he had been on the Vice President's personal security team. He had saved her from almost certain death in the Mount Weather disaster. Now that she was President, he was the head of her home security detail.

Just ahead of him, a dozen men moved briskly through the stone hallways of the West Wing, headed for the main entrance of the building. They were military men, in dress greens. At the head of the group was an older man, who Berg knew to be General Robert Coates, the Chairman of the Joint Chiefs of Staff.

"Copy that. We have them on video."

"On my signal," Berg said.

"Copy."

The group was approaching the doors. Outside, Berg knew there was a line of waiting SUVs.

"Now."

Instantly, Secret Service agents appeared from the left and the right, guns out, emerging from side hallways and doors. Another group came bursting in through the main entrance.

"DOWN!" agents screamed. "GET DOWN!"

The military men were not a combat unit—they were desk jockeys. They offered token resistance—some pushing and shoving—but soon they were all on the floor, face down, wrists clamped behind their backs. The Secret Service trained for these confrontations all the time.

Berg walked up to the group and found the general, his forehead pressed to the floor.

"General Coates?"

The old man turned his silver head to get a look at Berg.

"I'm Agent Charles Berg, commander of the White House security team. You and your men are under arrest, and will remain in my custody until this crisis passes."

Coates's eyes were venomous. "I am the commander of the entire Armed Forces of the United States."

Berg shook his head. "I'm sorry, sir. The President is the Commander-in-Chief of the Armed Forces. I think you must be aware of that."

"You're a traitor!" Coates nearly spit the words at him.

Now Berg almost smiled. "No, sir. You're the traitor."

Berg turned to the agents closest to him.

"Lock these guys up, including the general. Confiscate all phones, tablets, and electronics. No communication with the outside, and no leaving their cells for any reason. I want them dropped into a hole."

"I'll have your job," Coates said.

Berg doubted the general was going to have his job, or anything else, for a long time. Treason was something they took seriously around here.

"General, I'll deal with you and your men later."

"If there is a later," a Secret Service agent said.

Berg shrugged. "If there's no later, I guess we won't have to deal with them at all."

CHAPTER THIRTY EIGHT

2:20 p.m. Mediterranean Time
(8:20 a.m. Eastern Daylight Time)
al-Raqqa, Syria

They brought the prisoners, the ones that could walk, to the surface. They were fastened together in a daisy chain.

Ed cut Swann loose from the rest with a pair of bolt cutters. Swann's face was bruised and swollen. He was dazed, unsure—he didn't seem to recognize who Ed and Luke were. That was okay. It was shock. It was self-protective.

Swann was alive, and for the time being, that was enough.

But they had bigger things to worry about than Swann.

"They can't send anyone to Pankisi Gorge," Mika said in Luke's ear.

"Why not?"

"They're afraid that any American planes near Russian airspace will look like a first strike."

"So why don't they just call the Kremlin and tell them?"

"Communications are down."

"Ugh."

Luke looked out at the street and thought for a moment. There were running gun battles very nearby, maybe two blocks over. Everything here was dead. No, that wasn't quite true. Movement caught his eye below his feet and to the left—just in front of where they had crashed the truck. A man was crawling out of a pile of sandbags.

It was Nigel. He was still alive.

"Nigel! Over here! Get out of the street!"

"What?" Mika said. "What?"

Nigel made a shuffling run toward Luke, stumbled up the steps and into the building.

Luke's mind raced. There was still a chance they could get out of here, but that window was closing quickly.

"Mika, I need you to find me an airport, one with a plane parked there. It's got to be close to where we are right now."

"Luke, the Russians have the only airport in the city. It's just to the west of town. They've established a base there."

Luke shook his head. "No good. Find me something smaller."

To Luke's right, a block away, a small rocket whistled into a shattered building, blew another giant hole in it. A handful of ISIS fighters scattered, firing machine guns in the direction the rocket had come from.

The Russians are coming.

"There are no other airports, Luke."

Luke turned and walked down the hallway. Ed was there, systematically cutting the chains of the prisoners, freeing them from one another. Luke spotted Swann, sitting on the ground against the wall. His knees were up near his head. He was staring at the ground.

Luke went to his friend and kneeled in front of him.

"Swann."

Swann didn't even look up.

"Swann!"

He grabbed Swann by the hair, pulled his head up, and slapped him hard across the face.

"Swann, wake up!"

Luke sensed Ed right behind him. Ed coming up behind you was like a violent thunderstorm coming up behind you.

"Hey, man. Don't do that."

Luke raised a hand. "Ed, trust me. We need this guy. He has to snap out of it, if only for a minute."

"Swann!"

Swann's eyes finally focused on Luke. "What?" he said, his voice annoyed.

Luke nearly kissed him. "I need a small airport, an airstrip, anything like that, but it has to be close to where we are."

"Where are we?" Swann said.

"Al-Raqqa, Syria. The southern edge of town."

Swann seemed to think about that for a moment. "Sure. I spotted a tiny airstrip to the southeast of this town when I was going over maps… whenever that was. It's just a little scratch in the Earth. You'd almost never see it unless you were looking for it. There's no tower or anything. There's barely even a runway."

"How far?" Luke said.

Swann shrugged. "I don't know. Five miles?"

"I love you, Swann."

Luke popped up and moved back toward the front of the building. "Mika, did you hear that? Five miles to the southeast. An airstrip. I need you to find it on a real-time satellite map. Can you do that?"

"I'm already doing it," Mika said.

222

Luke poked his head out the front doorway. It was quiet out there now—dead quiet. He looked at the pickup truck. It seemed a little worse for wear, pockmarked and dented, but he wouldn't be surprised if it was still operational. The tires were intact, at least.

"I found it," Mika said. "I'm zooming in. It's just south of the highway on your way east from the city. There's something there. Right off the runway. There's a sand-colored tarp or awning, and it's covering something."

"Is it a plane?" Luke said.

"Sure looks like one."

* * *

Mitchell Baker had always gone where the money was. Until very recently, that had seemed like a good idea.

He had become a pilot because he loved to fly. It didn't hurt that there was great money in it. He had gone to work for the Chevron oil company in Saudi Arabia because that money was better than anything he'd get at the airlines. He had jumped to working for private Saudi businessmen because the money was even better. And he had taken a job with a notorious Saudi weapons dealer because that was the best money of all.

And that great money had brought him *to this*.

He sat in the cockpit of his boss's Gulfstream G-650, drinking whiskey to steady his nerves. His boss was Muhammad al-Kassab—a man who was calculating, uncompromising, rich beyond measure, and totally insane.

They had flown here this morning because Muhammad had been selling anti-aircraft and heavy machine guns to the Muslim religious fanatics. They had been paying him with oil deliveries. There was enormous profit in this for Muhammad—ISIS couldn't sell directly to the markets, so they transferred their oil to him at a steep discount. The guns were left over Soviet-era junk—essentially worthless. The oil had real value.

But ten days ago, the oil deliveries had stopped. Now it looked as if the ISIS government—the entire experiment—was on the verge of collapse.

So Muhammad (being Muhammad) had come here to collect his money. He had left the plane five hours ago with a dozen heavily armed men in four black armored SUVs. Now Mitchell was beginning to think that Muhammad wasn't coming back.

He raised the whiskey bottle to his lips again. The fluid went down smooth, giving him a nice warm feeling in his belly.

He could leave. And do what? Return the plane to Riyadh? He supposed so. Just land the plane, walk away, and catch the first flight he could find back to the United States. Change his name. Disappear. Because if Muhammad was still alive out there, and he found out that Mitchell had deserted him...

It wasn't something to think about.

Even so, leaving seemed like the best option right now. But the plane was covered by a sand-colored tarp—it made the plane more or less invisible from the air. The tarp was battened down. Leaving meant that Mitchell was going to have to go out there himself and remove that tarp. Stepping outside and revealing himself did not appeal to him at all.

He gazed out at the cracked and pitted runway—it was a scrape, a little bit of nothing, an echo from the past. It barely existed. Sand blew across it in weird snake shapes. Worse, there was some kind of truck out there—a black Toyota pickup truck.

How had he not noticed that before? He looked at the bottle in his hand—he had already downed half the booze.

"Drunk," he said. "I'm a little drunk."

As he watched, a big dark man in the bed of the pickup pointed a large mounted machine gun directly at the cockpit.

Mitchell felt his heart skip a beat. If he fired that thing...

A loud knock came at the plane's door.

Mitchell was so startled he dropped his whiskey bottle, shattering it. One moment, it had been an expensive, very kind buzz. Now it was just broken glass and amber liquid all over the cockpit floor.

The knock came again.

"All right!" he shouted. "All right, I'm coming."

* * *

"Where?" the pilot said.

"Georgia," Luke said. "Pankisi Gorge. And I need to get there fast."

The man shook his head. "This is the fastest private jet there is. But we'll never make it. We'll be lucky enough to take off without getting shot down. But if we do manage to take off, I recommend we fly south towards the Gulf. If we get that far, we

224

should be okay. We can land in Saudi Arabia or one of the emirates. But north? No way."

"We're going north," Luke said.

He was in no mood for arguing. The guy seemed like he was in a daze, and the cockpit reeked of alcohol.

"Sir," the man said. "The Russians are bombing everything. If we make it through them, then we're over Turkish airspace. They're having a coup, in case you didn't know. After that, Georgia? Really? They're on red alert because of the Russians. You're just asking me to get myself killed."

Luke shook his head. "Mitchell, right?"

The guy nodded. "Mitchell. Yeah."

"How about Mitch?"

The man threw his hands in the air, made a crazy shoulder roll. His eyes darted left and right. Mitchell, Mitch—what difference did it make?

Luke pulled his gun and placed it against the man's head. "Well, Mitch, I don't have a lot of time. You might think flying north is going to get you killed at some point, but I promise you that not flying north will get you killed right now. If you can't take me to Georgia, then you're of no use to me."

The pilot squeezed his eyes shut.

Luke looked back at Ed. He was standing a few feet away, at the front of the cabin. Behind him, Swann and Nigel were buckled into seats for takeoff. Ed had already cut away the covering tarp outside. The plane was naked—clearly visible to anything that passed overhead.

"Ed, what do we call things that have no use?"

"Garbage," Ed said.

"And what do we do with garbage?"

Ed shrugged. "We take it out."

Luke looked back at the pilot. "That's just our policy, Mitch. We take out the garbage. You understand. Now I'll sit in the cockpit with you and hold your hand, but we are flying north. Make yourself useful and you'll live a little longer. Okay?"

The man stared up at Luke with mournful eyes.

"Okay."

* * *

"Airplane, identify yourself."

They had been off the ground less than ten minutes. They were surrounded by Russian fighter jets—one directly to their right, one to their left, and one trailing behind. If Luke wanted, he could look out the window and wave to the Russian pilot over there.

The Russians had addressed them in three languages so far. Finally, language number four was English.

Luke picked up the mic. "We are Americans."

A blunt, deep, and heavily accented voice came over the radio. "Identify yourself, as I said."

Luke paused. What made the most sense here? A diplomatic mission?

No.

An aide mission?

Hmmm. Probably not in this fancy plane.

"Identify yourself or be shot down," the voice said.

How about the truth? Well, he could try it.

"My name is Luke Stone. I'm an agent of the Secret Service, and a special assistant to the President of the United States. I have high-value prisoners rescued from ISIS aboard this plane."

He paused. No sound came through the radio.

"And I know where the stolen nuclear weapons are."

The pilot Mitchell looked at him now, wide-eyed.

For a long moment, Luke thought maybe the radio had gone dead. He looked at the microphone in his hand. They weren't answering.

Nothing the Russians did now would surprise him. They could shoot him down in flames, or take him to Moscow and make him a Hero of the Revolution. Admittedly, the shoot down scenario seemed more likely, but...

"You will follow us," the voice said.

CHAPTER THIRTY NINE

4:30 p.m. Russia Time (10:30 a.m. Eastern Daylight Time)
Caucasus Mountains (near Mount Elbrus)
Southern Russia

They were very close to the Georgian border.

The last of the weak light was fading off to the west when they landed on the airstrip high in the rugged mountains. Nearby were snow-capped peaks. The five of them—Ed, Luke, Swann, Nigel, and Mitchell stepped off the plane, into the high winds and blistering cold. Mitchell, apparently sober now, had done a good job just setting the plane down in the heavy crosswinds.

A dozen men in winter uniforms and carrying submachine guns moved Luke's group across the runway toward a big steel door built into the side of the mountain.

Luke glanced at Ed. Ed was noncommittal—they were outnumbered, outgunned, and surrounded. There was no sense dying just yet.

A soldier poked Luke in the head with the barrel of his gun.

"Eyes front."

The door slid open and they moved through a wide corridor to an open elevator. A few seconds later, they were plunging deep into the Earth. Outside the elevator window, Luke watched yellow lights flow by at some assigned interval. They were moving very fast. They went down for what seemed like a long time.

They came out in a vast subterranean chamber. The ceiling was rounded and high above their head. The soldiers moved them along toward a group of men standing far at the other side. Luke glanced at Swann and Nigel—Swann seemed to stumble along in a dream. Nigel was limping on his wounded leg, wincing with every step he took. Somehow Nigel the ISIS recruit was on the team now. He had purchased his ticket—without Nigel, they never would have found Swann.

"Two of my men are wounded," Luke said to the soldiers around him, hoping his words would land somewhere good. "They need medical care, food, and rest."

"Keep moving," a soldier said.

They crossed the cavernous chamber. As Luke approached the men on the other side, one of them began to resolve into a familiar outline. The man wore a business suit, and was somewhat tall, broad, and balding. His facial features—forehead, nose, and chin— were prominent. His eyes were deep set, intelligent, and unforgiving.

Vladimir Putin.

Could that be right?

He stood with three other men in front of a giant video screen.

Luke came to within ten feet of him, then a soldier put his gun across Luke's chest. Luke stood, facing Putin, the President of Russia and the enemy of the West.

Putin's eyes were flat now, registering no emotion.

"You are Stone?" he said.

Luke nodded. "Mr. President."

Putin gestured to the man next to him. He was a young guy with shaggy hair. He wore a suit with a wide collar and an open-throated dress shirt underneath. He looked a little bit like a guy in a New York City disco during the 1970s. He and Putin made an odd combination.

"My able translator, Vasil. He is the very best."

"Vasil," Luke said.

Putin began speaking in Russian at once. Vasil listened for a few seconds before beginning.

"We know who you are. You and your partner are American shadow operatives. We lost a helicopter with six men on board last night, and we believe you are responsible for this. You must make a full accounting of your activities in Syria during the past twenty-four hours, and of your whereabouts during the past seventy-two hours."

"We lost a helicopter, too," Luke said. "Three men died."

"We are not interested in your men. Why were you in Syria?"

Luke shrugged. "We were looking for the missing warheads."

Putin laughed and said something to one of the men next to him. Then he addressed Luke again.

"For me to accept that," Vasil said, "I would have to believe that your government didn't know where the warheads went in the first place. But I don't believe that. I think they gave the warheads to the extremists. Then again, perhaps this is a game of charades the Americans play among themselves. With the right hand, they provide dangerous criminals the weapons to destroy entire cities. With the left hand, they send ignorant murderers like you to retrieve the weapons. So enlighten me, Mr. Stone. Where do you suppose the warheads are now?"

Luke stared at Putin. "Why are you here? In this place? And not in Moscow?"

Putin barked something at Vasil.

"Answer the question. No one knows where you or your men are. You could easily die here and your masters would think you perished fighting in Syria."

Luke didn't say a word. Putin stared back at him.

Who cares? Luke thought. *Who really cares?*

The bombs could go off and the whole world could end. Is that what this man wanted? Because if he killed Luke, or any of the people here with him, that's what he was going to get.

But then Putin smiled. It was a genuine smile, and even a warm one. He spoke to Vasil in a softer tone.

"I am here for two reasons," Vasil said. "They say to keep your friends close, and your enemies closer. Here I am very close to my enemies. They also say that when your enemies think they know where you are, be somewhere else."

Now Luke smiled. If a nuclear war came, the United States would concentrate on Moscow, raining death on the Kremlin and the surrounding area. The US Strategic Air Command would hit known underground command centers in that region with bunker busters, again and again and again.

But here, high in the mountains, a few miles from the Georgian border? Did anyone even know this place existed?

"The warheads are in Georgia," Luke said. "Pankisi Gorge. Not very far from here. That's what I've been told and it's what I believe. I have the coordinates and I can plot them on a map for you."

Behind Putin, the giant video screen came to life. It showed satellite footage of the Earth then zoomed in on the Middle East and western Asia. It settled finally on Turkey and then Georgia.

"I need men," Luke said. "Men to accompany me and get them out. There is no time for my country to provide these men— and I am not sure that they would, even if they could. They don't believe me."

Putin stared back, stone-faced.

Luke took a risk and took a step closer, needing Putin to believe him. The gun shoved him in the chest. No further.

Luke hardened his eyes to match Putin's. He recognized the killer in them, and he wanted Putin to recognize it within him, too. For as much as Luke had reason to hate the man a few feet away from him, he also recognized something kindred within him.

Something he hated to recognize, but had to admit. He was, in many ways, the same as the man a few feet away.

"My country did not unleash these weapons," Luke continued. "My country does not support ISIS. The last thing my country would want, believe me, is a nuclear war to cover the world. The last thing they would want is the shame of losing these weapons. In our defense, the breach of security was Turkey's fault, not ours. Nonetheless, they remain our weapons, however outdated, and thus our responsibility. I was sent to get them back."

Putin stared back.

"And you failed your mission," he said.

It was a rebuke, but at least in that rebuke, Luke sensed that he believed him.

Luke nodded.

"Thus far," he admitted. "But not entirely. We know where they are now. No one else on earth does. And with a few hours work and a few hundred men, we can complete our mission."

Putin stared at him, unflinching.

"Why would you, Luke Stone, care so much about Mother Russia?" he asked. "Why would you risk your life—and your men's lives—to save us from a bomb that you claim you did not unleash?"

Luke smiled. And he took a chance. A tough edge was not getting through to Putin; perhaps humor would.

"Must be the Russian in me," he said. "My grandmother was part Russian, after all. Did I mention that?"

Putin stared back for a full thirty seconds, as if stunned. Then finally, he smiled.

"I recognize something of myself in you," he finally replied. "You are a bit crazy. And I have to say that I like you. And even, for some reason, trust you. After all, the man who killed the North Korean leader is worthy of something in my book."

Luke smiled back, not knowing, in the long silence that followed, if Putin would not step forward and put a bullet in his head, or offer him a shot of Smirnoff.

Finally, Putin nodded.

"I will give you one hundred of my toughest killers, and I will send you both into the Gorge," he said. "You will lead them. I am putting the lives of my finest Russian officers in your hands. Lead them well, rescue these weapons, and do not disappoint me."

Putin turned his back as abruptly as he had entered, and disappeared back into the shadows, as immediately rough hands escorted Luke back to the elevators.

Luke turned and stared at Ed, who stared back, as disbelieving as he.

Finally, Ed smiled.

"Making friends in all corners of the world, are you?" he asked.

CHAPTER FORTY

5:50 p.m. Georgia Time (11:50 a.m. Eastern Daylight Time)
The Skies over Pankisi Gorge

Luke couldn't understand the instructions being given. His Russian wasn't good enough. It all sounded like one long word.

Soon, on a signal he didn't understand, the Spetsnaz paratroopers began to move toward the open doorway, their big combat packs strapped between their legs. Luke and Ed were last. Before them, each of the men waddled to the line, paused for a second, then jumped. No hesitation. They just went.

"You ever see these guys in a fight before?" Luke shouted.

"No!"

"They go right at the bad guys. They're worse than the Marine Corps. They could hammer spikes into the ground with their foreheads. When we get down there, let's see if we can try a work around. And let's not give them any reason to shoot us. I can't understand anything they're saying. For all I know, it's kill the Americans when we hit the ground."

Ed laughed.

When Luke reached the open door, there was nothing but darkness and open space, and wind. He couldn't see anything out there. It didn't matter. There was a time when he lived to jump. Those times had passed, but the feeling never went away.

He pushed hard with his legs, like an eager kid jumping into a lake.

He was out.

He fell away, and the plane was gone in an instant. For a few seconds, there was nothing but the wind and the darkness. He let it take him.

* * *

He hit hard in some kid of field, and dropped immediately to the ground.

Ed came in right behind him.

All around them, the Spetsnaz were up and running. Where were they going? Suddenly, they were taking fire from a dark tree line just to the west. Tracers whizzed past. Somebody over there was worried about all the Russians falling from the sky.

Luke struggled to get out of his chute. It was a Russian parachute, and he didn't know where the releases were. He finally kicked free of the thing and crawled away.

Spetsnaz troopers fired at the trees, lighting them up, blowing them to pieces. The sound was deafening.

"Ed! You with me?"

"Yeah!"

"You ready?"

"You know the answer to that."

Luke moved along the ground crawling like a snake, going south, parallel to the tree line, instead of directly toward it.

After a long while, he had crawled far enough south that he was outside the lines of fire. He and Ed were out here in the dark, all by themselves. He crawled even further, in case any lucky ducky might still have a bead on them. Then he crawled some more.

"What do you think, man?" Ed said. "We gonna crawl to the South Pole? The fighting is back there."

Luke pressed up into a crouch. Ed followed suit. The firefight was well to their right. The darkness of the tree line was just ahead. Luke indicated the fighting.

"The bad guys are holding the forest edge, right?"

Ed nodded.

"And Spetsnaz is trying to come in the front door?"

"Right."

"I'm thinking if we come straight up the spine of these woods, we might hit the bad guys on their flank. Could be they're exposed. I don't know."

Ed looked at the dark woods. "Makes as much sense as anything."

They stood up and walked across the open field toward the trees. Soon, they were inside. They walked deeper, feeling their way. The woods were dense and dark—almost black. They had to force their way through heavy underbrush and between trees that in certain instances were less than a foot apart.

At some point, they turned north again, back toward the sounds of the battle. Luke could see flashes of light from the tracers and the muzzle signatures of the guns. He could hear the explosions and the crunches of trees disintegrating. The militants were going to hold the Russians outside the woods as long as they could—they were buying time to launch the missiles.

They crept through the woods now, quiet like deer. Gradually, Luke became aware of a clearing up ahead. There were lights inside the clearing, and the faint drone of machinery. The shooting was now far to the right.

He and Ed moved to the edge of the clearing. They ducked behind the trees.

The clearing was extensive, perhaps a football field across—it was a clear cut that had happened recently. Broken logs and stumps were scattered throughout. There was a wide path leading out the other side, perhaps to a nearby roadway.

Luke took a deep breath.

There were at least fifty men in the clearing, many of them heavily armed. There were several aluminum huts and small wooden buildings. There were several truck-mounted anti-aircraft guns pointed at the sky. In the middle of it all was a large green tandem trailer. The front was a typical tractor trailer cab, large, very out of date. The back was a missile launch platform. The platform was raised, with four missiles in launch position.

Off to the left was an identical trailer, also loaded with four missiles, the platform raised and in launch position. Men swarmed like angry bees around the two launch platforms. At the nearest platform, a payloader lifted what looked like a beer keg in the air—it was a warhead.

They were still mounting the warheads on the missiles.

Very, very quietly, Luke checked the magazine in his MP5. It was full. He patted his pockets. He had six more magazines and four grenades. They were going to get exactly one chance at this.

"What are we gonna do?" Ed whispered.

Luke stared at the problem. There was no easy answer. It was two against the multitudes. To their right, the fighting was coming closer, but they couldn't wait for it to arrive. The missiles could be in the air before then.

"Triangulate," Luke said. "You got your blooper?"

Ed patted the M79 grenade launcher.

"Circle over to the left and hit them with everything you've got. Hit and move, hit and move. Take a couple of those buildings out. Get the anti-aircraft guns. Hell, I don't know, get the launch platforms. As soon as you start to work, I'll come out with the machine gun. I'll try to reach that closest platform, take out that whole crew if I can. If we can sow some chaos, we might be able to delay them until the Ruskies get in here."

Ed looked at him closely. "Not much of a plan, is it?"

Luke grunted. "No. Not much. But I'm not working with much right now. I got you, and me, and all these lunatics." He gestured at the men out in the clearing.

Ed nodded. He let a long breath exhale.

"I guess I'll see you after the game."

A moment later, he was gone.

Luke stood behind the tree, not moving. He watched the action out in the clearing. He tried to picture how it might go. Instead, he saw Becca, lying in bed, thin and frail, her skin hanging from her face, as though she were laid out for a wake. He saw Gunner growing to manhood, with no mother and no father.

He and Ed could die out here tonight. He knew it. He saw it in Ed's eyes. They were both beyond tired. And the odds were bad this time—really bad. Why did he put himself in these positions? Didn't he want to see his son grow up?

Didn't he want to live?

When Ed's first grenade hit the clearing, Luke was still deep in thought. He was so accustomed to hearing the distinctive report of Ed's gun—*doonk!*—that when he didn't hear it, he didn't even realize Ed was shooting.

The sound had been drowned out by the machinery in the clearing, and the firefight on the other side of the woods. All that happened was one of the aluminum huts suddenly exploded.

Luke watched it rip to pieces, a red and yellow fireball blow it out, the heavy aluminum making that thunderous shuddering sound as it flew through the air.

Then people were shouting, running in the darkness, firing into the woods where the grenade had come from.

Oh man! Ed!

Now Luke was moving.

He burst from behind the trees, running hard for the nearest launch platform. He had the MP5 up ahead of him, firing off burst after burst.

The men at the platform tried to scatter. Luke's first burst dropped one. His second burst dropped another. Now he was just running, and the men had disappeared.

Doonk!

He heard it this time.

BOOOM!

Another explosion lit up the night. A man was on fire, shrieking, screaming.

Luke reached the edge of the missile launcher. He crouched in the darkness, lit by the flickering flames. Could anyone see him? He didn't know. The beer keg nuclear warhead was right near him, still mounted on the bomb loader.

BANG!

A gunshot rang out, ricocheting right in front of him, and whining off into the night.

He dropped to the ground. Someone could see him—that was for sure. He slid beneath the platform of the launcher.

Machine gun fire strafed the ground bare feet from him.

Perfect. He was trapped under here now.

Doonk!

Ed was taking his life in his hands.

Another explosion, a long rolling BOOOOOM, as something else went up in flames. That was a big one, very nearby, and suddenly a secondary explosion came. Ed had hit something with a gas tank.

Luke lay still for a second and took a deep breath.

Oh well. The hell with it.

He rolled out from under the platform, jumped to his feet, and dashed around the corner. He fired wildly, looking for a target. One man was ducked down behind a large control console. He was trying to launch the missiles. Luke ran toward that man.

Another man jumped out from behind the platform, aimed at Luke…

BANG!

…and died as Luke shot him in the head.

Luke turned to the man behind the console. He shot the man once, twice, three times, but the man stayed on his feet. The man opened a box and flipped a switch. Behind and above him, the missile launcher came to life. Flame burst out from the bottom of two missiles.

Luke grabbed the guy and dragged him away. They landed in the grass, just as the missiles shrieked out of their launch tubes and streaked off into the sky.

Luke shouted in gutter Arabic at the man. He shook him by the shirt.

"Where going? Where going?"

"Volgograd," the man said. "Astrakhan."

"Are they armed?" Luke said in English. "The warheads—are they armed?"

The man's life was ebbing out through his wounds. A small sound of mirth escaped from him. He gestured with his eyes. Luke followed his gaze.

On a small mobile platform twenty yards away were three more beer kegs, just like the one on the bomb loader.

"The warheads," the man said.

And died.

Luke stayed on the ground near him. He could not stand up. Too many bullets were flying now—to stand up would be to get sliced apart and chopped down. There were no more reports from Ed's gun. Ed was gone—alive, dead, impossible to tell.

Suddenly, to Luke's right, the tree line exploded. Missiles, tracers, machine guns, all coming this way—the Russians had broken through. Luke lay nearly still, like the dead man next to him.

The only thing that moved was his hand—it reached inside his flak vest, looking for his satellite phone.

CHAPTER FORTY ONE

12:37 p.m.
The Situation Room
The White House, Washington, DC

Luke Stone's voice screamed out of the conference call speaker.

"There's nothing on those missiles! Repeat! There are no warheads on those missiles. Repeat! There are no…"

On the big screen, there was a map of the region—southern Russia, Georgia, the Black Sea. Radar had picked up two projectiles, one streaking almost directly north, one streaking to the northeast.

"Astrakhan!" Stone shouted. Explosions and gunfire were happening somewhere near him. "Volgograd! Repeat! There are no warheads on those missiles!"

The entire room was silent, watching the missiles streak across the early evening sky half a world away.

"Kurt?" Susan said.

"We called the Kremlin," he said. "We called the ambassador. We delivered the message. There's been no reply. It's the best we can do."

On a screen nearby, a digital map of the Russian landmass materialized.

As she waited, Susan imagined seeing blips begin to appear on radar as the Russian silos launched their nuclear weapons. If that happened, she would have to respond in kind.

Haley Lawrence was on a telephone. He looked at Susan. "Strategic Air Command and NORAD await your orders."

They watched as the minutes ticked by.

"Northeast-bound missile should hit Astrakhan in one minute or less."

Susan took a deep breath.

"Do we have imagery from there?"

Kurt nodded. "Satellite coverage. If it's big, we'll know it."

One long moment passed. Suddenly, the blip disappeared from radar.

"Was that it? Was that the hit?"

Kurt was listening to a wire plugged into his ear.

238

"We have an explosion," he said.

The entire room gasped. Kurt raised a hand.

"Wait! Wait! Explosion is consistent with a small conventional weapon. We're getting more information. It landed on the outskirts of the city. There's a warehouse fire."

He looked up. "It's not a nuke."

Susan felt all the air go out of her, like a tire suddenly deflating.

She looked at the board again. It didn't matter. If the Russians overreacted, if they launched, then it wouldn't matter. Still nothing on the board, though. No Russian missiles inbound. She kept watching, her eyes never wavering.

Still nothing.

The second blip disappeared.

She looked at Kurt.

"I don't know," he said. "We'll know in a minute."

Suddenly, the telephone began to ring. The big heavy red one, sitting on the desk, the phone from out of a nightmare.

She picked up the receiver.

"Vladimir?"

"Hi, Missus," he said. "We have a lot to talk about, wouldn't you agree?"

CHAPTER FORTY TWO

11:30 a.m. Mountain Daylight Time
(1:30 p.m. Eastern Daylight Time)
An Underground Bunker
Ketchum, Idaho

This was not going to work.

Her name was Denise Harker. She was a survivalist—a prepper was what she called herself. She'd had this fallout shelter built five years ago, in the sloping backyard behind and above her house. She had spent years slowly stocking it with food and equipment.

There was three years' worth of canned food in here—most of which could be eaten straight from the can, if it came to that. There were two thousand gallons of water. There were half a dozen first aid kits and an entire wall of vitamins. There were ventilator masks, guns, and thousands of rounds of ammo.

There were hundreds of batteries to run everything for as long as possible—the tiny electric stove, the sunlamp, the FM/AM radio, the short wave radio, the flashlights, the DVD players. Along one wall, there were more than two hundred DVDs, plus at least a hundred books.

She was prepared for the end—she had convinced herself this was true. And on some level she was prepared, but not the way it counted.

She was down here with her two small children now—Isaac and Linda—twenty feet below the surface. An hour ago, in the mad dash to get inside the shelter, they had forgotten some things. One of those things was the family dog, Cosmo. The crazy gray mutt was currently chained to the back deck.

She could hear him above ground, barking. So could the children.

"Rowf!" Cosmo shouted. "Rowf! Rowf!"

Where is everybody?

The three of them sat in the tiny living space, staring at each other.

That was another thing—the living space was way too small. How had she imagined three people were going to get along down here? There was nowhere to stretch out, except in the bunks, and even then…

Isaac had grown a lot since she built this place. He was going to grow even more, and he was as headstrong as his father—not a good combination. Denise herself had probably put on twenty pounds since then. The space was tight. Even if they got a chance to bring Cosmo down here, where were they going to put him? The bunker predated Cosmo by two years. It was not designed with a family pet in mind.

"Rowf!"

"Can't we just go and get him?" Isaac said.

"Honey, I told you half a dozen times already—"

"I don't want to survive without my dog!" he screamed.

Little Linda started crying.

"Baby, don't you cry now. We're all right. We just need to wait and see what happens."

"Mommy, I don't want to die down here," Linda said.

"We're not going to die," Denise said.

But was she sure of that? And if they lived, what kind of life was this going to be? How long would they be down here? If the communications were lost, how would they know when to go topside again?

A shriek of static suddenly burst from the radio, and Denise nearly jumped out of her skin. The damn thing hadn't made a sound in twenty minutes.

"This is the Emergency Broadcast System. In the past five minutes, the White House has announced that the civil emergency has ended. A direct call was placed between Russia and the United States, and the presidents of both countries have agreed to an immediate cessation of hostilities. Strategic Air Command and NORAD report no intercontinental missiles are in the air at this time, and at no time were any launched from either side. Civil air defense and military radar stations around the globe are monitoring the situation, and will continue to do so for the next several days. Repeat, the White House has announced…"

Denise let out a long exhale. It seemed that she had holding her breath all morning. She shut off the radio.

"See?" she said. "We're going to be fine."

She let the kids climb the steel ladder to the surface ahead of her. Isaac knew how to open the hatch. She worked her way up the tube, and when she pushed through out the hatch, she was surprised to see that it was a bright, sunny day.

On the sloping hill behind the house, Isaac was already running with the dog, little Linda trailing awkwardly behind them. Well behind her children, a mile away, the steep mountains towered over the foothills. It was if she were seeing that view for the first time. The whole thing was so beautiful that Denise did something she almost never did—she started to cry.

She slid on her butt and lifted her legs over the rim of the hatch. She stood on the spongy grass.

"I guess we dodged a bullet today," she said through her tears.

CHAPTER FORTY THREE

October 23
6:05 a.m. Eastern European Time
(12:05 a.m. Eastern Daylight Time)
The Presidential Palace
Ankara, Turkey

"I want to see him first," Ismet Batur said.

He walked briskly through the marble halls of the massive palace, guarded by a contingent of more than fifty heavily armed men. The corridors were so wide that they could easily accommodate such a large group.

Once again back in the palace. What a waste.

It was the handiwork of Ismet's predecessor—a palace so gigantic, so ostentatious, and so expensive that the public's revulsion at it was probably the reason Ismet had been swept into power in the first place. A house with eleven hundred rooms and so many amenities they were impossible to count, never mind make use of. Though it was expected of him, Ismet found it embarrassing to live here. He pictured the American President, living in a house a tiny fraction of this size.

He shook the image from his head.

Ismet was President once again, as he had assured Colonel Musharaff that he soon would be. In the end, Musharaff and his henchmen had toppled the government for less than twenty-four hours. Their lightning attacks had been well planned and carried out. But with no popular support, and only a very narrow slice of the military joining their ranks, their movement had collapsed very quickly.

The odd thing was that Musharaff knew this would happen. He said so himself. Anyway, how could he not?

Ismet shook his head. Musharaff had always been a baffling character.

"Just up ahead, sir."

They passed through a set of double doors into a large great room. Large didn't really describe it. Monstrous was closer. There were dozens of sitting areas, each with a sofa and chairs arranged around a small plush carpet. There were many fireplaces. The ceiling was three stories high. Ismet had never entered this room before. He had not been aware of its existence until now.

A man stood in the room, out in the open on the stone floor, away from any of the sitting areas. He had a thick white mustache. He still wore the uniform of the Turkish Air Force. Perhaps his intention was to have been a military dictator?

"Musharaff," Ismet said. "I see you are alone. What happened? Did your friends desert you?"

"Batur," the man said. "You are a dupe and a fool. The Russians have made you their instrument."

Ismet shook his head. Musharaff was insane, seeing conspiracies everywhere. There was no truth to this at all. Ismet was an enemy of the Russians. He'd had no contact with them except to lodge a complaint when they stole the Turkish islands. He had appealed to the Americans for help, but none was forthcoming.

Musharaff was dangerous, not just to Turkey, but to the world. Only a lunatic would launch the apocalypse over three tiny islands. One day the islands would be returned. Diplomacy would accomplish this. Perhaps every man in this room would be dead before that happened. Certainly one would.

"I will bring my case before the Turkish people," Musharaff said. "They will see you for the traitor, and the Russian stooge, that you are."

Ismet said nothing.

"I will have my day in court," Musharaff said.

Ismet finally shook his head. "No... you won't."

He made a hand gesture to the men nearest him. It was little more than a wave, and in ordinary circumstances wouldn't mean anything. Today it meant:

I'm done here.

A lieutenant stepped up to Musharaff, placed a small silenced pistol against his temple, and pulled the trigger. The colonel barely had time to flinch. Despite the silencer, the gunshot echoed in the vast space around them.

An instant later, Musharaff lay on the marble floor, a pool of blood spreading around his ruined head like the halo of a Christian saint. Ismet touched the corpse with his toe.

"Please," he said, as he turned to leave, "dispose of this trash. And make sure the room is made clean again."

CHAPTER FORTY FOUR

October 25
8:45 a.m.
9th Arrondissement—Paris, France

The man's name was Mustafa Zarqawi.

Sometimes, people called him Jamal, or even the Phantom. He thought perhaps he would not go by these names again, maybe not for a while, maybe not ever.

He awoke alone in his bed, light streaming in from the window above his head. A girl had been here, but she was an office girl, and must have arisen early and left for her job. Mustafa smiled at the sunlight. This was a modest apartment, but a beautiful one, in a lovely old building. It was a nice place to bring young girls.

He stood and padded barefoot through the living room and into the kitchen. He wore nothing by a pair of tight underwear and a thin T-shirt. The rooms he passed were green with plant life—the light here was perfect for growing things.

In the kitchen, he placed the coffee pot on the burner. There was bread and butter. A simple breakfast, but more than enough for him. He placed two slices of the bread into the toaster. His hand touched the lever to press it down.

Someone was behind him.

He stopped. There was a shadow back there, a wrong one. He had spent so much time in this place, even the shadows were his friends. But not this shadow.

Mustafa reached for the cupboard, moving slowly and naturally. Nothing out of the ordinary here. There was a large gun on the top shelf. He reached, brought it down, and spun to face his attacker.

A large black man stood there, in the living room, just beyond the threshold.

No, the man wasn't large. He was a giant. He was tall and his shoulders were massive. His chest must be a full meter across.

He wore jeans and a black T-shirt, both of which clung to his muscular frame. He was pointing his own gun directly at Mustafa's head.

"Hi, Jamal," the man said. "Careful with that gun."

Something moved to Mustafa's left. A man emerged from the bathroom, this one a white man with blond hair and a three-day growth of beard. He was tall and muscular, but nothing like the black man. He also held a gun, pointed at Mustafa's head.

"Triangulation of fire," Mustafa said.

"Yes," the white man said. "You don't even stand a chance."

"Do I know you?"

"Luke Stone," the white man said.

"Ed Newsam," said the black man.

Mustafa nodded. "Ah. That was always a concern. Am I off to prison now?"

The two men said nothing.

There was a choice here, Mustafa knew. There was always a choice, even at the end. When all other choices were extinguished, the last thing available was to choose how to die. Was he afraid of death? Yes, he supposed so. Was it because he was afraid to meet God? No, that wasn't it. If he was honest with himself, he was afraid that when he arrived on the other side, there would be no God there to greet him.

Even so...

He pulled the gun down and nearly aimed it at the big man.

He saw the flashes from the muzzle of the man's gun. One, two, three. Only later did he hear the gunshots, or feel the pain.

Then he was on his back on the kitchen floor. The two men stood over him. Mustafa thought briefly about his gun, but he no longer knew where it was.

The pain wasn't bad, and it was already fading.

As he went into the black, a last thought came:

I've never been shot before.

CHAPTER FORTY FIVE

October 27
11:03 a.m. Eastern Daylight Time
The Oval Office
The White House, Washington, DC

"The rats are still on board this ship," Luke Stone said.

Susan watched him sip the coffee an aide had brought him. They were in the high-backed chairs in the sitting area of the Oval Office. Outside the tall windows, it was a sunny fall day. Susan wore tan slacks, a white dress shirt, and a blue jacket—business casual attire. Her hair was in a ponytail. She felt good. Sleep would do wonders for anyone.

And things were looking up—they'd had a diplomatic breakthrough with the Russians. Right now, Kat Lopez was working with about a dozen planners to create a series of Russia—America Friendship Day events. Food festivals, sporting events, parades... Susan loved that kind of thing.

On a deeper level, both she and Putin had committed to talking on the phone one day a week, for at least fifteen minutes, even if there was nothing to talk about. They would talk about the weather, if it came to that. And on a frivolous level, next week's cover of *Time* magazine depicted Susan as the Great Negotiator.

"I'll take diplomacy over nuclear war any day," was the quote that would apparently go with her photo.

The most bitter Congressional campaign season in modern American history was set to end in ten days, and God only knew how that was going to play out. However, right now, at this moment, things were pretty first rate. Today was a good day to be Susan Hopkins.

But Stone? That was hard to say. He had just returned from ferocious combat, again. An old friend of his—Bill Cronin—had died in the fighting. He and his partner Ed had survived a helicopter crash. Judging from his report, they had gone on to kill dozens of opponents. These things had to weigh on a person, didn't they?

Susan stared at him. He seemed different from before. He had let his beard grow during the days he was away. His steely blue eyes peered out from atop a blond beard and mustache. His hair was getting a little bit long. He was retreating back to the caveman looked he sometimes sported, retracting into it. To Susan, that suggested he was about to disappear again.

Stay a little while, why don't you? she wanted to say.

"What does that even mean?" she said. "We have rats?"

"Two days ago, in Paris, Ed and I eliminated a man named Mustafa Zarqawi."

"I thought you two went to France on a vacation."

Luke smiled. "Call it a working vacation. A little business, a little pleasure. Zarqawi was a Pakistani, and once upon a time he was an agent of the intelligence services there. He went by the name Jamal, and was sometimes referred to as the Phantom. I have reason to believe he was the mastermind behind the theft of the warheads."

"Shouldn't you be sharing this with our own intelligences services?" she said.

"I would, but I also have reason to believe he's been working for our intelligence services. Elements of them, in any case."

"What reason is that?"

Luke's face was impassive, giving her nothing. He gestured at the walls of the room. "I wish I could tell you."

"Oh, come off it, Luke. There are no bugs in this room. And even if there are, you of all people don't need to worry about it. Everyone values what you do, and what you just did. Okay? I thank you. Everyone thanks you. The nation owes you a debt of gratitude, one that will probably never be adequately repaid."

She raised her voice and directed it to any hidden microphones.

"Do you hear that, dummies? Luke Stone is the best agent America has! We owe him a debt that we can never repay."

Luke said nothing.

Susan lowered her voice. He had her half-convinced that the microphones in his mind were real. "I go out on a limb for you," she said. "You do know that, don't you? My advisers… well, I'll just say I have advisers who are not in your fan club. They'd like to see you lose your job, and I tell them no, Luke Stone is too valuable. But then you do something like chase stolen nuclear weapons to Syria, when they've in fact gone the other way. And then you disobey my direct orders…"

"I went to save a friend of mine, who also happens to be an American intelligence asset, the best in his area of expertise that I've known during my long career."

Susan sighed, sat back in her chair, and placed her hands on top of her head. She stared up at the ceiling. The ceiling was a deep rotunda, and she sometimes felt she could lose herself in it. Luke Stone was a difficult person, and still… she liked him. She was even attracted to him, she realized now. He was intelligent. He was uncompromising. He was exasperating. He was unpredictable. He was about as brave as a human being could be.

And he was handsome. Not in a Tommy Zales way—no one in real life was *that* handsome. More in a rugged way. He was weathered—the lines of experience were written all over his face. He was a serious person, as serious as Tommy was silly. Luke could kill Tommy with one finger, of course, but would probably refrain from doing so unless it was absolutely necessary.

"Do you believe this man was working for the United States when he stole the warheads, if he actually stole them?"

Luke shook his head. "I have no idea. I certainly didn't say that, or even suggest it. I only said that he's done work for elements of the United States intelligence apparatus, and probably recently."

"And you killed him?"

He nodded. "Yes. It was the prudent thing to do. The guy was slippery."

"But now we'll never know who he worked for, or what he did."

Luke smiled. "I didn't say that either. That's you talking."

Susan took a deep breath and shook her head. This discussion wasn't going anywhere.

Luke seemed to realize it, too.

"Hey," he said. "I hear you threatened to shoot the Chairman of the Joint Chiefs of Staff. That's fun. You gonna go through with it?"

Now Susan smiled. "It was the heat of the moment. He was trying to seize control of the military, and that made me angry. Anyway, I've never fired a gun in my life. I've certainly never executed someone. But if anyone had it coming…"

"It was him," Stone said.

They both laughed.

A long pause passed between them.

"I could teach you," Stone said.

"To shoot a gun?"

He nodded. "Mmm-hmmm."

"Then I can kill General Coates if I want."

"Sure."

She pictured herself at a weapons range with Luke Stone. And she imagined the tabloid headlines when that little story leaked out. *President Handles Super Spy's Gun.*

"It sounds like fun, Stone. Let's do that some day."

He was already standing up to leave.

"I'll pencil you in."

CHAPTER FORTY SIX

October 30
2:45 p.m. Eastern Daylight Time
Fly Guys Indoor Skydiving Center
Baltimore, Maryland

That looks like fun.

Luke stood outside the glass wind tunnel, watching Gunner. The instructor, dressed all in white—white jumpsuit, white helmet, white shoes—held Gunner in a horizontal position as the wind ramped up. Gunner wore a red jumpsuit and blue helmet. He had thick goggles on his face and was grinning from ear to ear. His arms and legs were already splayed out.

The helmets were mic'ed, and the voices played through speakers mounted on the walls out here in the viewing area.

"Ready, Gunner?" the instructor shouted.

"Yeah!"

"What? I can't hear you!"

"Ready! I'm ready!"

"All right! One… two… three… GO!"

This was the fifth time Luke had brought Gunner to this place, and by now the kid was an old pro.

When the instructor released him, Gunner instantly flew toward the ceiling, three stories above his head. He did several somersaults before diving headfirst toward the ground, stopping bare inches from the floor. Then, upside down, the boy spun around and around the outside edge of the tube, as though he were in a giant blender.

Each move gave Luke a mini heart attack.

Luke had done more than a hundred real skydives in his life. He had dropped into enemy territory, sometimes under fire. He had been on high-altitude jumps, night jumps, free falls, and he had flown wingsuits. He had never done anything like the kinds of moves Gunner was making inside that glass tunnel. It looked like the kid was dancing in there.

Later, they stopped for hamburgers at a fast food joint. They sat in a booth near the window. The light was already fading from the sky. The days were getting shorter. Winter was coming on. It made Luke think of Becca. She'd had two chemotherapy treatments so far, and she was refusing to see him. Luke had to pick up and drop off Gunner at her parents' house.

"Dad, how come you never go in the jump tunnel?"

The question shook Luke from his thoughts. He shrugged. "I just like watching you do it. You're better at it than I'm ever gonna be."

"I thought you did a lot of skydiving."

Luke nodded and slurped his soda through a straw. "I have. But this is kind of different from jumping out of a plane."

"Can we jump out of a plane one day?"

"Sure."

"When?"

The kid was amazing. Always pushing, always pressing for more.

Don't ever lose that.

"When you're a little older."

Gunner seemed thoughtful at the idea of becoming older. He lapsed into a studied silence. He chewed on his double cheeseburger. He shoved a few fries in his mouth. Finally, he seemed to come to a conclusion.

"Things are changing, aren't they?" he said.

Luke nodded. "Yeah. They are."

Truer words had never been spoken. Luke thought of Mark Swann, currently an in-patient at a private mental hospital in Bethesda. Luke and Ed had visited him there the other day. He was in bad shape. He was on drugs to keep him calm, but even so, all he could talk about was his time in ISIS captivity.

The heads, man, Swann had said. That's the worst part. I can't get them out of my mind. I see them when I close my eyes. Those crazy bastards. They chop people's heads off. All the time. If you guys hadn't come when you did...

Swann had closed his eyes and started to cry then. Soon, he was just sitting there, abject, like a little boy, his body shaking, tears streaming down his face.

In Luke's experience, Swann was probably done. It took a long time for people to come back from trauma like that, if they ever did.

Trudy was gone, off in the world somewhere. Don Morris was in prison. And Becca...

Life, man. It just chewed people up, and it took them away.

"Dad, is Mom going to die?"

The kid and his questions—it was like being on the witness stand sometimes. "We're all going to die one day, Monster."

"Is she going to die soon?"

"I don't know," Luke said. "I don't think anybody knows the answer to that."

Luke watched Gunner's face, and his eyes. There was a lot going on in there, behind the scenes. Gunner had things he wanted to say, but he wasn't saying them. If Luke knew the kid at all, Gunner had about a hundred questions lined up, ready to be asked. And he wasn't asking them. His world had become a very dangerous place in the past year, and Gunner was treading carefully.

When he spoke again, he made a simple statement, one Luke wasn't expecting at that moment.

"I love you, Dad. I just want you to know that."

Luke, for the first time in as long as he could remember, felt his eyes well up.

"I love you too," he said. "More than anything."

Coming soon!

Book #5 in the Luke Stone series

BOOKS BY JACK MARS

LUKE STONE THRILLER SERIES
ANY MEANS NECESSARY (Book #1)
OATH OF OFFICE (Book #2)
SITUATION ROOM (Book #3)
OPPOSE ANY FOE (Book #4)
PRESIDENT ELECT (Book #5)

Jack Mars

Jack Mars is author of the bestselling LUKE STONE thriller series, which include the suspense thrillers ANY MEANS NECESSARY (book #1), OATH OF OFFICE (book #2), SITUATION ROOM (book #3), OPPOSE ANY FOE (book #4), and PRESIDENT ELECT (book #5).

Jack loves to hear from you, so please feel free to visit www.Jackmarsauthor.com to join the email list, receive a free book, receive free giveaways, connect on Facebook and Twitter, and stay in touch!

11540789R00144